IF YOU LIKED *NEUROMANCER, BLADE RUNNER*
AND *A CLOCKWORK ORANGE,*
TERRAPLANE IS THE BOOK FOR YOU!

TERRAPLANE is the breakthrough SF novel of an ultra-violent future by a powerful young writer who has taken the sensibility of William Gibson beyond cyberpunk — and the violence of A CLOCKWORK ORANGE into transcendence.

"Startling numbers of people die in TERRPLANE. At last one can stop muttering and looking over one's shoulder, and get down to the liberating basics of kill-and-be-killed."
— Bruce Sterling

"Utterly bleak and thoroughly convincing."
— Will Shetterly & Emma Bull

"Visions of commercial successes such as A CLOCK-WORK ORANGE and BLADE RUNNER may well have played through Womack's head."
— *The New Republic*

JACK WOMACK

TERRAPLANE

A TOM DOHERTY ASSOCIATES BOOK
NEW YORK

Reprinted by arrangement with Weidenfeld & Nicolson

A Tor Book
Published by Tom Doherty Associates, Inc.
49 West 24th Street
New York, N.Y. 10010

Cover art by Nick Jainschigg

ISBN: 0-812-50623-5

Library of Congress Catalog Card Number: 88-9656

First Tor edition: May 1990

Printed in the United States of America

0 9 8 7 6 5 4 3 2 1

FOR
CAROLINE,
FOREVER

TERRAPLANE

1

"A toast," said our host and contact, Skuratov. Like most of his countryfolk he flashed steel teeth, and resembled a car's grille when he smiled. He'd treated us to the Brotherhood of Money restaurant on Gorki Street. In Moscow restaurants the first decor systems noticed, once eyes unblinded beneath overhead flood's glare, were the enormous wallpapered ads. From each the long-rotted leader glowered at his descendants as they chowed. In twelvecolor holograph the Big Boy modeled furs, guzzled kvas, smirked at his reflection in freshly waxed Lenin, patted puppies' heads, spun the wheels of Hungarian sportsters and proffered tubes of holistic nostrums. If his icon was on it, Russians bought it. Stalin sold everything from laser printers to pantyhose. "To great general—"

"Spassebo. *Retired* general," I reminded. Retired, with reason. Twenty-seven army years proved overmuch. In business was no less danger but the pay was twice tripled.

"Of course."

Marx's and Lenin's dead pans were found, too: in the Buros, on apparatchiks' desks, in the wallets of workers for the Ministry of History. That team couldn't leg it like the Big Boy when it came to pumping profits. BBDS & S, Dryco's ad arm, discovered this through countrycrossed demoteering analysis done for Krasnaya

3

while Russian-backed Saharan forces assaulted a tenth, final time American-supplied Zairian troops. We sustained a personnel realignment of 275,000 in that entanglement—by chance, the same number of people who were surveyed. Didn't matter; the casualties would have never spent like the survivors.

"To great retired general, Robert Luther Biggerstaff," Skuratov continued, hoisting his complimentary glass of mineral water. I raised mine, examining it against the light; saw it unsullied clear, as in a stream, on a field nonbattle betrammeled.

"Na zdorovye," I said.

"Das vydanya," said Jake, for whom one lingua sufficed. I wondered how Skuratov saw my associate. Jake's first impression was glacierlike; showing as something immeasurably cold which crushed all before it. Skuratov smiled, hearing the error. Jake knew why he smiled. I activated the minicam sewn into my jacket, rolling the tape. Our host and guide drummed fingertips against the crimson tablecloth with a five/four beat, Morsing the code.

OVERHEAD CAM ANGLE DESTABILIZED. SHOOT.

"A young man still," he said. "Thirty when generalship conferred, yes?"

"Thirty-five," I said. Generalship conferred unwanted, lived with thereafter. "I lucked."

"Turnover rate in your army gloriously high at the time if memory serves true. We know great men take their place in history with little need of luck, even in America where you negritanski suffer such difficulties—"

"Black." Suffered little; my family held money bushelsful before the collapse. Joining the army was the sole method to thrive and prosper further at the time, and I joined as a second lieutenant. "Like Pushkin," I added. He drained his glass and rephrased.

"To all poets of color."

NO SIGN ALEKHINE, he tapped. I pressed knee against table's underside, muffling vibes to throw overaware readers. THREE WEEKS GONE. So long as the cassette spun anything misread could be decoded later, reviewed in-hotel. If you wished to plug Russian ears this was standard op. In Russia, even when trees didn't fall, they were heard.

WHERE? I wondered. Solid cover alluded to my meeting reps of our company's Russian arm, Vladamer—true, in a sense; Maliuta Skuratov, as he called himself, was our leading subcontractor. Jake came as my enabler, undesired by me, an extra ingredient to spoil the sauce. We were meeting none but Skuratov for none other than to effect Alekhine's transfer to our department.

HE WALKS THE WIND.

"Why aren't we knived?" Jake asked, shaking his *contagion-free*-stamped dinner packet. In his, as in ours, was but a napkin, spoon and fork with rounded tines. Said cutlery looked metal, felt plastic; was some unwarranted alliance of both, like that solid used in rocket-part production which always failed when most essentialled.

WE TAKE HIS ASSOCIATE.

"Too handy in event of nondinner maneuvers," said Skuratov. His crust of dark wool suit sufficed for daily performance, but his footwear betrayed the lie that lay always beneath truth; calfskin Italians in brown and white, handstitched by Neapolitan serfs, cozied his toes. His family was of the old nomenklatura, who had eased so fittingly into Krasnaya ways after the reimplementations (the Czara and Politburo answered to Krasnaya as the President and Congress answered to us, to Dryco). In younger life—he was my age—he was one of the *zolotaya holodyozh*, or golden youth. "So the belief is ruled. Risk of contretemps, yes? Russian food tender enough not to demand sharp utensils."

SHE IS A HOYDEN. A TERMAGANT.

From his white vest Jake slid his switch, flicking it open. Bladed, his utensil stood fourteen inches, appearing suitable for dropping trees. He gracefully slashed the packet as if lending a birthmark to one heretofore unblemished, spilling contents across his place mat. He tabled his knife to the left of his spoon.

"We hear so much that is interesting concerning Jake," Skuratov said, staring. Peacekeeping is my natural; wasn't Jake's. Our waitress happened upon our table just then, extracted her pocket computer from her filthy apron's crevasses, prepped to doublecheck menu availability. She gleaned my accent immediate.

"Ischo Amerikantski," she said, her voice rising, as if she'd found worms in the honey. *"Borghe* moy!" Narrow-minded Russians found state policy of businessing with America inconsistent with the existing thirty-three-year intercountry war, but held tongue upon penalty of removal. Krasnaya oversaw each and every: it fought the war in chosen countries; decided the output, traded the surplus; treated the adults and readied the children. The old way never approached Krasnaya's success. Two dozen species of police assured propriety; of all those units the most problematic were the Shnitmilit—translated colloquial, the Dream Team.

LEFT DUBNA TWO NIGHTS PAST. IN MOSCOW NOW.

"No coffee?" I asked.

"They're washing the cup," she said, stonefaced. Russians hated Americans as we hated Russians, to similar purpose and with like result. Thus the war continued, with negotiations essentialled only when time came to split the booty.

SENSORED THIS MORNING. NO MOVEMENT SINCE.

"There've been many trying efforts recently bringing cargo in from Indonesia," interrupted Skuratov, shrugging. "Nichevo; can't be helped."

"Under present situation, what have you?" I asked.

"Armenian cognac." Eyeglassing, she parroted her screen. "Tsinandali wine from Georgia. Milk. Pepsi in hygienic reusables. Pepper and lemon vodka, vodka with buffalo grass. Scotch—"

HIDING IN NORTH QUARTER. BAD NEIGHBORHOOD.

"Made from vintage Scotch grapes," Skuratov said, winking.

SHE HAS IT. UNDOUBTED.

Untabling his hands, he lapped them stomachways. His face lacked all but laughter; his smile's rictus certified caution. Whether someone truly fixed us or whether he only felt nerves was unbeknownst. Transactions within Russia problematicked; feasting with those who might moneyfy you or kill you with equal ease and reason poured no syrup over the already indigestible. My boss thrived under such. I always held out for honorability's illusion, if no more, had I choice.

"Pepsi," said Jake.

"Bottle of Tsinandali," I said.

"Jug only," she said. Russian staples came packaged economy

sole if availabled. Potatoes left stores only in fifty-kilo bags. Sliced
bread sold by the meter. If shoes wanted, you imagined yourself a
spider, and provisioned accordingly. Hereby overblown inventories
and farm surpluses left over from military application forever turn-
overed, and cash flow ran as rain.

"When does performance begin?" Skuratov shouted after her as
she stomped away.

"Soon." Skuratov's jaw muscles belied his grin's peace as they
drew up, throbbing, seemingly exposed to unexpected G-force. I
read the room's faces, hoping to nail whomever he'd spotted. Under
carcinogenic fluorescence profiteers dispersed vast rewards grifted
through the Second New Econ Policy; NEP II, it was officialled.
Barrel-waisted Ukrainians welded into dinner jackets rang crystal
with anorected Lithuanian women. Wiry Buryats guzzed cognac,
rewinding after long Gobi pipeline months. Dark Kazakhs and
Afghans, looking as if they'd been imprisoned for years in similar
tanning rooms, abandoned religious principle to attempt drink-by-
drink seduction of tight-skirted Finnish market analysts. Cubans
and Siberians pored over spreads, rigged Monday's margins, traded
inside rumors, at intervals tablerapped knuckles, spurring wait-
resses with the crack of gold rings. Jake and I, nonsmokers, sucked
in what oxygen remained in the fume.

Full-dressed Krasnaya lackeys bedeckled the crowd, so ignorable
and as appreciated as rocks in a salad. None but one eyed us
overmuch. Skuratov's respect towards him underwhelmed. "The
alert one there is Kidin," he said. "Grazhny brazhny. So ugly,
when he looks in window poor people inside think someone is
climbing in ass first."

"Is this subject proper?" I asked, stilling lips. Skuratov always
showed overmuch among his lessers, in my opinion, so used was he
to freedom of action befitting high command. In theory such
conduct was disallowed.

"I'll tell you secrets everyone knows. Not long time past he
oversaw drug company in Smolensk. Pharmaceutical Patrol called
upon all producers to manufacture more penicillin-ten capsules
for use in Iraqi refugee fraternities. Smolensk company produces
four times as much overnight to great acclaim. They make quotas

by putting no penicillin-ten in capsules. Russian inventiveness America's equal any day." Expecting a laugh, we received a shiny smile no warmer than the metal shown. "Now again he rises in Observance Buro as if from dead. Pushing shit deeper through bowels till one day all pours out. I know worse things he did than that. Thus, no worries."

Kidin studied the Kazakhs as they palmed warm Finnish hips. He looked as a type I forever assigned to disinfo; his eyes' look awared that he would never know joy so long as truth left his lips. Twenty polished medals secured his chest from gunfire's blessing. The ad above his head showed waterskied Stalin, drawn by hydrofoil. *Be Young in Yalta*, the copy read.

"Eyes and ears everywhere," said Skuratov, forwarding, flattening hands tableside, readying to pick up where he'd paused. "Stukachny; informers mad to further themselves while keeping Rus pure. You watch me watch you, we say. Once it was tried a plan whereby all newborn citizens would be implanted with needed sensory device to make future days more workable. Didn't work. Most died from—" He stopped. Skuratov's English sufficed, yet still he needed often to rifle his mind for suitably innocent phrasing. "Unforeseeables, yes. Technology carries us so far through the swamp, till we sink or float, depending. Dream Team developed more productive techniques later on in either event."

His fingers actioned anew. SAFE NOW. Never, truly. As the prop claimed, the Dream Team knew what wasn't known; saw what wasn't seen. They were termed the Dream Team because they picked thoughts even if thoughts emerged but in sleep. You never knew them; anyone might be one, though they didn't exist. If you spoke to yourself, the Dream Team heard. The Dream Team's reflection showed in your lover's eyes; their fingerprints smudged every soul. So, as said, the prop claimed.

"Here citizens tell all they know without nudge," he continued. "Krasnaya has prophylacted dissent of those eternally unsatisfied. There is backlash to this. People do right thing like maintenant without seeing that for them it could prove wrong thing. A six-year-old girl last June handed over her parents on political-irresponsibility charges and so they were delivered to Lubianka."

He drew finger crossthroat. "The right thing, no question. It followed, sure, that small devotchka then paid her own price for showing disrespect for essential family structures. She accepted punishment with "smiling heart.""

SHE DOESNT EXPECT ATTENTION AS YET.

"What punishment fit?" asked Jake, shielding his lids with his hands. "Gulaged? Steady-state tranquilized? Thirty years' labor at Baikal Chemical?"

"How cruel you think us, Jake," said Skuratov, shaking his head as if hearing a plea. "Certainly such things aren't done." Afterthought: "They shot her."

SURPRISE ESSENTIAL.

Muffled backstage crashes alerted me that the show readied to underway. Our waitress ripped her cart through the crowd's blanket. As dishes fell from bumped tables I whipped round, frozen, set to hit; over years control again settles over everalert muscles but some reactions always respond to the big red light. Jake, unmoving, lifted his eyebrows. As the waitress posted us Skuratov Amexed her; once promised, she allowed us our food. He penned in a fivepercent tip; repenning, she adjusted to twenty. After a moment's heat they settled at twelve. Receipting him, she plodded off.

SHOULD BE PUSSYCAT ONCE SECURED.

"Your first visit to Russia, Jake?" he asked, changing tone, his cig's smoke shunning him, seeking us. "How do you find us so far?"

Russians mastered paranoia, whether causing it or suffering from it. Eversuspicious of how outers perceived, they demanded constant reassurance as to their worth, no matter what bluster moved their tongues. I'd suggested applicable responses to such questions to Jake before we left. He proceeded unmindful, with his usual detachment; Jake was one of few I'd known who never vomited, before or after a kill.

TOMORROW AT EIGHT-THIRTY. DETSKY MIR SECOND FLOOR. The toy store; a toy, after all, was our ultimate catch.

"Schizo," said Jake. "One face lips, another voices."

"Americans equally accomplished in similar technique."

WE GO FROM THERE.

Jake smiled, showing rotting American teeth. "Channel official and the party line draws an old old picture. Econ equals. Europe's spectres loosed free. Toss the chain and run. Peace first, profit second. Worker's triumph as tradition demands. Fancies and delights, nothing more."

I WILL PILOT.

"Myths and legends passed from father to son, yes?" Skuratov remarked, popping a radish from his zakuski platter into his mouth. "As in America every child becomes President." My pirogi, ordered boiled, arrived fried. I wouldn't touch them. An actor behind-curtain screamed. Jake's lids pressed as if to squash; he despised scream's sound. "Our country remains the worker's state, it is said."

"Shopper's state, more like," said Jake. "Buy or die. Lookabout, blind boy. Every store passed teemed with mob. Peddlers hustling corners all. Heaven's Mall."

"Housing, free. Medicine, free. Essentials provided to all without taxes. Money earned must be spent, Jake. Most useful method in calming domestic tension is to employ best of both worlds." Skuratov held a lump of saccharin between his teeth, slurping his tea through its fabric. "Bourgeois liberalization has purpose so long as spontaneous movements remain minimalized, said Lenin, or so we now hear. Ergo, *sozializtkapitalizm*. Nation owns producers. Producers sell goods. Buyers sell goods to other buyers. A most productive state."

I TOO REALIGN PERSONAL SENSIBILITIES.

"And all money returns to Krasnaya," I said, "but for drips and drabs."

"Krasnaya invests big. Others invest small. In time small money becomes big. Thorough success."

"Which makes happier citizens." I unscrewed my jug's cap, pouring a cupful of wine. Varnish's smooth poison shellacked my mouth. The culpable grapes might have been Georgian; the bottler of this grand old label was Stolichnaya, subbrand of Vladamer, a Dryco subsidiary. Dryco—our company—convinced me to retire when I did so that I might join them in spirit, having worked for them in flesh since my first day at boot.

"That some become happier and wealthier sooner than others is

unavoidable dysfunction of near-perfect system," Skuratov said.
"Eventually monies reach all society members."

"Marvelous theory."

"Popular in America many years too, yes?" he said, laying the
saccharin on his plate as he would a pulled tooth. "Here it works.
Fresh techniques satisfy long-hindered desires. Russian people
have money now to buy fine products at last available in plenti-
tude."

"They *have* to buy," Jake said, lifting and twirling his switch
between his fingers as if keen to plant it. Russians failing to meet
their monthly purchase quotas were investigated by the Consumer
Patrol. If matters were beyond their hands, the Dream Team
settled.

"First-time Americans visiting our country find it always difficult to suspend belief in long-heard propaganda even when facts
beat them over head with shovel," said Skuratov. "In America,
perhaps, facts so hard to face propaganda is better, yes?"

"You haven't been in ten years," I said.

"Russia and America both bloody lands," he said, frowning.
"We transfuse ours. You spill yours. One day you learn as we did."

INTERCEPT THIS MORNING GAVE NEW INFO.

The curtain rose. The lights brightened. The orchestra's flac-
cidity drooped over a synthesizer bank, cracking knuckles, scratching himself.

"A toast. Na zdorovye!" cried Skuratov, lifting his cup, tapping
mine, rubbing it against Jake's box of Pepsi. "Tomorrow you do
business in best business place in world. To Vladamer."

DEVICE IS PROBABLY NOT WEAPON AS SUCH.

WHAT? I tapped.

POSSIBLE TRANSFERRAL DEVICE.

No set showed onstage. Two yellowed posters of New York's
skyline hung from the back wall; a green Statue of Liberty molded
from one of the lesser plastics stood at stage center. The Drama
Advisers chose to rouse at once; their production—*West Side
Story*—opened with "America."

"Songs left in original tongue to preserve purity of text,"
Skuratov noted.

TRANSFERRAL WHERE? I tapped.

WHERE ALEKHINE WENT.

The Puerto Rican girls wore nuns' habits and flapping wimples, and possibly came as if from a convent to attempt conversion of the male dancers, boys of Sakhalin shoeblacked to appear more tropical. Backgrounders repeatedly slammed together as if following choreography's demand. The synthesizist, orchestra's iconoclast, lent a sixty-piece unit's sound.

"They've punched up the lyrics," I whispered to Skuratov, noticing a variorum libretto in use.

"Public domain," he explained. The women tore off their black cloaks during the first bridge, prancing thereafter in glitter and G-strings, headpieces affixed topside. Bending, they wiggled towards us. Russians loved shoving acres of flesh into centimeters of cloth and studying the result.

"What *is* this agitpop?" asked Jake, unable to pull his look from the action. One of the nuns swung over the stage on a rope, felling the statue as she hit her mark.

"*Muzhiki!!*" came a cry rearward. At this alert Jake moved; we were up before the splintering rang. A Mongol shattered empties floorways. Before his bottle shards impressed full, the bouncers buried him beneath their tonnage. Onstage nuns wrapped young men around them as if to keep warm. The song concluded with an atonal thud. The clientele—Skuratov, too—stood, applauding.

"All was intentional?" I asked.

"How else?" said Skuratov, reseating with watchful look. Kidin turned his attention from us back to the Kazakhs. The principals onstaged for the next number. Tony seemed not to be of troublesome Polish descent in this adaptation. Maria's paint, mahogany dark, offset her blond curls. Neither danced; of good voice, they sang "One Hand, One Heart." Audience murmur supplanted audience roar. Looking up I saw Jake's face radiate as if lit from within. A tear dropped from his dead-coal eye, perhaps fearful that if seen it might be blown away. His pox-scarred expression fixed solid; he could have been zooing, watching baby ducks at play, or viewing that little girl of whom Skuratov spoke tumble as the echo faded. Hypnotized, I watched that tear shuffle along his cheek into darkness. It was like seeing a tank cry.

"*Ochen krasiva!*" Jake, drawn from his mourn, swiveled round; the commentator was already set upon by the bouncers, who entwined him like vines strangling a tree. Kidin perked; with fellow Krasnayaviki, advantaging the sitch, they leapt up to beat the Kazakhs with their heavy knouts. The room's tension peaked. The song's last bars were swallowed in curse's roar and crockery's rattle.

"Khulighani—" Rifles showed, clicked, weren't yet fired. The performers stepped forward to view the floor show.

"A delicious dinner," said Skuratov, rising. "Shall we?"

We jostled through the crowd, stamping the fallen when needed, until we exited. Between interior and exterior one hundred degrees vanished. My lungs rustled like paper when I drew in air. Snow powdered the long blue line of people awaiting entry.

"You're staying where?" Skuratov asked, thrusting hands into furry pockets. Trim as he was, the type of coat he wore, a shuba, impressioned his look as three hundred kilos heavier. Ten bears gave their lives to warm his final years.

"Sheraton Kremlin," I said, "on Kitajski Prospect."

"Not the Moskva?"

"My choice." A firetrap; too obvious, besides.

"Let me offer you warm ride." The wind scarred us. Skuratov's official car, a Chaika, was curbsided on Chudozestvannogo Teatra Prospect. Russian limos resembled America's; Gorki-Detroit factories built both and supplied both countries as a rare joint venture. Chaikas, Krasnaya's preferred vehicle, retained the styling of cars forty years old. The Czara, the Politburo, leading members of Krasnaya and old Heroes of the State, all prone to nostalgia in weak moments, rode Chaikas.

"*Look.* Perhaps we shouldn't interrupt such pleasure." The chauffeur reclined in the back seat, eyeing a movie on the TVC. A vodka bottle, full only of air, lay next to him. "Out!" shouted Skuratov, opening the door. "Do your duty." The chauffeur tumbled forth, slinking frontways. "Ten minutes, we're there." But in vidding time away the chauffeur had drained the battery. Switching from idle to drive, he stalled the car. Striving to restart it, he succeeded in making the engine wail as if it were being beaten. Even while armied I allowed myself to be driven but twice, during state funerals. I felt safer when I guided the wheel, once another started the engine.

"Let us have brisk walk, then," muttered Skuratov, decarring. "Call for new limo from hotel's comfortable lobby. Leave this zek here. By morning he'll feel ice below instead of balls. Come."

Frost ferns sprouted across the windshield as we cruised away down Gorki. Moscow's streets dichotomized after the sun fell from daily grace. Krasnaya sealed and patrolled all avenues holding government Buros, the homes of notables, banks and the larger business blocks. Gorki Street, so wide as to allow passage of five tanks tread to tread, was of the secular world, and provided trade's entertainment nightlong. It might have been noon, so peopled and trafficked was the boulevard. Most businesses on the main strips followed the seven/twenty-four plan, forever open to handle unceasing demand. Citizens passed as if on enforced parade, many pushing red carts topful with freezers, washers, TVCs, copiers; all manner of technologic flotsam. Staring into their puffy, bloodshot eyes disconcerted. Refugees' faces held similar looks in every land I'd troubled; the look of these fit naught but for breathing and running, forced by us to abandon home and race the roads before the other team, purposeful and timeshort, landed to steal their days away.

"What demands the wait?" Jake asked, spotting one store's queue running down Gorki and then Belinskogo to a length of sixty meters. "Bread?"

Skuratov perused the storewindowed posters. "Electronic food reconstitutors."

By using those one metamorphosed sawdust into bread; transmogrified dust into spice. So long as the machines worked, they enabled any semiusable to become the near-real. Russia, as did all countries, traded homegrown goods through standard barter, simultaneously balancing the unpayable debts and obtaining desired goods. With Krasnaya overseeing, the system's efficiency was twice redoubled. Peru needed no caviar in exchange for guano but that was what reached the Andes in return; Krasnaya ran the homegrown with equally just rationale. For every Odomovana dishwasher assembled, fourteen DL-50 mortars entered inventory as well; for every Chaika rolling off the line, thirty Turgenev rocket launchers showed on the field. By controlling all, Krasnaya kept all bottomlined, and all citizens, if not happy, then quiet.

"A lovely night," said Skuratov, sliding on sanded ice underfoot. "The stars are so clearly seen in our hemisphere."

Sparrows flocked solid on pavement grates, warming chilled feathers. Red stars apexed Kremlin towers downstreet as they had for a century, everstable amidst the nine floodlit domes of Blagovashchenski Cathedral, the Telespire and the three-pronged unistructure blossoming above the Hotel Moskva. Nature gave Moscow little light overall; Krasnaya compensated. Red neon delineated each building's form along both sides of Gorki. Centerlaned were long-legged metal bugs on tiptoe, balancing upon their backs huge arc lamps similar to those we'd used in our camps, lamps so hot that birds flying into them vaporized. At every second corner a searchlight slashed the sky. Each building's facade shone with fluorescence and plasmalight and argon gas; holograms and vidscreens displayed vast quantities of purchasable stuff. Signs' light-formed slogans never reiterated pedantic messages or anti-American saws but sent forth instead the world's standard litany: *Drink Pepsi, Use Bulat, You Deserve, This Is It.* Some few phrases showed in no place other than Russia; *We Know,* said one, *But Tell Us.* One vast screen hid eight floors; bore nothing but a frozen headshot of the Big Boy, drawn oldstyle, so that he looked to sit not at the hand of God, but on it. The eyes didn't follow your progress, but if you were guilty—you always were—you thought that they did. The letterscroll continually running beneath read: POSTBIRTH-DAY MADNESS AT GRIGORENKO FURNITURE MART. The birthday was three months past.

"Stalin vsegda s nami," said Skuratov, looking upward, safe from the lure.

"Pardon?" Jake asked.

"He is always with us," he translated. "That is terrible difficulty with our new mutual friend." By his squints and winks I secured that, for the second, we might freespeak.

"Difficulty in what way?" I asked, my lips so stiffened by cold that their vague movement could show nothing.

"Krasnaya knows value of symbiosis. The Big Boy suits our purposes so long as his like never again arrives. But our friend is— current phrase? Retrovert. Unnatural love of the past. Commercial images seen as those of great beings, rather than of useful idiots."

"That problematicked?"

"Certainly. She believes he was—" Skuratov danced across possible phrases. "She digs him the most, we said as teenagers. I myself was great fan of Abba and of your own Dean Reed. Our policies work too well sometimes."

The Czara served as figurehead for imagined popular affection, but no one knew, or cared, how he, or she, manifested; every fool knew every pore on the Big Boy's face.

"*Watch!*" said Jake, drawing us close as a man passed full tilt downstreet, two others heeling close, bearing in. "Politicals?"

"Chuchmiki," said Skuratov. "Asian trash."

Moscow was no more dangerous than any American city. Between the restaurant and Marx Prospect we traveled six blocks, passing seven robberies, three assaults and something of gray nature, half spat and half rape. Unless political infractions evidenced, on uncontrolled streets all was watched and nothing stopped. Though their vehicles' sirens forever sent their synthetic pig's squeals across the dark, no police—not the General Militia, the Krasnaya Guard, the Consumer Patrol, the City Druzhinhas, the Okhranha, certainly never the Dream Team—interfered with hooligans' free enterprise. As in America, one of Russia's myriad charms was that you could be murdered without reason and not even God would notice, or care.

"We cross under here," said Skuratov, pausing before a stairway that led to a tunnel below-street. I considered situational inherencies. "We will miss terrible Marx Prospect traffic. Follow."

The tunnel's bone white walls seemed never to have suffered the human touch. Concealed vents at each end deflected the piercing wind rushing through from above; the tunnel light cowered along the ceiling's edge. At the halfway point someone marched down the cracked, stained steps we'd hoped to approach.

"Possible problem," said Skuratov. The one new-appeared wore checkered trousers, a cloth cap and a knee-length leatheresque coat, and looked to be of the southern mountains, perhaps from Armenia. At five meters distant he extracted a blue-metal long-barrel Omsk .44, a make availabled only through official channels. Most Russian guns reaching citizens' hands were poptoys, worthless even if usable, and illegal in any event. An Omsk could bring down a small plane.

"Public defender," said Skuratov, which was local slang for such a mugger. "This might be final moment, friends. Beg for mercy if you wish."

"Zdrastye," said the man, in shivering voice. "Such fine clothes. Shuck them, please." His Russian was inept; his wrists, where visible, were no larger than mailing tubes. "Off!" Skuratov slipped off his shuba, tossed down his astrakhan.

"Do as desired," said Skuratov, eyeing me with calm. "If we don't live it will not matter if we freeze."

"It will," said Jake, doffing his own, lighter coat, showing the white linen three-piece he wore yearround, standing in apprehensive reverence as if the national anthem rushed through his ears. Jake wasn't big, though he impressioned such; wasn't slow, though he moved so deliberately that he seemed forever to be gliding across gelatin; wasn't stupid, though until you believed you knew him you wouldn't have figured. He didn't seem dangerous at all.

"Uncoat! Please obey, please."

Our terrorist seemed unnerved and amateurish; any delay might suffice. "What gives, friend?" I asked, wording Turkish, a language unfamiliar to both Skuratov and Jake, but not, I hunched, to him.

"Asian brother," he replied, in like tongue. "I regret." Interesting; but before more might pass Jake raised his foot, kicking the pistol downtunnel. He shouted and brokeaway.

"Don't scream!!" yelled Jake, his voice ringing along the walls. To see his rolling flip was to watch an angel descend from heaven. Leaping up, Jake heeled him twixt the scapulae, felling him

timber-style. Jake booted him onto his back, then swung his fist
sharply against the Adam's apple. The fellow's limbs thrashed as if
on motor overload; spasms blurred his features. Close in, he
showed fewer than twenty years agrowing; reminded me of one of
my many lost sergeants. Jake kneeled over him as if to pray,
smoothing the boy's long hair away from his brow.

"Let's go," said Skuratov, recovering his hat and coat, managing
to appear both more and less bothered than I felt he should have
been. "You are as we hear, Jake. Come now. Babushki will sweep in
morning before commuters arrive. Don't delay." His voice
betrayed no unreasoned emotion.

"*Hold.*" Jake spun the retrieved pistol twice round his forefinger,
testing the balance.

"Leave him," said Skuratov. "He can consider the errors of his
life."

"Never need to suffer overlong," said Jake, unclicking the safety.
Pressing his thumb and his fingers against the boy's jaw, Jake
squeezed open his mouth, inserted the barrel. "Hurts?" he asked,
his voice soft, as if confessing to uncaring mother. "Here. Peace."

I shut my eyes; once retired it no longer necessitated that violence must be watched. Air's whuff sounded loud as shot's blast as
the boy's breath left his body. Maybe too many field trips left me
unwilling; maybe too many takeouts left Jake hungry for more.
When I reopened I saw him examining the lacy pattern of blood
beneath the boy's head, pondering the flowery petals of brain, as if
considering form and texture. Art knew its fashion, whatever the
season.

"So pretty," Jake whispered.

Less blood reddened Skuratov's face; he looked to have heard the
woodcock, in Russian phrase. Had he expected? To enter Russia
was to enter a world but roughly correspondent to the one known, a
world whose logic demanded that seeds would grow in sand, that
plants there grown would look right once paint made their colors
more natural. Had he expected? I decided not. There was no
greater reason for him to have served us so well over the years.
Subtlety was all; there was no subtlety in having us termed in that
tunnel.

"What'd he call you, Luther?" Jake asked, pocketing the Omsk for future frolic. Some mutterance sufficed his curiosity as we hoteled ourselves, taking leave of Skuratov until the next morn. Too rarely I'd had men such as Jake with me in combat—over Mexico, in New Guinea, along the coast of Turkey; Johnson was with me on Long Island's Martianed dunes, in the old days, and Johnson was the only one who neared Jake's level. Still, only with Jake siding me would I always have won.

2

JAKE SLEPT, LOOKING NO MORE HARMFUL THAN A BABY COBRA. That night I waited till he bedded safely before linking up the TVC's monitor and the telephone. Upon transmission override's directive the screen glowed skin white, a grateful relief. Our room's media—as in all Russian hotels, American owned or not—were adjusted, and could be ordinarily neither switched off nor turned down, so that advertisements might at least subliminally sink through the murk of travelers' brains. That the phone, too, was tapped made no difference. Inserting earphones, hooking my vocal scrambler to my collar, I ran the codes; tied into the New York mainframe to contact Alice, my company's computer. Unsullied info essentialled, and if Alice didn't have it, no one did.

"Alice," I said. "QL789851ATM. Safeguard. Closed channel sole. Audionse per basic." Ocean blue washed the white from the monitor's screen.

"All secured," she voiced across the waves. "I was concerned if you could transmit, Luther. Have you decided how I might be of help?"

"Info needed pertinent to Oktobriana Osipova. Target residence city Dubna. Present whereabouts unknown. Possibly Novy Marina Roshcha, street unknown. Krasnaya file 9320005441—"

"Hold."

Hearing an unexpected creak, I flattened against my chair's back, sealing my breath. Jake lay deathstill, his pocket-player's phones tightclamped, the old sound he adored massaging his mind. No lyrics shook their speakers but those of Robert Johnson, the blues singer of the century past. His words came as whispers through the muffle.

"I sent for my baby—and she don' come—"

There came no further creaks; the sound of the building aching as it aged, I decided, though the walls' wrinkles looked no deeper. The purr of cameras recording our lack of movement grew so familiar as that of a loving pet, so long as you removed yourself from lensview.

"Luther," said Alice after a five-minute absence, "Krasnaya's limitless files accessible only through local retrieval modes account for my delay. Please forgive."

"They'd roadblocked overmuch?"

"Using false headings, standard codes, the usual chicanery, they had buried her file quite deep."

"What's shown?"

"Oktobriana Dmitrievna Osipova received special tutorials at the Fourth School of Physics and Mathematics. While attending classes at Moscow State University, under Krasnaya supervision, she also took courses at Lumumba Institute, studying the use of scientific theory when applied to political objectives. A fruitful field, as we know—"

"No editorials, Alice."

"Her senior thesis on Lysenko was never published, having proved acceptable but inappropriate to Krasnaya objectives. Copies move through the samizdat matrix network to this day under pseudonymous listing. After she was graduated she was assigned to the Leningrad Selective Service Program, receiving doctorates in theoretical physics, environmental engineering and neurological bioadaptation."

"Bio," I repeated. "Learning to make pigs glow in the dark—"

"As her thesis in that particular field, she created the recombinant gene plasma that eliminates neurofibromatosis. In physics her

study on the military applications of Tesla coils remains
unpublished."

"What's a Tesla coil?"

"An air-core transformer with primary and secondary coils tuned
to resonate," she said. "Converts low-voltage high current into
high-voltage low current at high frequencies."

"English, Alice."

"They produce usable electricity and small ones are in common
use today though they were invented over a century ago. Their
inventor, Tesla, was brilliant but prone to develop theories years in
advance of possible application. One of his ideas concerned the use
of enormous coils harnessed to high towers so that through means
of resonation electrical power might be drawn not only from the
sky but from the earth itself, creating a source of perpetual energy
as well as a potential instrument of enormous nonnuclear destruction. I infer that she was working with that concept in particular."

"What else have you?"

"She holds six thousand hours in pilot time, is an accomplished
artist with a fine eye for perspective, performed gymnastics
throughout her teenage years. She received perfect scores in every
class at every school she attended, even when completed work was
denied acceptability. A unique accomplishment, it seems."

"Generate her picture, if possessed." An image rose from the
blue. Oktobriana Osipova stood in Red Square, in summertime,
judging from her lack of wrap; she showed as a very young woman.
Her dark hair was short in back, long in front. Her gymnast's
training evidenced in her overdeveloped shoulders, her muscular
thighs and her high, round buttocks. Scaling, I sized her to be no
taller than a meter and a half. "There're no shots more recent?"

"This is a near-contemporary," said Alice. "Taken two years ago
when she was twenty-one. Dependent upon date of testing her IQ
fixes between 253 and 280, Stanford-Binet, not to automatically
infer that such arbitrary scores are indicative of empirical intel-
ligence."

"We've no record of her in-house," I said. "Why isn't she riding
the whale with such abilities as possessed?"

"Prejudice," said Alice. "She is a woman, and Georgian as well.

More immediate to the situation is that her political opinions and Krasnaya's differ sharply in several areas, though not so much as to warrant exile or ultimate control. Following an unrecorded incident two years ago she was ordered to assist Doctor Alekhine and sent to Dubna. I infer that they more easily compromised their differences."

"What shows in regard to experiment records?"

"Nothing."

"They must exist."

"They did."

"What's meant?" I asked.

"Files pertinent to experiments during these two past years were entered in such a way that not even Krasnaya could uncover the information within."

"Impossible—"

"Obviously not. Through unknown methods secret entries were filed as required without standard dupes, using a remarkably complex encoding program. The code employed remade itself when outside penetration was attempted. I raped the system in one minute thirty-one and five forty-sevenths seconds, during which time the code adjusted to block intrusion one hundred and eight times. Upon final entry all records self-erased in accordance to program directives."

"All lost?"

"All," she said.

"One question further, Alice. The Dream Team's awared of our directives?"

"Of course," she said. "Continue as you have. The Dream Team is the most incompetent of all covert surveillance and corrective units."

"Closing time, Alice. Pass word topside."

"Luther," she added, "wait until airborne before renewing contact. Though words go unheard, they know a signal passes. Take care."

"Good night."

Her blue rinsed from the white; she was gone. In memory my ex-wife's voice sounded almost as Alice's, and the match would have

exacted had she had spirit like Alice's. Mayhap I was wrong; it
possibled that as time's lobotomy settled over years, that which
seemed most unexpectedly familiar became the recipient of all
long-bound pain. It was the hour's least attractive and most oft-
occurring thought, and as on every night I bade it leave my mind.
Once unlinking, feeling the usual sadness at taking leave of Alice,
I didn't bedaway immediate; I sat staring into the screen's milk,
attempting to hear the radio strains of *Gayaneh* over the toilet's
perpetual gurgledeglurp. When ease enough to allow sleep
returned to me, I bedded, settling into troubled sleep. Eyes over-
looked my dreams, eyes watchful, eyes alert; little-girl eyes,
dimmed by pain. From the sandy bloodred dune upon which I
stood, panting, catching breath, the sound of breakers scarring my
ears, Johnson rose, dragging me into his depths, where I so surely
belonged. I awoke, screamless. Jake, safely earphoned, slept on.

At morningside we attached scramblers previous to wording. At
check-in we'd bug-run, stopping the count at forty-seven within
the living room alone. If we'd searched and destroyed all, we
would still have been eared, through the radio, the phone, the
window, so long as our words rang free. With scramblers and
phones, we communicated sans worry.

"Seven-forty," said Jake, reading his watch, collapsing before the
TVC. As heard scrambled, his voice sounded as a tape rewound at
hypermode. "We've an eight-thirty set to toystore it?" I nodded.
"Why such earlybirding? Heavy action expected?"

"No," I said; he frowned. "Washes idle speculation. Recall that
as cover goes, we move toys. Just two businessmen keen to measure
product. That gives our check hours to clear."

"Transporting footways or on rubber?"

"I've called for a cab. Eight o'clock arrival."

"A cab sans media?" he asked. "The background racket gave me
splitters nightlong." The room's radio, by daytime, blared no clas-
sical, as I would have wished, only American apocalypso or Euro-
pean postwave redone *con tempo*. Over TV's air showed whatever
its wires sucked from the sky. Backgrounding us as we spoke was a
Leningrad exershow called *Jump, People!* Russian television, no

less enjoyable than America's, bore one demonstrable diff: those televised here were ugly, therefore close-to-real; people on American air always seemed alchemized from some unnatural clay.

"Alice's info enlightened as to whether this associate's worth the bullet?"

"She's the catch of the day," I said. "Good as Alekhine."

"Can't viz this fucker half a minute till the throb digs in," Jake said, eyeing the screen, rubbing his temples violently. I recognized his problem. Taking a hotel-provided blank, inslotting it, I taped a minute of air. Rewinding, I paused and pressed superslo playback. White blurs imaged midscreen. "What goes?" he asked. "Jam session?"

"Of sorts. Here's your pain's excuse."

Pressing freeze, I showed the words whole as they emerged, four frames per phrase, and translated. *"Go now and buy. Money is life—spend it. Thrifty are traitors.* They've run these onscreen yearslong. It must affect over time."

Jake shook his head as if to reattach his brain. "Where's our takeoff?"

"Near her living space."

"Which is where?"

"Maliuta knows the route."

"Him you trust?" Jake asked. "He's secured proper and tight?"

"One of few," I said. Under circumstance it was like trusting Jake; there was no choice if accomplishment was expected. "He delivered last year in Leningrad. Gave us our visit's reason this year."

We'd connected while crossing the bridge to Vasilovski Island. As we walked Skuratov had worded me of developments in areas long studied. Through the military Krasnaya funded projects studying potential application of parapsychological battle methodologies. To American eyes such implausibilities showed as corrupt idiocies befitting a spirit's world; compared, Freudianism seemed scientific. The dropping sun drew thin shadows over the river; he told of how, in the Dubna science colony north of Moscow, hard evidence had recently showed during experiments performed under Alexander Alekhine's guidance. Alekhine,

Russia's leading theoretical physicist, oversaw the Academy of Sciences. We had generated photos; knew he was four times a Hero of Socialist Labor, twice winner of the Lenin Prize. All else involving him was as fog. In that first success of which Skuratov spoke in such nonspecifics, what had manifested? The bending of forks? Control over the tumble of tossed dice? No one knew.

"I'm hunching there'll be no backtrack," I said. "Essential yourself."

"Essentialled," Jake said, slapping hands coatways, relishing his arsenal's embrace. He'd retained our attacker's Omsk as something more than a keepsake. "Suitcase me."

"Nonessentialled," I said, slipping on my own coat, heavy with minicam's weight. "Appear all as if we've stepped out for a breath. Lead to astray."

"Three linen whites I packed," he said, his face drawn.

"Wear what's worn. Come on."

The potential stupefied. If someone worked such ability into skill, he could, in time, properly trained, think tanks to a stop, dream planes out of the sky, wish that rockets would stray from their targets. Were an improper cue be then employed, the spin might purposely forever scratch the ball. What beasts resulted from domesticating wild talents? By Skuratov's word Krasnaya reactionaries wished to apply Alekhine's discoveries, whatever they were, to military purpose sole. We American optimists were awared that such blessings as scientists brought were most effectivized when deployed by the private sector, so that our world's delicate alignment might not be unduly tipped by governmental mischief. Only in recent quarters had the profit/loss forecast stuck when thrown; only during recent years did our economies boom again to levels where recovery for those still living seemed at last possible to consider straight-faced.

The hotel's elevator was broken; we crept down six darkened flights. From the lobby ceiling downstairs hung chandeliers, each bearing a dozen monitors showing unceasing vids of goods available in-hotel, at every shop from McDonald's to Smert'Muzham—the latter a women's store whose name, translated, meant Death to Husbands. The monitors never dimmed or blew.

"Traveling where for how long?" asked the hostess: as concierge, she lent help; as *dezhurnaya*, a licensed tattler, she eliminated hope. She fisheyed our entrycards, looking to see if we'd remagnetized them to untoward purpose. Upon approving us, she unsafed our passports and visas, handing them over, again lending our presence more weight than dust.

"To town. To shop," I said. Her smile stretched earways at the ring of that ultimate word, revealing a kilo of metal embedded in her mouth.

"Shopper's Line provides continuous helpful guidance," she said, patting her monitor, reading its announcements. "Excellent deals on jeans and samovaramats at GUM today during Noontime Madness Hour. Vibrant springwear on display at Zinoviev Fashion Mart off Mayakovsky Square. Sultry yes, shameless no—"

"We're taxied or no?" Jake asked, pushing forward, palming the desktop as if prepping to leap.

"Da. Returning when?" she asked, her smile but a memory.

"Uncertain," I said. "Business meets after."

For record's sake she entered my response into memory in case of belated inquiry. "Enjoy Moscow hospitality," she snorted, staring through us as if we were glass. The hotel guards, awared by Krasnaya of our Guests of State status, steered us past the metal detectors. We hit the street, inhaling pure, painful air. A pasteboard Big Boy directed Intourist groups away from the main entrance to the side, next to the disposal area. Ignoring the cold were sixty-odd vendors, ready and spreadwared, set for tourist reveille.

"There," I said, spotting our cab, a lipstick red Volga Supreme Wagoneer carrying as driver a stub ruffed headround with wiry hair and beard. Dashing rearward, he opened the tailgate.

"Interested?" he asked, attempting English. In his taxi's flatbed lay a bulky oak bureau swaddled in animal pelts, resembling a coffin built for six. As he slid hands across his furs, I noted several fingertips lacking. "Finest ermine and mink from my Kamchatka native home."

"Terrier and mastiff," said Jake, copping his own feel. "Roll us, hack. Blow."

"Best prices for British friends if you reconsider," he said, jerking about as if guided by strings, heaving himself wheelways while we boarded. His cab's interior called to mind an unlicensed souvenir stand at an unsuccessful resort. Glued to the dash were plastic icons, pipeholders and holographic badges. A green skeleton dangled from the rearview. Rubber hands affixed to the front seat's underside impressioned that deportniks desperate for breath were hauling themselves up through the oilpan.

"Ya Amerikanets," said Jake, unfortunately using one of his few accurate phrases.

"*Americans!*" the driver said, beaming, stunned by fortune. "See what I have wholesale for you experienced hard bargainers." From the glove compartment he slid velveteen-covered trays layered with paste jewelry. Jake, drawing his powerdrill, set the bit against our driver's cranium, fingers itching to trigger. "Toystore me," he said, so softly I barely heard. The hack heard; lipshut and floored. We bug-ran before reaching the first stoplight, discovering multiple infestation as expected. Wiping mist from my window I eyed a black Marx DeVille pacing us.

"Travel buddies," I said to Jake as I waved their way. They waved in return. Another carload drew up, keeping several carlengths rearward. "They trail all but the chaperoned," I explained; Jake gave them a moment's attention. "They'll drop once our stability's proved."

"Will it be?"

On rightward, a third black Marx came along. All, undoubted, tuned in to hear our confessions. Desuspicioning, I noted local glories; Jake yawned. The sun, a pink ball skulking along the horizon, threw faint heat and little light. St. Basil's multihued domes, brushed clean of snow, radiated morning's lavender hues. Edging Red Square and the Kremlin's inquisitional walls and steeples we saw the touristline awaiting their moment in Lenin's box, his tomb dyed in dried blood's color in this season's light. At distance, Moscow attracted; close in the city forever bore the look of a sixth-generation dupe: details fuzzed, colors weren't true, images bled at the borders. In the middle distance, wedding-cake skyscrapers from the Big Boy's day screwed heaven while awaiting some long-delayed celebration. We reached the store. I slapped our furrier a fiver.

"They even ad the green?" Jake asked, examining a ten-ruble while I took my change. Debilling him, I perused the ornate designs wreathing Akhmatova's debeaked profile.

"Coins, too," I said. "Stamps, stocks and bonds." The ten-ruble's message was *Hoarders Bleed Our Nation*. Small-print credit thanked the unequaled Zolotskova shopping mall. Our cab sped away, seeking fresh capital. Jake snapped back his money.

"We're going shopping or rioting?" he asked, looking storeways. Hordes massed behind heavy metal barriers topped with high sharp spikes. Adults lifted babies above the crush as the mob awaited their cue to rage and plunder. Elderlies swatted unpeopled pavement with birch brooms, sweeping sparrows from the grates. We tossed time glancing nearby newsstand's wares. Stacked alongside *Pravda* and *Izvestia* were Russian mags, bright with untrue color, pulp laden with chemical scent. There too reposed American mags no less reliable than Russian journals and so Krasnaya censored nothing but their ads, keeping expectations no higher than ordained to rise. The store's siren roared as if to beckon firestorm; we filtered through the crowd, trailed by our newest fans.

"Where's the meet and greet?" asked Jake.

"Interactive Strategies department," I said. "Level two."

Russia loved the children it didn't have to kill. Detsky Mir sold as Russian the toys of every nation; the ones homegrown evidenced by their tendency to break beneath the weight of dust settling upon them. The ancient interior, transplanted with fresh organs as fashion demanded, resembled the post office's central auctionhouse. Upholstered mothers, toddlers bundled into immobility, men of disconcerted mien and ill-tempered babushki shuffled like lost ghosts through the aisles. One wizened hag, eyeing Jake's bare head and slick hair, shouted: "*Shapkoo propil!*" Before he made his grab I grasped his arm, guiding it to his side as I would a cannon.

"Her attitude shows plain," he said, his face purpling. "Translate her slur."

"Ignore, Jake," I said. "She said you must have wasted so much money you can't afford a hat."

"Nosetroubler." As he spoke, he fumbled a coin between thumb and finger; bent it double, flattening it as his color drained. "These stragglers close in. Should I react?" Those trailing showed through the crowd so plain they might have been spotlit. From the ceiling above cameras focused, keeping angels' eyes on us.

"Ignore," I repeated. All escalators to level one were broken and so we climbed. Summiting, Jake looked, and let free, unexpected laughter burst loose.

"No wonder you're so eyed by all locals," he remarked. A carmine scroll draped overhead announced HAPPY GOLLIWOGS ARE HERE. Displayers held a regiment of dolls shaped in the form of squat black women, staring with leering eyes, grinning with lips like Brazil nuts. "Heavy sellers, you'd guess?" Jake asked.

"They talk," I said, reading a less prominent descriptive. Lifting one of the clammy little things I activated the cassette housed within. "Eat your veget—" it began, in Russian; the tape jammed. Coils oozed from the doll's mouth as if it vomited forth its intestines. I repiled it quick. The escalator to level two worked for a minute, then broke; our pursuers huffed casually behind us.

"Aisle E. Over here."

The Interactive Strategies department's goods could have kept the Red Army supplied for centuries had they worked so well as their models; as was, they gave the young ones opportunity to practice until their draft day. Toy guns of every caliber, from peashooters to those that might splatter elephants' heads, glistened beneath glass. All required easily obtained Krasnaya permits for toy gun purchase; then, were the possessor to suffer mistaken identity situation, the police might be secure in knowing that such had occurred through victim's choice.

"Alert yourself," said Jake; likely suspects browsed every side, crowded every aisle. The worst places were those where the children might offer so much danger as the adults. I spotted Skuratov striding towards us, his twohue shoes bright against the colorless floor.

"Gentlemen," he said, wrapping round me like an anaconda. Jake distanced, loath to know the human touch. "Forgive my lateness."

"No need to forgive," I said, loudspeaking to allay cats' curiosity. "We were perusing these marvelous toys."

Skuratov smiled; palmed a miniature half-track from a nearby rack, rolled it across his coatsleeve. The wheels fell off.

"Shouldn't we head?" I asked. Jake, on point, circled round on his heels as if to measure the room's footage. A well-bundled father dragged a swaddled lump towards the cashier desk nearest; the child pleaded for goods denied. Skuratov pressed fingers to lips.

"There is no hurry," he said, meaning there was, and by his inaction demonstrating that the sooner could not be bettered. Several newcomers appeared some distance down, sauntering with flamboyant disinterest, each garbed in basic black, which, by rumor heard, was Dream Team's choice. Our prospects seemed evermore evanescent.

"Eyes alight," Jake murmured. The father haggled details with the cashier; as each computer transaction was required in retail to be doublechecked by abacus, a certain confusion always resulted during the delay. Our voyeurs shelved toys recently fumbled, slowly starting in, holding respectable distance still. "They're readying."

"Certain product is quite impressive," Skuratov said, gesturing towards a wallcased rack as if to sell me. "Miss," he said to a clerk scuttling near, holding up his Krasnaya ID so as to be seen, "pass over Turgenev item there for my examination." Unlocking the case, she handed it across; a half-scale dupe of the Turgenev B95 rocket launcher. "Made for us in Yugoslavia from lightweight polymer. Fires genuine explosive shell. No more harmful than cap pistol, certainly—"

"My *change*," said the father. "Give to me." The overhead whirr's tone descended a half note in the scale; I looked upward.

"I have no coins," said the cashier. "Why do you harass me so?" All ceiling cameras rotated, focusing our way. Our troupe moved in for the finale.

"Thirty kopecks," the father shouted. Other customers—there were many—grew testy. The man's toddler, recovering from his mourn, bored by his father's pleas, looked at us. Skuratov, the plastic armament nestled in his arms, smiled at the child.

"No coins," the cashier screamed in reply. "Take delicious candy bar I offer you as suitable change equivalent." Jake unclicked something within his coat's cover. My stomach dropped as I felt the nausea of the about-to-be caught. "Be happy, citizen."

"Small boy," Skuratov said, grinning, bending down, handing the boy the toy. "Aim that way away from people like brave army man. Press trigger underneath for big fun."

"Da," the gleeful tot rumbled, needing no further prod. Laying paws on tight, he fired with sharpshooter touch. The faux-Turgenev's sun yellow projectile shot across the floor, with deafening boom shattering a carefully stacked pyramid of plastic grenades molded from sky blue resin. Tumbling floorways they flashed and banged and threw smokeclouds of evil scent. The father struck the boy; the cashier struck the father for having struck.

"Shall we move briskly to down elevator?" Skuratov said, linking arms with us, leading us from the smoggy melee. "I am conveniently parked outside in free zone. Let us attend important meeting."

Untrailed by any, we heaved our way through the crowd. The cries of mothers, the shouted threats of the store's in-house police and the yaps of a thousand children drowned the icerink music playing over the store's hundred hidden speakers.

"They fold so easily," I remarked as we twisted through the exit doors.

"True," Skuratov sighed. "Dream Team always formulate perfectly conceived program of action. Slightest unforeseen circumstance leaves them groping to find their own backsides. They are never trained in spontaneity, for security reasons. Here is my fine machine."

Skuratov's car was a navy Mercedes with black mirrored windows. He opened the trunk, retrieving the detachables: wipers, hubcaps, the hood ornament, the sideviewers and the aerial, all favored barterables on the Black Market. We climbed in as he reattached all. Jake settled into the back seat. It took Skuratov one or two minutes to close the trunklid, I noticed; a frozen lock, mayhap, or a need to reshuffle still-trunked accessories. As we bug-ran he climbed in; our sensors showed no ears within, and at last we were almost secure.

"Impressive, Mal," I said. "How'd you obtain?"

"Suitable reward for many good works," he said. "Note hand-worked details and stylish instrument panel design. Gently rub butter-soft leather upholstery." The car's skin was filthy, but every Russian car needed a scrub. For its two million autos Moscow was provisioned by Krasnaya with ten carwashes. "Leave windows slightly open, please, to disrupt easily read glass vibrations. Engine, drive us to destination one."

"Done," replied the dash's voice; the motor ignited and revved. Skuratov took hold of the wheel and we entered traffic, passing red streetcars rolling down the side lanes.

"What's the ETA?" I asked.

"Half hour. You are familiar with our friend's neighborhood?" he asked as we rolled down the Sedovoye Koltes, or Garden Ring, which supported fourteen lanes of fullbumper traffic. Glasseyed towers lined the road, some nothing but Potemkin facades cloaking defensive missile-launching sites.

"No," I said.

"Novy Marina Roshcha is a trushchoba," Skuratov continued. "Slum of most terrible kind. Their look is quite American. Krasnaya reactionaries have long insisted that their existence is necessary evil, so that nonconsumers and ex-soldiers with problems adapting to nonarmy life might be suitably housed. Social order is thus preserved by keeping together all bad people holding much hurtful resentment. Many carry dangerous contagion. Be careful the podonki do not touch you after we leave car."

"Podonki?" Jake inquired, wiring his ears to his pocket-player's phones; the long thin yellow cords impressioned that he was being intravenously fed.

"Scum," Skuratov translated. "That is official term only, meaning no disrespect."

"Why would she hide in such a place?" I asked.

"Is self-evident. From such slums individuals come and go as pleased," he said. "Choice places for those unwilling to perform responsibilities. Favorite hideouts as well for vicious criminal element. Provides area from which suspects may always be plucked. Krasnaya lives with drawbacks."

"Do many scientists fall into criminal element's heading?" I asked.

"Depends on their science," he said, smiling. "Miss Osipova takes chance of losing life, living among uncivilized trash, but is chance she evidently wishes to take—"

"Where's her choice?"

"With Alekhine," he laughed. "No matter. Her new residence will be free from fear of random hooliganism." He pressed on the radio; the scherzo from Shostakovich's Tenth played. Only a few bars passed before he switched to a station playing songs rich with twang and blurp.

"We've addressed her precisely?"

"Her street is Raisa Row. With handy implement of mine we locate with ease exact address." From underdash he extracted two thin barlike devices no larger than TV remotes; he handed one to me. A liqrystal screen made up all of one side; on the other were a number of minute buttons and unlit lights.

"Only the Dream Team has trackers so advanced," I said, examining his face for reaction, but none showed. Our side had obtained one, by accident, only months before, but I'd had no opportunity to employ it. "How's it work?"

"One of my many confidential sources was very accomplished," he said. "Turn it on with red switch. Then touch button marked M."

Moscow's street grid imaged on the screen; innumerable glowing dots winked in unpatterned formation, each white but for a single blue spot.

"Blue one is myself. Press V, which is tuned to her coordinates." As I did, only two dots remained, his and hers. A light flashed green. "That signals her continued viability."

"She's implanted?"

We pulled from the Ring onto Gorgoko. "Certainly. Standard microtransmitter in thick muscle at back of neck, inserted without pain or knowledge. Transmits thereafter over two-hundred-kilometer range. The Dream Team always knows where to send party invitations. Keep that one, please. Within one hundred meters beeping will begin. We will close in."

It long puzzled certain of those in our organization why Skuratov, suffering from no political disaffiliation, unneedful of clandestine finance, should have chosen treason as his hobby, but nothing suspicious ever showed; his files, triplechecked twice, even cleared Alice's approval. Political motivations are no more explicable than sexual fetishes, and not nearly so employable in quotidian life; thus my mind remained untroubled by idle speculation. Skuratov, eyeing the rearview, noticed Jake sunk seatways, lost in his tunes.

"Jake is great music lover?"

"Some music," I said. "Mostly the blues."

Jake's tape bore no music other than that of Robert Johnson, by historical agreement the past century's greatest blues singer. A single photo remained to give his voice form. Murdered before he was thirty, he left but forty-odd songs recorded under the most primitive conditions; Jake knew each by heart. So many Caucasians enjoy the blues, even when they'd have trod across the blues singer were he lying cold before them in the street. Jake knew a more elemental kinship whose nature remained a mystery to me; I could only infer that whenever he felt himself touched by unearned peace he would dive beneath phones to scar himself anew with long-lost sound. Mister O'Malley mentioned occasions when Jake picked up an old guitar in his office and strummed chords as if to play, but I could never viz it. In Jake's hands musical instruments seemed correct only if he might use them to transpose others into death's chorale.

"How much info of results exists?" I asked. "There's no weapons potential seen?"

"Not as such. Their findings appear to involve nonaggressive device of unspecified purpose."

We entered neighborhoods built up with workers' palaces: uniform rows of concrete shoeboxes dropped down in sidewalked morasses. In front of each complex-unit stood sculptures recognizing the abilities of those who designed and developed; those not graffitied were usually decapped. Beneath the modern overgrowth showed old Russia's spoor: huddled wooden houses top-heavy with intricately carved gables and eaves, Orthodox churches bearing five crumbling domes, sprays of birch and evergreen sprouting amidst the billboards. Jake began vocalizing along with Johnson's tunes as they flowed from player to ear.

"*Gonna get deep down in this connection—keep on tangling with your wires—*"

To hear Jake sing ached bones and cooled blood; his warble held neither tune nor tone.

"*—when I mash down on your little starter your spark gonna give me fire—*"

"What use has a nonaggressive," I asked, "considering what Krasnaya must have intended?"

"Enormous use depending on nature of nonaggressive," said Skuratov. "Alekhine tested and developed as he saw fit. Basic essentials of prime discovery were known but to evershrinking circle as success approached. Every time Krasnaya inquired he made general remarks, refrained from telling specifics, at all stages promised complete report upon project's finish. Three weeks ago, he disappears. We find out three days ago that Miss Osipova prepared her own departure."

"Why weren't we advanced?"

"Makes no difference from whom information is obtained, correct?"

"Alekhine was surely implanted," I said; Skuratov nodded. "So where has he gone? Where's he showing?"

"He isn't showing," said Skuratov. "Our friend is nowhere found."

"In Russia?"

"In world. We have thorough coverage in all locales, as you know. Nowhere do we find evidence of his presence. Alekhine's implant is like mine, in brain instead of neck, and impossible to remove without—" He paused. "Terrible mess. Either he has discovered way to jam signal, which no one else has ever done, or he has gone somewhere beyond our range, which is to say, no place."

"Inferences must have been possible," I said. "What lines were followed?"

"From Dream Team reports we ascertain that device as perfected must involve paraphysics rather than parapsychologics."

"What's meant?"

"After long years of study we find no truth in so-called parapsychologics in traditional sense. Forecasting future, calling up spirit of dead mother, reading thoughts of strangers; such foolish things are as dreams. Minds are thick as Kremlin walls unless Dream Team methods are employed, and then only generalities may be inferred. Employing such methods we know that paraphysics are involved, that major experiment succeeded. Otherwise, no more."

Dream Team methods involved modified implants, so that those so adapted might not only be at all times located but, in some as-yet-obsure way, have thoughts' track mapped without derailing the train. "What falls under paraphysics' heading?"

"Inexpressibles," he said as we entered a bleak avenue carrying four rutted, scarred lanes. Putty-colored ten-story towers were stuck like arrows along each side. Cars' shells lined curbs, covered sidewalks, piled high upon yards as if left by guests at a technological clambake. Rats raced streetways, daring us to strike. "Poltergeists and telekinetic effects. Sonar showing large animals in lakes where limited food supply prohibits such from existing. Wild cougars in London suburbs where no one has lost cougar, and grown alligators in Canadian ponds in dead of winter. Why frogs fall from cloud-free sky." He pressed a button, shifting to slower drive as we rounded a turn. "Plane crashes and little girl's body found, unburned; no little girl on board or on ground reported. A silver coin in a chunk of granite. The look of a sinner on the face of a saint. Growth of hair on a mummy's head." He flashed his steel. "Why one sock of pair always vanishes in dryer."

"What's meant by transferral device?" I asked. "Transferral where?"

"Over rainbow, perhaps," he said, his eyes glistening, as if flash-frozen. "Soon we discover. Novy Marina Roshcha, gentlemen."

Eight-wheel crowd compromisers, steel skins gleaming, guns and gas jets shining, guarded each end of a twenty-man soldierline blockading the avenue. On either side of their wall, the worlds appeared similar in look. The formation broke to allow our passage; none cared that we didn't slow, none halted us to check ID, none questioned our intent or purpose or plan.

"Residents come and go freely, you said," I reminded Skuratov. "Hasn't the army more immediate situations?"

"Individuals come and go free, I said. Army is here to prevent attempts at simultaneous escape of many. Krasnaya prefers to certify safety of even these citizens, for great loss of life would be unavoidable if such problematic situation occurred."

"Krasnaya prefers this?" I asked, seeing Russians of decidedly unpropagandistic value.

"As also mentioned, Luther," he said. "Not everyone prefers fitting into fine-running system just as not everyone rises to appropriate level during lifetime. These neighborhoods offer suitable surroundings for—how is it put—"

"Casualties of the system," I said. Their great-grandparents suffered under the nobles, their grandparents under the Big Boy, their parents under the nomenklatura and so they suffered under the supervision of the great Krasnaya multinationale. Inheritance they provided forever grew, no matter who borrowed against the trust.

"They prefer to live in such way, after all," he said. "It is hard to remember at times." The street sparkled with broken glass as if diamond paved. Cardboard blocked wind blowing through broken windows; newsprint curtained those yet unshattered. Dunes accumulated at building corners where concrete devolved into sand. There'd once been trees; rotting stumps remained, the rest recycled into cold night's fuel. We rolled downstreet sans sound within or without, past residents' dead stares. Children at play scrambled over those rust red cars, yanked rodents' tails to hear the squeak; women indistinguishable from potato sacks squatted beside building entrances. Groups of men huddled over trash fires. All but the children were drunk. Russians, no matter the prohibitions, drank alcohol as they breathed air. As those of Skuratov's class guzzed beverages suited to their status, so these citizens surely poured down their raw throats formaldehyde, eau de cologne, varnish and liquid heat. Jake slipped his phones from his head, his attention seized. I supposed that he suddenly felt more at home.

"How close?"

"We are on Raisa now," said Skuratov, eyeing his own tracker, "and she is but a short ways further." The beep began, a steady pulse. Jake readied. Between two eight-story hulks I robbed a glimpse of the center's faraway spires and pastel domes, hazed soft in morningshade.

"Locals' interaction expected?" Jake asked.

"None should harangue," said Skuratov. "Fine car such as mine can belong only to high Krasnaya member, or so they will fear. Therefore they understand not to give hands-on treatment in untoward manner." From undercoat he drew a slim black Shrogin machine pistol, an item impossible to procure at any level. "But if podonki approach my crowdtickler will hush them. Jake, be fully prepared. These people very temperamental around those they unavoidably see as their betters."

Raisa Row's two-story structures held separate entrances for each flat. Littered mud served as yard, parking lot and playground. "Destination reached," said the car; he cut the motor. People faded into the buildings' dark. Skuratov's fears, as suspected, overblew; I'd sized all surrounding as too nubworn to offer threat.

"She is on ground floor rear of right-hand unit. Proceed without rush around side yard. Keep weapons always visible. Pause at corner to await signal. Once signaled, approach door. Wait. Count three." He unclicked his gun's safety. "Hop in, showing big smiles."

When we decarred we were all nearly muckered flat by the smell, an inescapable blend of bathroom and grave that not even frozen air subdued. The locals, eyeing our ordnance, scattered like roaches in sudden light. Skuratov led, moving as if twotoned feet barely scraped the ground. Midway across I stepped wrong, squashing a teddy bear lying unburied amidst debris. The neighborhood children were rich with imagination beyond their years; the bear's eye sockets stared blindly towards the sky, its tummy was slashed open and degutted in amateur's autopsy. America's touch showed in every land.

"Her windows," Skuratov whispered, motioning at cornerside to a pair of draped eyes. Gray clouds drew across the sky as a front neared; we threw no shadows over the terrain. He pointed us ahead, and we edged over, skirting the building's wall, Jake now heading our line.

"One," Skuratov murmured, "two—"

Before the last number came, before my next breath passed, I noticed the door's ajarness as a scream rang within. Jake—no bullet flew faster.

3

"CAREFUL," I SAID, AS IF TO OFFER ADVICE, BUT JAKE WAS DONE before we'd crossed the threshold. Skuratov bore the vision better than I'd have guessed, seeing Jake slash away, tearing the man's flesh as his burlap and polymer clothes were already torn; Jake doublelooped his chain within his hand to attain double result.

"*Jake!*" I said. "Enough's enough. Step away."

Airborne, he came down heels-first upon the interloper's head, completing his task; stepping off of his leavings, he began his descent into calm. I sensed adrenaline's vibrations pulsing through his slim frame. Sucking down a long breath, he stood silent, letting temper fade, shaking his head as if awakening and still finding himself within his dream. His voice returned before he did.

"Women's rapists try all patience, Luther. Forgive overzealotry."

"Was robber," she said; whipping round, she fisted him true at mouthcorner. "Not rapist. I handle you as well."

Red constellations spotted Jake's pure white; small, but compact, she slung mean. My mind blanked with instinct; vizzing our objective slipping through our grasp through in-house action, once Jake's temper reseized, I threw myself between them before he might respond.

"No, Jake, calm—!" Heaving me floorways, sidestepping, he seized her, yanking her close, pressing her against him. As he

41

unclasped, she spat. Ineffable peace lit his wet face from within, and as he closed his eyes, he smiled, his face reddening beneath its glisten. Ungatherable Georgian obscenities fluttered from her mouth like bats from a cave in the night. Jake rounded her armways, holding fast. Skuratov stared on, as if watching a gameshow.

"Priyatno. English, please, Miss Osipova," he cheerfully said, wiping shoes free of the mess with which they had been splattered. "American friends possess little fluency in such vernacular."

"*Chort!*" She banged feet against Jake's knees; he took her upward, ungrounding her.

"Ah," said Skuratov, paying respect to Jake's takeaway. "The boy next door."

"Rip him raw," Jake said, bloodfuried anew.

"You did, Jake," I said. "Possibly he's not so local, Mal. Krasnaya running deep water, or worse."

"I'll examine," said Skuratov, dropping to his knees, drawing away the fellow's shirt to onceover the left arm's underskin. Evidence received awarded that Dream Team members wore tattoos; images of a softedged cloud overlain with an everstaring eye.

"What is wanted?" she screamed, serving English laced with heavy accent's spice. "Go begone."

"Be peaceful during playtime," said Skuratov, not looking up. "*Zhrini sapozhnik!*"

"Are sedatives wished?" Jake asked; she caught his nose with the back of her skull, but he still smiled, and stroked her waist as he gripped her. While Skuratov pawed the lost one's belongings, I bug-ran; nothing showed.

"Nullified the first morning here," she said, seeing my actions. "Americans expect constant stupidity from Russians?"

"Friend of deceased?" asked Skuratov.

"When soot is white." Driving elbows into Jake's sides, loosening his hold; pitching forward, she butted me chestways with enormous force, employing those powerful legs and shoulders, staggering me. Jake, wrenching her arms behind her back, applied the cuffs he carried. "*Ai, bolit!*" she screamed as he drew his bracelets tight against her wrists. He clasped her once more, focusing eyes on hers; as if reacting as bird to snake, she settled at once. My heart's normal rhythm recovered from its forced solo.

"Pacify or we'll ride rougher roads," he said. "Sorry but true."

"Luther," said Skuratov, his mood unchanged, as if nothing more had occurred around him than a change of weather. "As judged. Identifications prove him to be ex-army. Lives—lived, to be most accurate—three buildings down. A local alone. A zhid, undoubted, judging from patronym. No surprise."

"Unmarked even in protective mode?" I asked. "Not Dream Team?"

"Freebooter," he said. "Nothing more."

"Why do you khulighani bother me?" Oktobriana asked, her face's excess color draining. She looked so young but for her slight-slanted eyes; wrinkled bags dropped below her lower lids, weighed her uppers down. "I am facilitator. I don't retain substance."

"Does snow retain water?" asked Skuratov. "You are great with substance."

"There is nothing I can do for you. Please leave me. I wish aloneness."

"We wish good company. Sound of voice holds ring of truth. But let us see for sure." He depocketed a small red box; on its surface was a smaller screen. As he shoved it against her cheek lights flashed; she cringed, as if its touch burned. "Stress analyzer sees truth when it creeps out. Let us have useful conversation without tiring repetition or undeliverable threat. Something of interest is here, true?"

"No." She shivered whenever he pressed his box against her; Jake looked on him deadeyed but kept her still, aware of his job description's duties whatever his inner preference.

"Yes. Useful tool developed by trusted mentor Alekhine, correct? Resembles videocassette of unnatural make, I believe."

"*Vranyo*. Lies and rubbish."

"Quite unlikely. What have we brought with us in rubbish lying about room? Shall we see?"

"Don't burrow through my soul," she pleaded as he pocketed the analyzer—a small red dot remained on her face—and began his search, drawing out dresser drawers, tossing clothes floorways, sending her life ascatter. "What brings you here to plunder?" she asked, still fighting Jake's embrace.

"To help you," I said.

"*Gospodi*. Americans always claim to help when they come to steal and kill."

Oktobriana's miserable room was contained by four gray walls, pierced by two doors, one leading out, one leading to the attached bath, and held two broken windows insulated with gum and cloth. Floorboards seesawed skyward when one's ankle hit the wrong spot. The decorator's hand showed only in the Big Boy's portrait hanging above the bed's dough-thin mattress, an oldstyle print from the period proper, done while he lived, demonstrating his form as he wished to be shown. In the rendering he stood erect in worker's cap and army greatcoat, on bare promontory, storm-racked heaven backdropping full. Lightning raked all but his watchpoint. With fixed eye he considered the plain beneath his mountain, the great city rising upon the veldt below: Lucifer regarding his kingdom, Kong appraising his jungle. In his own years the Big Boy had sold nothing but himself.

"Who awared you of form and substance?" I asked Skuratov as he busied himself. His lips kept still, as if inferring protection of ones highly placed. Reaching underbed, he extracted a hard cloth-wrapped lump.

"What have we here?" he said.

"*Dlya zhizvi!*" she screamed, thrashing against Jake as if to set him ablaze.

"Life threatening?" Skuratov repeated. "Hush, little loud one. Nerves strung tight like violin strings. Let me wander without guidedog."

Skinning a pillowcase bound tight round a black plastipak, he pried its lid open, revealing what at immediate viz showed as a vid therein nestled. Uncasing, in full light he flashed its lapis lazuli color, its featureless face.

"Too heavy for usual dupe of classic film, I believe. Perhaps useful just the same for—timeshifting, should we say," he said, palming it as if judging produce. "The Alekhine machine, friends. Many brains at play make marvelous item. Operates on same principle as model, true? Slide into appropriate slot, press appropriate button. Behold wonder."

"Button and slot of what?" I asked, expecting the answer given, to this day disbelieving.

"Of average home TVC unit," he said. "Imaginative recycling of existent technology."

"And what happens upon use?" She gave no response. That this dull plastic slab proved to be the object of our search was so anticlimactic as climbing Everest to buy a cheese sandwich. Presenting findings to the board would be easy, but Mister O'Malley wished hard result; wouldn't be pleased otherwise. Reflecting a moment on the thing's subtle guise, Skuratov recased it, rewrapping the pillowcase.

"Quick movement now is of utmost importance," he said. "Pack her belongings, Luther. We must not linger." Into her suitcases, without search or seizure, I tossed her clothes, her pens and books, her picture of the Big Boy, such papers as lay scattered free. She stood unmoving, watching our rush; unshaking, unspeaking, almost as if she'd hypnotized herself into acceptance so as to ease her kidnappers. Perhaps Jake's presence lent moment's peace, for he held her as friend, not prisoner—the cuffs notwithstanding—his grip all-enfolding, his face's sudden color appearing to make him, almost, warm.

"We're airport-near, then?" I asked, pounding the cases shut.

"Airstrip," he corrected. "Is on my dacha. Twenty minutes from here normal speed. We should make in ten." Holding the cassette box underarm, onehanding his Shrogin, he glanced the room over to see if anything missed firsttime showed at second look.

"Your estate's airstripped?"

"Convenient small one for vertical-ascent craft."

"Plane's readied?"

"Destination programmed as desired."

"Pilot's secure?" asked Jake.

"Pilot you see before you." His question hung, unanswered. Oktobriana gave sudden word, as if waking from coma.

"Where are we going?" she asked, staring up at Jake with eyes great with fear, eyes alit by oncoming headlight's glare.

"On lovely vacation," said Skuratov.

"To America," said Jake. "New world life awaits."

"Jake," said Skuratov, not looking at him direct, "put suitcases in trunk. We shall follow."

Jake's paranoia ran deeper than mine but usually for greater reason; he trusted its touch, like a caress from a perfect lover. Unnoticed by the others I vizzed his eyes tighten. If Jake readied, I knew I should as well; in such event, I followed his lead as I followed any commander.

"Porter's life isn't mine," he replied.

"Forgive sharp method of asking, Jake. The language is full of pitfalls."

"Key me," said Jake, retaining grip on Oktobriana.

"Trunk is unlocked. Is simple to open."

"Why don't you lend hand?"

"Purpose of my delay is quite reasonable," he said, turning towards the bath. "Before leaving I must walk hand in hand with Stalin. Luther, keep strong hold on small friend in Jake's absence."

Jake, winking my way, passed Oktobriana to me, hoisted the cases and slipped through the front door as Skuratov opened the bath's, pulling it shut after. Holding her I felt no struggle, which worried. In times past, during prisoner retrieval, there always came a moment early on when one or two would, without warning, tumble earthward, pulses stilled, dropping down dead as if their unwillingness to be held so strengthened that they drove away their souls, dying by will, sans symptom, sans blow, sans threat. That often occurred on Long Island, during those long campaigns. Oktobriana's seeming peace, so expected and so unnatural, wondered me if, consciously or not, she prepped to do just that.

"Mal," I shouted, growing anxious; Jake's odd behavior hadn't helped. "Hurry and exit soon—"

In the outer world something blew; someone with it, undoubted, at first listen. My stomach felt as if it were trying to claw free of my flesh. I rounded for the front door; Skuratov stepped into view again, his Shrogin leveled. As I fingered the doorknob, he spoke.

"Such a rush," he said; my spine went rigid. "Concern is hereafter unwarranted. Our flight will be smooth and uninterrupted."

"Slavic humor, Mal?" I asked, straight-faced. Drawing my hand from the doorknob I pocketed it, involuntarily reaching for the gun that we both knew wasn't there. "There was a noise outside."

"Is on occasion necessary to be more Russian than Russian to enjoy things Western," he said. "Mercedes, for example. Exceptional automobile. German executives are so often lost that bombproof trunk on finest models is standard accessory. Bomb explodes, leaving irreplaceable corporate valuables unharmed so long as they are in trunk. Conversely, small bomb may explode within trunk, leaving excellent machine unharmed. Harm results only to hooligan opening trunk."

Jake would have known, I knew; had seen, did know.

"Dream Team employs no wasteful folk. We prefer contacts warm and breathing without question. Rare people such as Jake are so adept and so unpredictable, however, that only one option is available when longterm schedule is considered. Your people's loss is so great in this circumstance that I should later submit to Krasnaya letter nominating him to receive honorary Hero of Labor award posthumously, perhaps making amends."

"Questions'll rise with my loss, Mal," I said. "Business hostaging is forbidden—"

"As is capture of scientists," he laughed. "Is full accounting necessary? We know of your organization's troubles. Those petty backbitings and dark conspiracies. You should employ Kremlinologists to observe such Byzantine struggles. As with all complexities, a simple lie suffices. Under tragic circumstance each of you suspected other of danger and took action accordingly. Possibly to make story sit better I should obtain honorary award for you, too, Luther. So. Condolences go out, your people briefly note and as soon forget. No room for sentiment in American business, true? Of course."

"I'll be missed—"

"And mourned for proper period. Then your name will go on small plaque in lobby. Meanwhile we obtain valuable scientist of our own country and at last possess gifted American equally expert in business and war. Two-for-one deal, true? Dream Team, like everyone, is always on lookout for bargains."

His estimation of response was accurate. Twice before we'd lost Russian contacts, one homegrown, one lured later. Both times it was as if they'd suddenly slipped into nonexistence, leaving neither clue nor trail. Both times the reaction in the main office was that a hostage liabilitied, and therefore cut losses healed all the more quickly.

"Little one, will you at last tell us what your great discovery is? Alekhine was so careless in preparing reports."

"You'll hear nothing from me," she said, standing at my side, aiming her look towards his feet; facing him eyesdown, as if pretending reverence. At any second, I knew, Jake would show.

"That is not strictly correct," he said. "Later we have much time for stimulating conversation among friends. Discuss rumors and puzzles we hear. Inescapable rumor that Alekhine machine is time-travel device. Impossible, without question, yet this is what we hear."

"Time travel completely impossible," she said. "Rules of causality cannot be broken."

"So we hear. But what marvelous uses such could serve for mankind. Go back into time, kill Hitler at birth, let Spanish Armada win, prevent Rome's fall."

"Mischief making at best," she said. "Means of ultimate destruction at worst. But such is not and cannot be possible."

"Go forward in time to see how glorious the future shall be." His smile disappeared beneath lips' blankets. "How miserable. There remains question, then, of where Doctor Alekhine has gone."

"He is not far," she said, holding eyes downward. Skuratov's Shrogin was set to fire; had we brokeaway, we'd have been peppered before taking feet from the floor. Through my mind ran a dozen possibilities, none workable without Jake. Where—?

"Far enough, little one. One moment all instruments show his presence. Moment later, they do not. Day goes by, his light reappears. Week passes, he goes again. Does not come back. After three weeks no evidence of continued existence anywhere reachable. Peculiar thing if he is not far."

"You won't find him," she said.

"Dream Team finds living and dead," he said, stepping to his left as if to come behind us; we turned as he moved. "Is possible, perhaps, that he is neither? Whether you tell now or later is unimportant. In course of history all becomes clear. But to speak without time-consuming and unpleasant prodding always improves mood of situation."

"Not in long run," she said.

"We take moment to moment," he sighed, stopping short of the intruder's drying husk in his rotation round the room, his back now to the apartment door. *Jake*, I hoped, I wished; there was no Jake.

"But these are doubtful surroundings in which to have pleasant conversation. We will pick up after our comfortable flight."

"We're still flying?" she asked.

He nodded. "You are ready to go?"

"Ready," she said as the door banged open. When Skuratov began to turn she stamped her foot floorways; the board below him lifted as if motor driven, striking him with terrific force between the legs. He dropped like an ox in the butchery, his eyes vanishing beneath their lids; the cassette box and his Shrogin tumbling as he collapsed. I leapt for the gun; Jake leapt over me, onto Skuratov, wrapping paws round his head as if to test for ripeness, readying to do the twist. Gathering full, if aging, strength I shoved Jake off, interposing myself between them, unthinking of consequence in thwarting Jake's rage. Clutching me underarm he dug iron fingers into my muscles, set to rip them free of the bones.

"Let me take him!" he shouted.

"No," I said, hoping to repress. "If you do his lights'll fade—"

"*Desired!*"

"Tracker's lights!" I shouted back. "If they see his lights go dead they'll move and quick. Sustain viability and—"

"He tried to *ex* me, Luther," Jake said, returning my feet to earth, flashing the mudstains on his jacket. Still, his hair was in place, his features showed clear even of shaving scars. "My *suit!*"

"Reason's needed to kill—"

"No kill but reasoned kill," he said, lowtoned, heart's truth spoken. Somehow I continued blocking his lunge. "With him there's reason twenty times full."

"*No!!*" I screamed, mindlost myself; it startled all, and Jake loosened from his coil. "Under circumstance he's our exitcard. If his signal steadies true his friends won't come out to play. Keep him whole and we'll pass as wished until we breathe free air."

"Once we bordercross," Jake said, "let him drop and fly."

"He's prime target, Jake, *Dream Team*. We've never had a quick one before. We'll take him all the way. Bind him tight. Once home we give him to Alice. She has her own techniques. Feeling's appreciated, Jake, but logic it out."

Skuratov lay wailing on the floor, rubbing his injuries as if for joy. Oktobriana stood unbudged, hands yet fastened. She eyed Jake updown, her lips parted, her face flushed with new-transfused blood.

"Understood," he whispered, recovering. "If I'd snapped him I'd be better now. Excuse."

"I began to worry you'd been blasted after all," I said. "How'd you foresee?"

He unpocketed a tool recognizable from mine patrol; when blasts were expected, one used the giz by tuning the proper frequency, detonating from beyond harm's path.

"His look and stance alerted me from moment one," said Jake, "no matter your fancies of trust. This is my business, Luther, remember. That tunnel of love last night awared me full. Then when he stripped the car in town's safeness but not among these ruins I knew all was up. So when I took the bags out I stood back, ran my spark's channels till the proper tone blew it. The whoosh sent me mudways—"

"Why the delay coming in?" I asked. "Were you knocked loose for a mo—"

"I had to straighten," he said, adjusting his necktie's knot as if for the hangman. "Essential."

"How's the car?"

"Trunklid sailed off like a great blue bird," he said. "Driveable otherwise." Jake's anger kept underlid only until time boiled it over again. Following the automotive condition report, he spun round unexpectedly, booting Skuratov in the back full-force; not to crack the spine, simply to raise the pain anew.

"Nobody takes me out," Jake shouted at Skuratov, fetuscurled floorways, issuing the soft cries of one aborted too late. "*Hear?*"

"He heard. Strip him clean before we buzz. Roll over, Mal."

"Why take off my clothes?" he asked, scraping words past teeth.

"Time and place for all," said Jake, speaking low, as if in a library. "Let's see how prison love is liked—"

"*Jake!* Keep clothed, Mal. Property's desired. Let's have."

"Please," Oktobriana said, wriggling, jerking her arms. "Remove these from me. I will not run."

"I've only the pair," Jake said. "Better him than her."

"Agreed. Cuff him," I said. "Roll this way, Mal."

When Jake uncuffed Oktobriana we both spotted the fire red welts ringing her wrists. Hers shortly faded; Jake intended Skuratov's to last, and he drew them on till he squeaked. As promised, Oktobriana kept to where we left her as we rifled Skuratov's goods, her look held fast on Jake's slippery form. Skuratov carried five passports of four nations; a thousand rubles and numerous credit cards, along with his personal ID, all of suitable innocence.

"Two trackers," said Jake. "Take?"

"Take one. He'll not need." I pocketed his stress analyzer, hoping later to apply it to him.

"It's candyland, Luther," said Jake, diddling the ordnance, loading my coatpockets with most, selecting some for his own future use. "Christmas in March." The Dream Team awashed with postmodern flash. Jake, who followed such developments more closely than I, demonstrated the safer toys found, told of the more hazardous. Skuratov's keys shot poisoned needles; his cigarette lighter carried X75, enough to bring down the neighborhood around us if a crystal was hooked on. In his belt buckle were biologics that Jake refused even to touch; by their color, I estimated them—being more familiar with items of this sort—to contain microampules of recombinantized anthrax. We pulled his cyanide tabs, cracking them between our fingers like fleas.

"We've lost time, Jake. Drive as capabled and we'll get there in eight."

"Get where?" Jake asked. "His airstrip? What if no plane awaits?"

"When he felt assured, he let slip we'd still be airing it," I said. "We'll call up the map on the car monitor."

"His airstrip's secluded?"

"His estate's road is Krasnaya owned. They know we're coming, though they won't know of the new arrangements. We won't see trouble. Come on." I retrieved the cassette box from where it fell; wondered if it could possibly prove so useful as our larger confiscations. In any event the trip would now prove cost-effective, so I lost fears of having to deal with the accounts later on. Jake heaved Skuratov across his shoulder headdown; as his pain lessened, his complaints grew.

"Carry me properly," Skuratov shouted, kicking so much as his position allowed. "I hurt."

"Not enough," said Jake, swinging so as to slam Skuratov's head against the doorframe, calming him once more; a scalp cut drizzled blood groundways. Jake, a puritan in heart, never allowed true personal pleasure to enter the work that fed him, though passion for perfection of the work performed was another matter; even when he actioned irredeemably it was always to purpose and never with glee. But vengeance, not one of his specialities, perhaps a feeling least favored, too had time and need.

Locals rounded as we appeared, curious as to visit-motive; we moved so unobtrusively as possible to the Mercedes.

"Where're her cases?"

"Backseated," said Jake. "As he'll keep. Keep him locked."

Whether the haze fuzzing the air remained from the blast, or from whatever the residents burned for fuel, its smell struck metal-harsh, as what lingers after chemical attack. We would have hauled Skuratov trunkways during transport but under circumstance he would have shown plain; Jake backseated him headfirst. Our outside viewers remained to watch our unexpected, unexplainable performance. Gripping the cassette box tight I rested myself between the cases and Skuratov's carcass, finding no comfort. Jake wheeled himself; Oktobriana drew herself close to him so that he might more easily prevent her escape.

"Drive at slow pace within neighborhood," she said.

"Known," he said. "Can't hurry without drawing wonder—"

She shook her head. "Many children at play here, Jake. Do you understand the controls? I realize you seem unfamiliar with Russian language—"

"The fucker starts how?" At times Jake seemed as unfamiliar with his own.

"Check the programmed destination," I said. Oktobriana pressed two dash buttons; a map rose on the monitor's eye. I recognized. "His place, undoubted. Aim there without change. Drive, Jake."

"Engine," said Oktobriana, "drive us to next destination."

"Done," said the car; we rolled upstreet. Oktobriana pressed next to Jake as if to meld with his flesh; he edged her away.

"Worktime," he said.

"Closeness necessary for effective rapport."

"We're kidnapping you," Jake said, not looking her way, astonishment plain in his voice. "You enjoy?"

"Is not unpleasant now that initial surprise is done with. And you did assist me in preventing my assault. I am very grateful."

More than grateful. I'd been affection's object for those falling into the Swedish syndrome several times myself, but that affliction never showed symptoms this soon. Firstsight lust was common enough, yet what unwound before me seemed a more complex phenomenon, one of rarest sort; like star's visible birth, or seeing a picture fall, unaided, from a wall. That she chose to shed suspicion so easily—if she had choice—I accepted as good fortune. Jake, as ever, seemed dubious. She stroked her hand over his hair as if to test his existence; he jerked back.

"Touch isn't essentialled," he said.

"You are cold observer of life, Jake."

"Taker," he corrected. No further messages of import passed our lips until we'd cleared the soldier line safeguarding the neighborhood from the bitter world without; even then we spoke little and said less, as if by wording overmuch the world might shake down upon us. Jake centerlaned upon hitting the main road, floored and sped free. Traffic's quick colors smeared our roadsides as we shot along.

"We're tracked?" Jake asked, eyeing a light flashing at middash. "Should we evade?"

Oktobriana judged the readout. "Refrigerator needs defrosting. Let me examine all systems," she said, fiddling with dials, peering at screens. "None follow. Safe thus far."

We passed apartment crops rising forty floors from concrete pastures; unlike American cities Moscow rose highest at the borderwall, shielding the low center from ground assault. True land showed but briefly amidst the blight, pale gray mat poking from a long-worn carpet. The expressway narrowed to fifteen lanes at the outskirts; on our roadsides now were nothing but brown evergreens.

"We take trip to America after all?" Skuratov asked, coming to full consciousness. "You are apt at impromptu response."

"We try," I said.

"Many try," he said. "Few succeed. Is sad thing."

"That fellow in the tunnel," I said. "In your employ?"

"Indirectly, perhaps," he said, shifting to take his back's weight from his bound wrists. "It was needed to see if Jake, ah, truly required devitalization. Jake was as heard. Stories passed mouth to mouth tend to exaggerate. In this case, no—"

"Wire his jaws, Luther," said Jake, keeping eyes roadward, flicking looks into the rearview. "Use his tongue for sandwiches."

"Had truth proved rumor, Luther, there was no need to fear. We had no wish to harm you too soon."

"Here at right, Jake," said Oktobriana. The car guided us downramp onto a service artery curling away from the mainline. Several hundred meters more and we righted again, onto a rutted dirt road, its winter's mud permafrosted. Entwined treelimbs overhead sheltered us from airview.

"This road's not fit for horsetrade," said Jake as we bounced along.

"Servants' entrance, I suspect," said Oktobriana, staring at Skuratov as if she might sear the skin off his bones. He took all with disconcerting peace, now that most pain had retreated.

"Neighborhood's not soldiered?" Jake asked. "No army boys required?" Oktobriana had again slid closer towards him.

"To guard people of best type?" asked Skuratov. His was an attractive neighborhood; the houses and grounds, where visibled, dripped with the subtle taste expected of Krasnayaviki. Amidst wooded hills so fully treed that the forest seemed, impossibly, of original growth, homes' fragments appeared briefly before vanishing, passing like dream's vague-remembered shards. High stone walls lent further peace to the fearful minds secluded within the shadows. Neither person nor vehicle evidenced. Our car swung onto a graveled drive, and coasted down a gentle-graded hill running half the length of Skuratov's estate. His house evidenced by its near-absence; squinting between branches, I saw a dome, a chimney pot, a window lit from within.

"If I hunch true," I said, "the plane'll need reprogramming."

"If a plane is readied at all," said Jake.

"Soon enough seen. Oktobriana, you've experience. You can adjust for flightpath override?"

"Depends on plane," she said. "I should think so."

"Once we unground," said Jake, "won't we be trailed on high?"

I wasn't prime for catechism, and chose nonresponse. Trouble would trail us oceanover, I feared; surely Jake held like mindset, and his vocalized uncertainties only disturbed me more. We entered a clearing, bare as if it was defoliated weekly.

"Presto," said Jake as we bumped onto a concrete thread centeraimed. The field, as stripped, covered several hundred square meters. At meadow's core a blasted circle sheltered the earth from the sun; thereupon, a plane was provided, an eight-passenger sweepwing GBL97, its glossy black skin free of number, mark or flag of originating nation. Jake cut the engine at landing pad's edge.

"Let's plan," I said, forwarding so that I might sound clear, gripping the cassette box, keeping close eye on Skuratov. The plane sat thirty meters distant; the car might blow on takeoff if we pulled closer. In the surrounding forest, undoubted, badger and rabbit and boar were supplanted by cameras and monitors and every species of ear. "Either of you flown this type previous?"

"A playtoy," said Jake, looking towards the plane; towards Oktobriana. "Translation's needed. Wouldn't wish to confuse rudder with aileron."

"I fly well myself," she said. "Will be no problem there."

"Let's shift all in one trip doubletime. Oktobriana, case yourself if you're so assisting," I said, handing her one of her grips across the seat. "I'll lug the other as well as our little gift here—"

"Treat that with great care," she said, opening her door.

"Jake, stroll Mal across. Secure him but don't expend force while we're outside, AO?"

"What if he so demands?" Jake asked, rubbing knuckles as if to sharpen them. "If he keens to suffer I'd hate not to oblige—"

"Once planed, abuse as wished," I nearly said; realized in time I'd only freerein him. "Keep him close till we're onboard," I said. "Just that. We owe more time than we can afford. Let's."

Frost glazed wings and fuselage; as the deicer activated, discerning our approach, all melted off. While crossing the tarmac I suspected Skuratov might breakaway, no matter his chance, but as ever he unpredictabled, striding happily beneath Jake's wing to the plane. The gangplank lowered as we neared.

"Certify our passage," Jake said, shoving him ahead, nearly tumbling him upstairs. We planed; flipping the closure I listened to the comforting hiss of pressurization as the door sealed. Jake and Oktobriana cockpitted as I tied Skuratov onto one of the seats, having retrieved a plastic line from the galley.

"Not so tight," he complained. "You cut off my blood."

"It'll flow soon enough, Mal." The cabin lit up; the plane, adjudging the interior, could have belonged to any megacorp. No portraits of the Big Boy evidenced here.

"No trouble locating override," Skuratov noted. "No trouble with controls, I would think."

"Good."

"Trouble, perhaps, keeping plane in air," he said, smiling. Once he was immobilized I headed upaisle. Jake gestured towards the surrounding one-way glass when I entered.

"We're seen under fine lens," he said. "Check there at woods-edge."

Where forest greeted field several observers clad in Dream Team's basic black stood so obvious as ravens against a summer sky, eyeing our plane in resigned silence, as if waiting in the terminal lounge to watch their lovers' planes crash on takeoff. They carried no evident armor.

"Judging stance and position assault isn't intended," I said, sizing the range; interpersonal assault, at least. "Front's cleared?"

"Bug-ran proper," he said. "Safe as mother's bed. We're armed?"

"Whether with working arms is question," she said. "Their controls should be near." She examined the big board's uncountable dials, gauges, screens and knobs. "Start switch here, Jake. Throttle before you. Altimeter here, powerfeed here, rudder here. Radarscope to right. Here is control for ailerons and here for landing gear. *Here*, now. Security systems."

"What's the firepower?" Jake pressed the ignition and the motor's whine came up.

"I will tell you when I know, please," she said; he quieted. "These two switches, the blue and yellow. Blue shoots flame. Yellow directs machine guns, twelve housed in two phalanxes under wingtips. Five hundred rounds per second."

Jake grimaced. "No glorious Fourth there. What effects climax?"

"For sustained attack press—" She eyed something she'd never seen before, to guess from the terminology employed. "This clickerlike object here. Is basic setup."

"We'll make do. Prepped, Luther?"

"Go." The engine revved, sounding as a beeswarm; exhaust billowed from the riser unit below, enshrouding us from our deforested onlookers for too-short seconds. Vibrations massaged my feet through my soles as we lifted skyways.

"Do they wait until good striking position is reached?" asked Oktobriana; that thought reached me the moment we spotted them.

"We'll discover," I said.

"Aimed ready," Jake said; he nodded rearward. "Tied him tight?"

"Drumtight." It took a minute for one of these midgets to attain altitude suitable for horizontal mode. Ascending above the cloud we'd made, leaving the gray-brown Russian ground, escaping the grasp of spider-fingered treetops, we vizzed below, seeing the bad boys still paused at the brink of the field.

"Movement'll show when it's realized we're not following expected flightplan. What was the destination as programmed?"

"Yevtushenkograd," said Oktobriana. "On Arctic Circle. A terrible place, we have always heard. Most troublesome go there, disappear like fog in morning."

I'd heard secondhand stories; shuddered to think of giving ear to ones heard firsthand, and to imagine the chance to acquire personal anecdotes—impossible; the most painful death would be preferred. "How low can we go inside the border without detection?"

"If we flew below the ground we'd still show onscreen," she said. "Jake. Green button, third from your left, sixth row. Hit it and send us on our way."

"Pull up and hit sonic soon as possible," I said. "Motorize."

When Jake pressed the button we lurched upward, our altitude rising so fast as our speed increased. As we entered the opaque cloud cover above I read understandable screens, judging that clear air would show after eight thousand meters.

"Anything radared?" I asked.

"Nada," said Jake. Russian-accented static exploded from a speaker concealed somewhere on board, shattering cockpit's cool silence; best ignored, I thought. "What's inquired?"

"Some people are unhappy with our behavior," she said. "We violate secure airspace."

"Nothing more?" I asked. "Once we're aced they draw up the covers."

"Identity already ascertained, I am sure," she said. "Planes cannot simply zip from ground to sky in seconds. Be assured they will come. Let us hope older models pursue us." She redoubled effort, assisting Jake, her spirit aglow with healthy pessimism. Leaving the grip of cloud's mud, we shot into clear blue sea. Jake forwarded the throttle and we leveled, our speed reaching the point where the feel of forward motion disappears.

"How long till borderlined?"

"Twenty minutes for complete safety," she said. "Mach one approaches. Prepare yourself." The plane shook when the boom shot; we drifted again into seeming stasis. "If velocity can hold we perhaps can reach—" Something on the radarscope snipped her thought. "Our attendants are here."

They showed through the window. Minutes distant, gliding like barracudas through water, two fighters broke the cloud's turbulent bed. As they banked towards us, into direct sunlight, blinding flares of light reflected off their silver fins.

"What's topspeed?" asked Jake.

"Mach three, it would seem," she said.

"Theirs?"

"Newest models," she sighed. "Mach twelve." Fresh bursts of static broke our troubled peace. Oktobriana gave close ear and frowned. "Our immediate return would please them," she said. "Otherwise we receive immediate attack."

"We land, we lose existence," I said. "Fly on."

"Isn't your friend theirs as well?" Jake asked, following Oktobriana's lead as she played the board's buttons.

"Not since our hands took hold. By his capture he forfeits privilege. To keep him would serve their use no further."

Our plane wobbled when theirs roared past, one over, one under, coasting by at some two hundred meters' distance. There'd come another pass; if no answer drew by then we'd be plucked like ripe apples.

Jake reached boardways, to defend. "Let's send our regrets."

"We haven't range for high-altitude interaction," I said. "Those dillies are latetech. They could shoot the moon from the sky. It's a no-go."

"We've something they haven't," said Jake; we looked at Oktobriana. The planes swung left and onrushed in their penultimate display before mating. Whether Alekhine had entered a more problematic situation than ours seemed questionable. Oktobriana read us clear.

"You don't *know!*" she said, trying to ignore our stare. "Is dangerous and unpredictable. No one should use it."

"Transferral device," I said. "Your boss used it."

"Nor should he have," she said; I uncased the thing from its box. "We cannot—"

"Three minutes more and we'll be cloud and vapor," said Jake, throttling full. "That's desired?"

"You don't understand—"

Leaving the cockpit, taking up my coat from where I'd left it, I unpocketed my cam. "By transferral device I infer we go from here to elsewhere, true?"

"Luther—!" Oktobriana rose, and followed.

"Still bound for America?" Skuratov laughed, seeing us. "I fear we will not get so far as that. I feel shock of passing planes. Accept fate, Luther. We are dust now, nothing more."

"Not quite," I said; the cassette inslotted easily. Skuratov's grin faded as he realized my intent, and he drew tightlipped. Oktobriana continued unavailing attempts to wrestle the cam from me.

"You do not know situation—"

"I know this situation," I said. "How's it work? Tell me—"

"No," she said. "I can't. Luther—"

"Will they transfer too?"

"No. All contained within surrounding closed environment transfer. No one else. But we cannot—"

"There's no choice, Oktobriana," I said. Our pursuers roared past again, drawing nearer on repeat run so that the currents thrown might send us spinning. I heard them sail off across the sky, unable to see their turn when they chose to reapproach, enroute to take us out. "I wish there were. Tell me what to do."

For the longest second she stared at me, her eyes nearly throwing out sparks. "Very well," she said, sans tone, wordchoice deliberate. "If there is no choice then I have none either. Is very simple—"

"Luther," Jake said, his voice no more full of fright than ever; it was softer, as if such fate were ultimately preferred. "They're readying."

"So what do I do—"

"Press rewind," she said. "Nothing more."

"Where are we transferring?" I asked; afterthought.

"It will not be as seems—"

"*Incoming!!*" Jake screamed.

As if thumbed shut by angels my eyes closed when I hit rewind.

Our plane shuddered as though windsheared; through my lids' skin I discerned the cabin disappearing within blinding white light, and in my mind I vizzed oblivion's paint covering us over. Fearing I'd moved too late, I nonetheless crushed my sobs away, refusing to leave life with wet eye. After splintering into uncounted burning fragments, the explosion blasting our souls' ears, what we were would plunge down in a quiet hail of slag and bits of skin, pattering onto the roofs of thousands, sending them into untroubled sleep, lending gentle dreams. I looked again, feeling no plunge, no splinter; the light faded, and we flew on.

4

Skuratov sat as I'd left him, bound as if for pleasure. "Is transferral into space, Miss Osipova?" he asked, unnoticed blood trickling from his nose. "Plane is perhaps not suitably equipped for such adventure." Our on-ground flight, and our chase on high, nervestrung me so that when his words raked my ears, I reckoned him to be but dishing out unwanted sauce; I swung round to hush. "Temper, Luther," he said, feigning horror, yet drawing back within his ropes. "Jake rubs off on you after time, friend. I ask reasonable question. Look round you."

Beyond the now-dim cabin illumination, through the portholes, showed naught but blackest black. "Sanya spoke of no such effect," said Oktobriana, said to self rather than others. By her use of the familiar—Sanya was the friendly form of Alexander, as in Alekhine—I reconsidered how close they must have worked together, supposed politics notwithstanding.

"*Luther!*" Jake shouted.

Before cockpitting I yet hoped that from forward vantage day might still brighten our path. Across Jake's shoulder, through the window, I saw only the same in wider screen: night sky starred from horizon to zenith; unbroken clouds below, moonglow shading their crests and pools as they blanketed the world.

"Who took the sun?" he asked, deadpanned. Oktobriana took

copilot position once more, scanned dials and readouts, entered mainframe commands. Without answering Jake, she continued her monologue with herself.

"No change in locale mentioned," she muttered. "Possibly due to simultaneous velocity increase at moment of transfer—"

"Some transfer," I said, running my own theories. "Two-thirds round the world in ten seconds."

"Explain!" Jake commanded, his usual aplomb on leave.

"We must be Pacificked," I said. "It wouldn't be night elsewhere. Altitude and direction. What are they?"

"Eight thousand meters," he read. "Westward movement, unchanged speed."

"Coordinates at hand," said Oktobriana, scanning as it rose from screen's murk. "Gospodi!"

"What? What shows?" Already she was repunching, testing anew. "Where are we?"

"Readings place us at longitude seventy-six thirty, latitude forty-one fifteen," she said. I couldn't place exactly, but realized the general locale.

"Impossible."

"But remains fact nonetheless," she said. "All other readings showing unflawed accuracy. Without question these are present coordinates."

"Then where are we?" asked Jake.

"Eastern Pennsylvania," I said. No expression came at once to his mask.

"How?" he asked, keeping eyes front, fearing perhaps that to look into hers would assure confirmation. "At liftoff it was near twelve by Moscow's clock. Look. No sun fore or aft. In jumping miles did we jump time?"

"Do you know?" I asked her.

"Impossible, as proven," she said, beginning a new monologue underbreath. "Earth angle shifts, evidently—"

"Evidently," I said. "Descend without landing, Jake. We need visuals. Eye the radar close."

"If Pennsylvania's below," said Jake, "shouldn't we turn and bear east?"

"Contact ground stations while I hook in with Alice," I said. "Make the turn."

"Alice?" Oktobriana asked, slumping into her seat. "Superior or wife?"

"My computer. Pass the modem." With morgue attendant's look she handed it over, its attached wires wrapping snakelike round all they slid across. My stance tilted from vertical as Jake banked our plane, recircling.

"You won't reach her," she said.

"Alice's signal reaches God," I said, unslipping myself from the wires, at last linking up.

"Uncontacted yet, Luther," said Jake as I entered codes into the board, watching the monitor for signs of her blue. "Cloud cover's like a lead sheet. After we breakthrough I'll bounce the signal ceilingways—"

"Alice," I said, praying for response. "Alice, QL789851ATM. Emergency prime. Respond. Contact essential, Alice. Come in." The screen's color remained ice green; no response came from she who heard all. "Spot me, Alice. *Alice*—"

"When Sashenka passed over," she said, "we retained contact till moment transfer concluded. Nothing thereafter. Cybernetic messages seem not to pass between worlds."

"Worlds?"

"Forgive misstatement," she murmured. "There is no way to communicate with your computers or with mine from where we are."

Her latest elaborations puzzled, but before I could consider we dropped below the final layers of strata; across the form of the void winked a thousand fireflies, lights of home and hearth. Leaning down between the seats to viz more clearly, ducking to keep my head from striking the sharp-curved roof, I tried and failed to spot larger gleams.

"Luther," said Jake, "location coordinates suggest Delaware Water Gap below us." A river down there evidenced, its surface agleam with night light.

"Where's I-80? If that's the Gap it should shoot right through there."

"The wires're fuzzed, Luther. Give ear," he said, flipping earphone vol into open mode; decibel-rich static breakup brainracked me. "Overmuch sunspot activity, mayhap? A like sound—"

"This month's clear for that," I said. "Try FM. New York or Philly might show. Someplace might show." As he switched bands the racket settled into electrical crackle and whoosh; no other evidenced as he ran the channels. "Try AM, then. There must be something to hear. Altitude's safe?"

"Three thousand. Nothing's radared." Static mugged us again while he swept and reswept the AM band. Midway along the spectrum, amidst flutter and hiss, sounds of controlled design flickered like aural lightning.

"Oktobriana, where're the toners? Defuzz it." She digitalized, hitting switch after switch; Jake centered in and locked on for those few seconds prime transmission reached. Even at full-clear remaining static obliterated all but vague musical passages, the sound of stray notes wandering from their chords. Dissonant signals blasted repeatedly, rocking the hold we held on the signal. Then, without warning, human voice rang forth.

"—that concludes the musical portion of our program," said the voice, "and now a word from our sponsor." For a moment it seemed lost again, and then:

"*Beeeeeee—*"

Foghorn?

"*Ohhhhhhh!* Lifebuoy—" Then, drowned in static's riptide. The fragment heard unsettled my mind, in undefinable but not unfamiliar ways. At a highlevel strategy meet in Argentina, ten years past, I met a VLF technician; she spent long days tallying unending ribbons of location numbers sent from her nation's deep-running subs. Before, she'd worked at Jodrell Banks; for some years at New Mexico's big dishes in the desert's reserved acreage. She anecdoted me nightlong with tales of unexpected sounds gathered by those listening to the air's constant call: stories of whistles received with Aldebaran's signals; fast-read numbers bursting over dead wavelengths, the ones not even used by intelligenceries; Indian war whoops transmitted from the far side of the moon

during the old Apollo flights. For brief seconds on still winter
nights, she said, if the clouds were right, the dishes sometimes
caught audio waves of decades-old radio programs, returning if but
for once to their origin before bouncing again back to the space
between stars. The sensation I felt as she told me those tales was the
sensation I now knew again.

"Where was fuel when we took off?" Oktobriana suddenly
asked, shattering my reverie.

"Full," said Jake, gliding the knob across the band to retry
pickup. "Why?"

"Blinking red light shows auxiliary tank now in service."

"Auxiliary?" he repeated. "We couldn't—"

"Twenty-five minutes remaining flight time," she said. "Cut
speed."

"Is Newark reachable?" I asked.

"Just," said Jake. "If it's there. We've no evidence it will be."

"Switch back to shortwave, Jake. Take any response. Keep trying. Oktobriana, talk is essential. Let's cabin ourselves."

"Yes. You will be all right, Jake?" she asked, rubbing her hand
across his shoulder; he nodded as he drew away.

"Thank you," he said.

I looked downplane, towards Skuratov. He remained placed,
grips taut. Here in the antechamber separating cabin and cockpit
distance and overriding sound prevented all eavesdropping.

"What's down there?" I asked her. "Where've we gone? Alekhine
must've detailed something."

She looked away; began talking in lowvoiced monotone, as if
recalling a crime's progression. "Before completion of device
Sashenka took over last steps entirely to assure team's security
and my safety. Having spent previous nine months overseeing
proper installation of essential Tesla coil for project, I was ready for
rest."

Tesla coil, again—

"Coil served to energize device in way Sanya never told. We
discovered presence of this other . . . place early on. Original plan
was to bring others across. We discovered soon enough that others
could transfer from here only if someone went to bring them back."

A secret showed amidst her enigma; Sashenka, which she had used twice now, was a very familiar form.

"He said he would be guinea pig in test and so he was. He steps into compartment built for purpose and he went across at four in the morning. I was only one present. As planned he came back, but not until midnight the next day, much later than planned. I was so worried. When he came back he seemed to have seen face of God, if there were God. Sat wakeful all night, not talking, though I insisted to hear. At last he said he had to go back. He said there were things that had to be done."

"What things?" I asked. "Where'd he emerge?"

"He answered neither question," she said. "For five days he shut himself in study with two cassettes we made. When he emerged on sixth day he gave me cassette we have now, one he had adjusted. Took other and returned to compartment with me late that night. We had eliminated our spies long before but still took such precautions for safety's sake, as said. He told me he would be back within three weeks. Said if by then he had not returned I should take cassette left with me and go underground for long as possible." She sighed. "As you know, he didn't come back. Krasnaya sent people round to look for him. We said he had been exposed to dangerous virus and was in isolation. Was foolish story but they pretended to believe."

"But did he say where he went?" I asked, nearly pleading. "Where've we gone?"

"Not often he spoke in riddles, but when I asked he told riddle. Said none should go. If anyone did they would find frightening beast easily tamed, he said. After beast was tamed, he added, it would shed its skin without expectation and show new form of dragon—"

"*Luther!*" Jake shouted, interrupting. "Sustained contact."

Upon recockpitting I eyed the unwinking fuel readout. "We've landing time?"

"Nearly just." Having answered, he switched on his mike. "Landing permission request directive prime op Dryco priority. List proximates for vertical craft descent pad guidance setup. Directives required regarding incoming pattern. Over."

"Holmes Field here," hollered a nasal voice whose clarity surprised. Such a field's name was unfamiliared; I wondered if it was one of Long Island's rogue strips. "Please identify yourself and your airplane. Over."

"Uncoded flight, origin Moscow. Priority Dryco. Over."

"Moscow, Idaho? Over."

A thin pink glow silhouetted the earth's long line; the city of New York. No lights evidenced Newark International's site.

"*Negative*. Moscow, Russia. Fuel availability crisis at hand approaching mayday state. Advise approach, entering incoming pattern prior to descent. Over."

"Russia?" asked the voice. "What are you flying in? Over."

"Teterboro Field here," another voice said, breaking in. "Identify yourself and your aeroplane. Over."

Jake drew deep breath. "Advise suitable approach immediately. Pilot name nonessentialled sans plan filed pro forma. Instrument GBL97 sweepwing, VTOL model A741—"

"What?" asked our first contact. "Speak English, man."

"Flight destination Moscow, Russia?" the second inquired. "This Wrong Way Corrigan? You're way off course, buddy—"

"We're unfueled," Jake said, overloud. "Drytanked. Emergency top leading to mayday situation. Advise suitable approach. Over!"

A sharper, gruffer third cut in. "Floyd Bennett Field here. Hey, who the hell is this?"

Jake palmed his forehead, shutting eyes. "*Priority Dryco!*" he screamed, as if to rain down law. "Online, Newark, understood? Respond, Newark, respond—"

"How'd you get onto this line?" asked our newest correspondent. "This is an army channel, you son of a bitch, get off the air. Over and out." He clicked off. Jake fisted the board, sending up a harmless bouquet of sparks as the radio shattered. I reached across, held his shoulders.

"I'm losing *control*, Luther," he said; he felt strychnined, his muscles tightened so. "I despise to lose control—"

"Eye the radar and the locator. When we sight the stadia, descend into the parking lot. If Newark's seen—"

"No signs show," he said, his color red as the fuel readout. "I'll hold this altitude until centered and then lower slow."

"We'll make?"

"Maybe," said Jake. "Your friend's secure? Interrupt his solitude. Idle minds stir boiling pots."

"I'll have to untie him in case of problem landing in any event."

"Keep him cuffed."

"How long's left?" Separate towers distinguished themselves amidst the cityline. How short, I should have said.

"Three minutes. Two," he said. "Uncertain."

Oktobriana settled seatways besides him, anxious to calm and comfort, to lighten his face's dark. As I aisled myself towards Skuratov he looked at me, rich with smiles. His look was so bloated with craft and mischief gone wasted that I couldn't keep back a desire to knifetwist.

"Prep for landing, Mal," I said, kneeling near him, unknotting ropes securing ankle and knee. "Could be rough and tough. I could retie you into crash position—"

"Your superiors shall receive improper-treatment complaints," he said. "Standard violations of human rights. Where are we now? Switzerland? Czechoslovakia, perhaps, if I am lucky. Such good time we make in the dark."

"We're entering New York approach," I said, watching his eyebrows lift above his glistening eyes. As I ungirdled his stomach he gasped, gaining free breath.

"Such romance," he said. "Is such quick travel possible?"

"Must have hit a good tailwind," I said.

"Then machine worked *very* well. You must feel proud of great mission's success."

"Very," I said, unbinding his chest; only two knots holding his neck remained placed. "Your failure certainly adds to our success."

He shrugged free shoulders. "So we land and you ship me to one of many American Lubiankas. I am but dilettante in these matters and have nothing of interest to tell. I have no worry. America is not nation that often tortures to death."

"Not to death," I agreed, slipping undone his final knot. "Dream Team's but boys at play if you're a prime example, Mal—"

"Prime?" he said. "The best." Pulling his left hand from behind his back, he flashed a wrist ragged with bloody skin, and a hand whose thumb bent awkwardly inward; he'd broken his thumb, somehow, to free his paw and loosed it before it swole. He swung with his right, cuffs dangling from the still-secured wrist, knocking me full faceways, over the seats opposite. Red washed my sight; I heard him scramble, and blinked blood away in time to see him land atop me as I struggled upward, throwing his cuffs downward, towards my eyes. By jerking my head away I took no more than a glancer.

"Jake!" I shouted. "*Help!*"

He hauled himself away; feeling warmth comfort my forehead, I saw him make for the Shrogin, which I'd pitched at cabin's far end, cockpit-near. To slow him I fell forward, falling close, snaring a trouser leg, tossing him aisleways. His twotones heeled me underchin while I gripped. He kicked repeatedly, never catching me full. "*Jake!*" Skuratov's fingers, stretching for handhold, brushed the gunstock closer, into seizure distance. Shouldering it quick, kicking loose, he rolled, raised and aimed my way. I dived into the trench between two rows of seats. Whether in moment's heat he forgot rapid depressurization's effects, or whether he cared no longer, I never knew; the latter, I suspect, for he showed no amateur's touch to my mind. Before he could fire more than a single burst he was felled by Jake's foot as it landed at skull's base.

"Fool!" Jake shouted; Skuratov fell forward as the plane hissed, its breath blown; his barrage had punctured the plane wall. I brushed back the oxygen hoses tumbling forth as I rose, seeing no need for them at our low altitude. Depressurization's effect, however, only sent us down with less control toward the grand slam sooner.

"What happens?" Oktobriana screamed as our angle declined; the engine song ascended five octaves. Jake threw Skuratov's Shrogin into the antechamber; dragged our friend from the floor and shouted instruction to our aviatrix.

"Engage stabiles," he shouted. "Glide us. Cut the engine and drop the tank if there's time. Settle us between buildings if able."

Jake then walloped Skuratov twiceover as if to barefist his skull ashatter. As my head itched with fluid's trickle I looked onward with stranger's eyes, calmed by the sight of newflooding blood, watching as if seeing a film preview. The plane settled into horizontal drop; Jake pulled Skuratov's limpness rearward. In still engine's fearful silence I heard the sound of his cuffs scraping the floor. Jake opened the side exit. With pressure's equalization there came no further outrush when the world beyond appeared. Jake, keeping inside, lifted Skuratov onehand, clutching a frame support so as not to overbalance. "*Out!*" he wailed, pitching. "Flyaway!"

"Don't—" my voice cried. Even had I pleaded, there could have been no change; Skuratov entered an unclaimed airspace. Jake pounded the walls as if regretful. We struck, bouncing airways once more. So many structures stood quadrant-wide through here that I bore no doubt that one would surely slow us down too quickly. Hitting seemed like tumbling from a height onto a haystack; the impact was not nearly so great as that for which I'd readied, but it was great enough to sail Jake frontways as I headed to the floor. Coming ultimately earthward, spinning as if on a carnival ride, the plane skidded along something much more than soft. As thought slipped free I heard the recognizable sound of splash, the liquid hug, the kiss of water.

Consciousness crawled back minutes later; I vizzed Jake stumbling downaisle, Oktobriana slung across his shoulder, his left arm adangle. Emergency lights cut cabin haze; ozone's scent sweetened the smoke like lobby fragrance. The plane tipped downward thirty-odd degrees. No fire evidenced; the smoke was obviously electrical, and no danger showed from asphyxiating fume arising from the safety padding.

"Luther," he said, eyeing my rise; I shook my head, jarring sense into correct place. "You movable?"

"Sure," I said, my legs buckling when I stumbled aisleways. My vertebrae seemed supplanted by roughened bricks held fast by layers of stone.

"Gather and grab. It's not prime to blow but I've no will to chance." With delicate motions, he seated Oktobriana, taking her from his shoulder with onehanded care. His left arm kept its hang. She murmured soft Georgian phrases. Retrieving suitcases nearest, he stroked her head, smoothed her hair.

"How bad?" I asked, feeling my balance return.

"Concussion's guessed." He swaddled her within blankets seized aboveseat. "A miracle she's preserved. I shot her full with Extamyl. That'll sedate." His face shone as if flame-glazed. "Shock's forestall essentialled. Hospitaling's sole certification."

"Her other case's frontways?"

He nodded; eyed me updown. "You'll need stitching, judging the flow."

Moving upaisle I touched hand to head, and felt as if I'd drawn knife through brain; detected, still, that my wounds weren't over-large, and had ceased to bleed. "What's with your arm?" I asked, finding her stray case.

"Shoulder's dislocated," he said; looking at his pale-lit features, tightdrawn as if embalmed, I saw how more bloodless than usual his face showed. "Let's exit first. Assist me, popping it back once outside. What's sought, Luther?"

"My cam," I said. "It's gone."

"Gone?" ·

"While he was upright," I said, "he must have plucked it. Kept it on him. After he slammed me the first time I heard him scrabbling." I tossed aside debris and nonrecoverables, hoping for its reappearance.

"Then it went with him," Jake said, eyeing the door. "We weren't too high when I birded him. He swipe the tracker you held?"

"No." Feeling it in my jacket pocket, I pulled it, switched it on. Two dots blinked thereon: hers and his. Underscreen the green winked bright.

"Survived?"

"Looks so. Whether cam and cassette did is another matter—"

"Will not matter," Oktobriana said, shifting beneath blanket's wrap, her face frost's color.

"Why?" I asked.

"Sanya adjusted cassette I had," she said. "In event of capture and abuse by unapproved."

"Adjusted how?"

"Ours takes us over. Will not bring us back." Jake and I stared at each other momentslong.

"Can you readjust?" I asked; if we had it still, I should have added.

"Don't know," she said. "Sanya was only one to work out final principle." She blinked her eyes quickly, as if signaling. "Caused great rift between us, his paranoia—"

"Why didn't you tell—"

"No other option at time of use," she said, barely audible. "Correct? Your option. Mine. We live with unavoidable decisions—"

The Extamyl took; she nodded, and slept. For the moment there was much to do and naught that could yet be known. Jake pressed her hand as if to warm a fallen sparrow, so that it wouldn't be cold when it died. "Sleep," he said, winding her blanket closer about her. "Sleep now." After a moment's silence, Jake laughed.

"*What?*" I asked, wishing to be home; knowing we wouldn't be soon.

"Your friend's trick retricked," he chuckled, his laugh slowing every few seconds, whenever shoulder pain overwhelmed. "Hoped to strand us and return to glory, undoubted."

"We *are* stranded," I reminded. Jake, excluding logic's sobriety, ignored. Under circumstance his was surely the wiser reaction. "We've got to hospital ourselves. He'll stay where he fell, surely. We'll return for him. You've the Shrogin?" Freehanding, he flipped it from undercoat. "I'll do the cases. Hoist her. Let's exit."

Cradling her onehanded beneath her hips, he downaisled towards the door; I trailed, heaving cases. Feeling greater warmth, I left my coat behind, estimating to later retrieve. Shallow water lapped entranceways; sauna's air beaded us with sudden sweat. Jake peered outside, and deadstopped, his thinned smile gone.

"Fucking O'Malley—" he said, barely heard. I looked. To the horizon showed nothing but an ocean of grassy waves, in which our plane floated like a great stabbed whale. Night breeze rustled the cattails, sending forth modal notes; insects buzzed and chirped and peeped as in entomologist's dream. Laying foot in ankle-deep water, we circled our sight. Southwestways deep orange evidenced Newark's poison sky; eastways, beyond the ridge safeguarding Jersey's ports from inland attack, rose the Empire State Building. South direct, kilometers distant, I discerned a trestle rising above the limitless marsh. A train rolled over its length, wailing its warning; the call split the darkness with long-whistling whine, echoing through the wet, still night. Northward, a few hundred meters away, was an ill-lit road; the whoosh of speeding cars rose from its body as breath. Overhead's full moon cast shadow across the swamp. Tracing distance by the Empire State—something in its look was wrong, though I couldn't say what—I estimated that our standing point should be occupied, so far as I knew by what now seemed but dream's logic, by PriTel's twenty-floor parking unistructure.

"Where've we come?" Jake finally asked.

"Home," I said, wishing to hold further speculation until fully facted. "There's New York. This must be Jersey. We've come down in the Flats Preserve"—that is, the old Jersey Flats acreage remaining, set aside by the government as a public park, where buried wastes made the tumorous foliage especially lush.

"I've been," said Jake. "It's not wide enough to spit across."

"Road's there. Let's make for it. Get ourselves citied quick."

Jake lay Oktobriana on the plane's wing, leaned against the fuselage and sighed. "I need a fix," he said. "Take my arm. Foot my side solid to lever proper. I motion, you pull."

"You won't stand."

"I drew two hundred mils of Diodin from first aid early on. The pain's settled. Prep and set, Luther, you're experienced."

Diodin or no, he slipped a bullet between his brittle teeth before we operated, quickly, as if I wouldn't see. He signaled; I tugged. The grind heard loud assured our success. His lips kept still throughout the transaction.

"You're AO?" I asked; he nodded. With good limb he touched the bad one.

"It's happened before. After she's hospitaled I'll have it

onceovered. Let's move." Checking Oktobriana for look, for respi-
ration, for temp, he lifted her one-armed; I struggled with over-
loaded cases, slogging through the reeds, feet sliding in the mud.
After thirty meters Jake's whites were black from collar to cuffs.
Mosquitoes grew fat on our flesh as we splashed through the chest-
high growth.

"Estimate that Alekhine"—as ever, Jake mispronounced—"is in
Russia. We seek?"

"Might have to. He's implanted. Should be easy to track once
we're ranged near."

"If we recover the one we had," he said, "think she can reset?"

"Sounds as if her boss had the know in that instance," I sighed.
Something in my back felt rubbery. "Possibly, though. I think the
one out here's our quickest bet. Wish we could search tonight—"

"She might term," Jake said. "I've no X-ray eyes to clear her
innards." I wondered if there were snakes about; wished I wore
boots into which pants might be stuffed. "We weren't over twenty
meters high when I pitched him. Dropping onto this'd be like
tumbling on a sponge if he landed right." Jake shook his head free
from mosquitoes' pinch, if for but a second. "If I hadn't allowed
emotion to operate I wouldn't have thrown—"

"Unavoidable, Jake," I said. "What's done's done."

"Always avoidable," he said. That he had permitted feeling to
enter his most sacrosanct action ripped him through, I saw, though
such feeling only made his action more spectacular.

"If he's still viable he'll emerge in time. If not we'll return and
retrieve. For now—"

"We need repair."

"Exactly. All we can do tonight is earplay." Lifting his head, Jake
examined the sky's starry bowl. "This heat's killing," I said; where
the swamp didn't soak, sweat did. "What's seeable?"

"Summer stars," he said. "Orion's missed. So's Hydra and Gem-
ini. There's Scorpius, Libra and Hercules. Post-ides of June, I'd
hazard—"

"It's March—"

"Not here."

We neared a nesting ground; a birdflock scattered airways before us, two meters near, shooting from the fen, throwing my heart into overdrive. Coming soon after to the highway's dry embankment, we ascended. A rest essentialled topside under any circumstance; what we saw made us as statues.

"This isn't," said Jake, kneeling, propping Oktobriana with care against a post. "Can't be, Luther—"

We faced a macadam road holding four narrow, empty lanes. The guardrail against which Oktobriana slept was nothing more than short wooden posts driven earthward, connected through their run by three steel cables. A waist-high divider separated roadways with concrete barrier. Along the roadedge, aligned rows of high wooden poles of two types stood. Long metal pipes attached at right angles to the shorter poles hung overroad; hooked on to the pipe ends were low-watt globes. At each taller pole's peak two crossbeams were affixed; between the poles, attached to the beams by small glass caps, stretched dozens of wires. From their strands rose the hum of a million bugs in eveningsong. A pole-posted sign said ROUTE 3 *Weehawken 7 Mi. New York 9 Mi.* The Route 3 we knew carried twenty-two lanes of neverending traffic. Another sign bore an unworded symbol: an orange peacemaker and single stone, outlined in black, with directing arrow beneath. Beyond the far roadside the swamp continued on into darkness. On the road embankment facing east stood a high billboard, its wooden planks scraped paint-free, its advertisement new-posted. In the scene's foreground was a headshot of an oddly familiar, historically unplaceable face; backgrounded was the White House, radiating as if it burned. EVERY MAN A KING, the sign's legend read.

"Causality prohibits," I said, attempting to convince rather than enlighten. "It's impossible."

"But true," said Jake. Eyeing the Empire State afresh, common sense's block having now worn away, I spotted at once the difference missed. Its pinnacle's TV tower lacked; the building stood as hypo sans needle. Running view along ridge's brow I saw the absence of considerable: the Trade Towers, Battery Spire, Battery Park, One Coliseum, Cititower, Lincoln Park—all gone. "We've disconnected, Luther."

Downroad west, two thin white shafts lit the path ahead. As the car drew close I roadsided, aiming to hitch; anxiety's hands pulled me away so that I might size the locals at near range before direct contact ensued. The car passed, its driver giving us a second's onceover. We'd camped directly beneath one of those dim lights; when his vehicle had its moment under spotlight, it first hit me odd to see something so old look new and used simultaneously. The car resembled a colossal potato bug, with bulbous abdomen, narrow thorax, wide round eyes; its hue showed briefly as a dull dirty yellow. A timekeeper in our day, of hostage ransom's worth; here, it looked as if it sat overlong parked in the rain. Its taillights flew away, toward New York.

"Flag the next, Luther," said Jake, crouching beside Oktobriana, his trousers rolled knee-high as he plucked leeches from his legs. "She needs doctoring quick."

"We all do," I said. "We've got to play this proper."

"Proper for whom?"

"For us. And *them*. If we're where we seem, circumspection in word and act is essential."

"To what purpose?" He tore one last black strand from his skin. "We'll show like snow on ice to their eyes, surely."

"Unproven," I said. "Our look and sound may cycle odd in these surroundings, possibly in ways unforeseen. We don't want to be mentaled without trial. We could show as institution's dream and not even know."

"Recommendations, then?"

"Keep profile low. Don't react as trained. Don't show surprise at their behavior, or their tools, or their uses. Move without rudeness or sudden shock. These are demands, not suggestions, Jake."

"Act as if traipsing Third World scenes?"

"You've got. We're in innocent days, Jake. Remember that we can infect worse than they."

"New lights showing, Luther. Flagaway."

Standing on the gravel shoulder, I overheaded arms, semaphoring oncomers. A truck rumbled past, dark miasma's cloud spewing behind; its full load of glass bottles rattled, shaking against one another and against the flatbed's wooden walls. Two more cars trailed: one's shell flowed in unbroken curve from bumper to bumper, its sinuous chrome seemingly designed by wind's wish; the other showed age, and resembled a boat estranged from the sea as it bumped along on spoked wheels. Its ripped cloth roof sheltered its passengers like a fallen sail.

"One should have stopped," I said as they vanished.

"To be poked and yoked by nightcrawlers?" Jake asked. "Deep-dish dread, undoubted. Other's expected by the king of fear?"

"Stop projecting, Jake," I said. "No call to drip our time's paranoia here."

"Wise words, I'm sure. Here's another." Placing myself again, I waved; the driver flashed lights as if signaling hello. Cheered to see my point proven, I turned to nod at Jake, only to see him drawing himself and Oktobriana behind the guardrail. The car accelerated and swerved, its tires throwing gravel from where I'd stood before tossing myself downhill, rolling into clammy safety at embankment's base. They laughed, skidding away; I heard unexpected cries.

"*Nigger!*" came their call. "Got 'im." Bile burned my throat as I hauled my aches to the road again, shuddering with fresh pain racking old winces. Jake and Oktobriana had returned to their seats; he appeared unsurprised. The road was still and quiet again, a river frozen by night.

"You see?" I asked. "You *hear?*"

"As forewarned," said Jake. "Losers roam night roads, Luther."

"You heard his call?"

"Another approaching," he said, eyeing the horizon's white glow. The oncomer needed no gesture to halt it; slowing as it passed, the car pulled onto the shoulder two hundred down and reversed.

"Prep yourself, Jake," I said.

"Prepped and doubleprepped," he said, sliding his good hand undercoat, standing at guard before Oktobriana's small bundle. The car paused beneath the light and the engine cut. The car's husk rose slablike from the enormous bumpers, curving only at fenders, roof and trunk. The license plate, fastened within a bracket set above the left taillight, read *New York World's Fair 1939*. The driver's door swung free from the front, rather than middle, allowing clear view of the driver as he emerged. A faint click awared me that Jake's safety was off.

"You fellows need some help?" he asked, voicing a deep baritone. Beneath his thin jacket, below his dark hat's rim, he showed
as tall, wide and black. A mustache's caterpillar slept above his
upper lip.

"Essentialled," I said. "Medicare's a must. Assist, please."

"Hospital us multitime," Jake demanded. Oktobriana moaned
as drug's comfort faded. The newcomer onceovered us, standing
without move or shake, looking as if he posed for a portrait.

"Got a woman with you?" he asked. "You boys trying to beat the
Mann Act or what? Going to get in mighty hot water that way."

Jake straightened himself, his hand still hidden. "*Transport* us.
She's pained overmuch. Help now or help never."

"*Jake!*" I said, hoping to preserve and prevent. "Hospital us if
possible, please. We'll reimburse. It's urgent twiceover."

Laughter cracked his face's wax; was it my look or sound? I
wondered, and feared how badly we showed. "I'm a doctor," he
said, kneeling beside Oktobriana, holding her wrist to try the
pulse, patting her face to stir her. "Miss, can you hear me? What's
wrong? You hear me?"

"Da," she slurred, newborn pup's eyes unopened. "Govoritye li
vy porusski?"

"*Russian?*" he said. "Good Lord. Ya govoritye," he said, "a
little." She slumped again, and no conversation ensued. He doc-
tored: ran hands about her neck, touched her toes, prodded her
ears. Unpocketing a small flash, he shone it into her dilated eyes.

"No bones broke," he said, gently pressing her abdomen, seeming to look for her liver. "Took a hell of a lick on the head, looks
like. What happened?"

"An accident," I said. "We're travelers."

"What kind of accident?"

"Our plane descended," I said. "Out there." Peering into the
swamp's acreage, he scanned for several moments.

"Think I see it." He hefted himself upright with fatman's grace.
"She's got a slight concussion. Mild shock, that's expected. When
was the accident?"

"Thirty past," said Jake.

"Past what? Good thing you kept her bundled up. She oughta be all right, long as we get her into town soon." As if to self-flagellate, he slapped his neck three hard strokes. "Damn skeets. Get malaria hanging out in this damn swamp. What about you two? Looks like you took quite a licking yourself," he said, flashing his beam over my forehead, sighting my slices and bumps. "Hurt anywhere else?"

"All over but nothing of import," I said. "Jake dislocated his shoulder, but we readjusted."

"*Shit*. You're walking around?" he asked Jake.

"Diodin holds antishock agents. If I sit overlong I'd fade to black. Standing's necessaried during the first fifteen minutes."

The man's look puzzled; possibly Jake's phrasing confused. "You all are some bunch. Damn lucky you made it. How high were you flying?"

"We glided groundways," I said. "Freefall, nearly." The man's own voice fascinated; I wondered if we sounded so strange to him as he did to me. The way his phrases wrapped themselves round his words, his odd pronunciations, his remarkable tone and pitch; all amazed. "We've ridden rough roads," I said. "We're hospital-near?"

"We'll go back to my office," he said, pushing his hat back upon his head, dejacketing, showing a drenched shirt. His under's line showed clear. "Little bird tells me you all may not want to get too involved with too many strangers right off. That a good guess? Give me a hand getting her into the car. We'll hash things out later on. Those your bags?" he asked. "Toss 'em in the trunk." Lumbering over, he unlocked the lid, pulled it up. "What do you go by, brother?"

"Excuse?" I asked. "Uncomprehended."

"What's your name?" he asked, sounding miffed.

"Luther. That's Jake. She's Oktobriana."

"Man," he said. "Damn Russians. I knew one once called Glory of Revolution. My name's Norman Quarles. Call me Doc. You two carried her out of the swamp?"

"I did," said Jake. Stooping, he encircled her shoulders with his good arm, placed his hand beneath and lifted.

"Careful—" Doc said, then realized Jake suffered no trouble in

his act. Still, he took hold of her legs, to relieve the weight. Shortly
they backseated her, Jake sliding in next to keep her upright.
Certifying the roadside clear of our holdings, I grasped the trunklid, startled by its weight as I slammed it down.

"Your car's plated?" I asked Doc, seeing no call for such density
but for security's sake. He stared, again.

"With what? Silver or gold?" He laughed. "Jake, you want some
morphine for that arm? I can't believe it doesn't hu—"

"Morphine contraindicates Diodin," I said. "We're fixed."

Doc shook his head, and wheeled himself. Opening the shotgun
door, expecting to descend, I climbed instead, seating myself on
worn, tape-patched upholstery; fine leatherette upholstery, nonetheless. A ceiling incandescent buttered us with yellow light. On
the unpadded, polished-metal dash were but six gauges and the
glove compartment.

"Isn't much traffic, this time of night," Doc said. "We ought to
make it in no time."

"What time is it?" I asked, fumbling for nonexistent seat belts.

"Clock's right there," he said. With a key, he ignited; when the
engine caught it roared and pounded loud. Finding the clock, I
found too that it bore hands. Seeing me count off the divisions,
Doc said, "One-thirty." He jerked a steering-column lever
knobbed with speckled blue, and drew up his left leg. Only on old
cars traveling the streets of Kabul or Ankara or out on the Island
had I, since childhood, seen such a system. Twohanded, with
evident strain, he steered us roadways.

"Usually I'm not running around this time of night," he said.
"Ever' Friday I'm assigned to work over at East Orange Colored
Hospital. Poor people out there need all the help they can get."

"Colorful hospital?"

"You could say that," he said. "I'll tell the world it's a hell of a
mess on weekends."

In the rearview I saw Jake inserting his pocket-player's phones so
that for short minutes, through long-sung songs, he might ascend
free from all surrounding. He drew Oktobriana near, despite the
heat; Jake generally showed affection only to the unconscious, but
his hold was a different hold that night.

"Where's the AC?" I asked, vizzing the dash; there wasn't even a radio.

"AC?" Doc said. "You mean electricity?"

"No. Air-conditioning. Sorry to misunderstand."

"In a Terraplane?" Reconsidering, I surreptitiously handcrept the doorside, hoping to find the window button. "Packard, maybe. Not in this car. You want some air?" he asked; paused, as if to rephrase. "Use that little crank with the knob on the right. Don't yank the handle, you'll fall out the door." Finding it, I rolled; leaned into the breeze's hot sting. "You and him aren't Russian," he said, "but you're not Americans. Where you all from?"

"We're American," I said.

"Been out of the country a long time?" he asked.

"Not long." Doc's car seemed suspension-free as we bumped and banged along; when he shifted again we settled into cruise. We passed a small house on road's righthand; two thick stanchions stood in the dirt lot fronting. Seeing their hoses and dials and globes marked HESS I realized they were gas pumps. A sign on houseside told that within could be bought ice-cold buttermilk, live bait and Moxie. Between house and bog a billboard announced a sale on DeSotos.

"What's Moxie?" I asked.

"Spunk," he said. "Oh, you mean the drink?"

I shrugged.

"I tasted it once. Tasted like tar. Creosote."

How often did he drink creosote? I wondered. "DeSotos are a car?" His look shifted, towards me, to the road, towards me again.

"Not often you see a mixed group like yours in the country. Some people get a little upset."

"One car tried a hit," I said. "Missed." We reached a narrow, arched bridge that crossed, said a sign, the Hackensack River. The roadway hummed as we hit it, startling my heart into extra beats. The buzz was as a plane speeding down to spray.

"You in any trouble with the law?" Doc asked, lowvoiced.

"We've interacted no legal modes improperly, as I gather."

"Level with me if you're on the lam, friend. You got something to come clean about, you come clean now for my sake just so I'll know what's going on. I'm not going to rat on you 'less you give me reason to."

Paranoia's oddest feature is that those closest are least trusted, and a stranger may prove the safest confidant; still, there was no trusting this one yet. If we tarried overlong round him, and under circumstance I knew there might not be choice, he'd have to be told unless he guessed beforehand. I nearly spoke then, but feared he would cast us away so soon after catching us. At present need for doctoring outweighed need to inform; I stilled my tongue.

"Stand in my shoes a minute," he said; why should I want to? I wondered, but didn't say. "I'm driving 'cross the Meadows in the middle of the night. Catch you three just crawled out of the swamp. Negro man, white man, white woman. *Injured* white *Russian* woman. Ever' one of you beat-up, filthy dirty. Covered with blood. You think people aren't going to do more than just rubberneck? Tried to run you down, hell. You all're lucky nobody tried to shoot you, just on general principle."

"Why'd you assist if we showed so strange?"

"I'm a doctor," he said. "God helps fools, doctors help people. If God helped people 'stead of fools, world'd be a perfect place, wouldn't it?" Extracting a cigarette from shirt pocket he stuck it in at mouthcorner, pressed a dash button and tossed a crumpled pack atop the dash. LUCKY STRIKE, its green and red colors told; Christmas colors. "Think you can salvage your plane?"

"It's demolished," I said. It wasn't, but none here could effect needed repairs. The button clicked; he pulled it out, lighting his cigarette with its glowing end. Noxious fog sucked the air's oxygen away.

"What? Never seen a lighter before?"

"Doctors never smoke," I said, staring.

"Maybe not the doctors you know. If I didn't smoke I couldn't afford to eat," he laughed, slapping a hand stomachways. "Much as I can put away." He blew smoke as if pumping a bellows; I faced the window's wind, gulping Jersey air. "Plane, huh? Just like old Lindy. I went to the aerodrome out at Holmes Field last year. Those Negro pilots from California, you know the ones. They put on a hell of a show. Something to see, brother. Made you walk out a proud man."

"We wished to go homeways," I said. "Only that."

"Ever'body's wandering these days," he said. "Travel if you got plenty, travel if you're busted. If you're getting by, like me, you don't get around much. Lots of people wind up in New York. It'll take most anybody. Better here than most places, brother, believe you me, especially for our people." He patted my shoulder. I wondered about his own suspicions; he'd not inquired as to our specific origin. Whether I read overmuch in, or whether he wasn't yet sure if he wished to know, I couldn't guess; only fear. "Take a long time getting here?"

"Years," I said.

The swamp vanished behind us; we ascended the low grade leading to town. Above the crest ahead the azimuth brightened above New York's everrising skyline. Through the car windows the panorama without washed rich with detail's rising tide until all flowed together into a torrent bearing an America horrifying in its course's inferred innocence. The flood carried ragtag tourist courts, airflowed chrome diners, tile-roofed gas stations hawking Sinclair at twenty or Getty at eighteen, sprawling roadhouses with dance floors worn bare. Lamplit billboards sold the Kiwanis, Ruppert's beer, Silvertop bread, Hudson automobiles, Mazda bulbs, Crosley radios. One big sign announced, beneath a drawing of a carborne family, grinning madly as if driving into sweet, sweet blast, that *There's No Way Like the American Way*; the other showed nothing but that silhouette of prick and orchid ball, this time with overlain legend proclaiming VISIT THE WORLD OF TOMORROW.

At ridge's peak the road swept downward; across the road's open cut, over the black river, stood lost New York, its ornate steeples rising as a host of sparkling crystals, freed from the looming flooded walls of our day. We passed into the tunnel below the dark, house-shingled hills, shooting into the city as a virus enters the blood, forever changing the body entering as it changed the body entered.

5

"GET YOUR FLYERS SET, LUTHER," SAID DOC, MIDTUNNEL. So glaringly white the lights within glowed that I felt to be speeding through a fluorescent tube. "Friday night, so they'll still have the watch up. Hey, Jake!"

Jake, deaf to normal call, softly serenaded himself, eyes lidhid from this world's grotesqueries, ears pitched sole to history's song. Oktobriana fastened limpetlike onto his slumped shoulder, sleeping safely unaware. As if by instinct he stroked her face, brushing her skin's canvas with new color. Under music's influence, I fancied, mayhap Jake's soul returned; heretofore to my sight in his life's art he brought to his palette no hue save red.

"Jake!"

"Don't scream," he muttered, de-earing his phones, moving nothing else; I relaxed minuteslong.

"You hear better without that deaf-aid than you do with it, Jake. We're coming into town, friend. Better look sharp."

"Doc," I said, "translate flyers. I'm uncertain."

"Oh, you know. Your pass papers. Get 'em handy."

"Pass what?" Giving suitable ear impossibled when such unfathomed slang proposed to cue. By my incomprehension, anger's cloud shaded his face, though his temper's worst kept at deep run; his wheel grip tightened and his knuckles paled as blood drained from hands to head.

85

"Your pass papers," he repeated. "You don't have them on you?"

"Haven't them at all," I said. "What's meant?"

His voice's organ loosed all stops. "Buncha damn lulus, you are," he said. "You know that? All of you just follow my lead, then, till we get through. You *especially*." With pointing finger he emphasized my attention's need. "Let me do the talking. I think I can pull the wool over their eyes." Dehatting himself he topsided his brim onto my head, rubbing clotted wounds raw. It settled upon my ears, rather than skull. "Good thing you got a small head. Now keep that yanked down low. They get a good look at your bean and they'll want to know who went down for the count."

"Who're they who await?" Jake asked, his voice dawn-calm.

"Police," said Doc, emphasizing syllables oddly. "Keep your traps shut. Less they hear, the better. Any luck at all and I'll know the ones checking."

As if awakening from a midnight dream we entered the city, moving onto Dyer Avenue's stretch as it funneled us to Forty-second. Scattered over the dusty lots alongstreet were boxes roped together, cars' rusting frames, a bedouin's camp of patched tents. "Burnt out this Hooverville a month ago and now ever'body's back," said Doc, referring—I gathered—to the settlement around us. Long bundles lay in rows as if set out for survivors' identification. Looking closely, I saw the bundles stirring, thrashed by dreams as they were by life. Glimpses of river flashed between cartonlike buildings to our left. Down at waterside, beyond a highrise road, darknesses rose which could, by their form, have only been ships. On the right, past the refugees, Ninth Avenue's unrenovated tenements showed only their worn facades' cornices and boarded stores. Down avenue's midlane stood a row of metal trees. Along its unified branches entwined above a train snaked uptown. Blocks away stood some few recognizables: the Empire State, Chrysler's tickler, Dryco's old slab, now as it once had been, RCA's. In the sky above, so much broader than in our day, there seemed to be stars.

"Shit," said Doc, eyeing frontways. "We're in the soup now. Don't start gumbeatin' about *anything*. Got me?" A twin-bulbed streetlamp at Forty-second's corner burnished two cars' smooth black hulls with pale gold; upon their roofs red spots revolved, throwing bloodlight. "Jive's on," he said, his whisper closer to ventriloquist's mumble. "Hope I can bamboozle these clowns."

We stopped and idled. The policeman ambling our way radiated vulnerable danger. Moon white, barrel broad, over two meters tall, he wore an unplated cloth cap and dark uniform bejeweled with silvered buttons. His sole tools were pistol and club; the bovine look his face held suggested that their use came naturally to him. His like usually bagged it homeways by first week's end in my old field. Tapping carside with his club, he reclined, resting elbows roofways until we answered. Doc, flashing three gold teeth in his smile, rolled down his window.

"Headin' somewhere, boy?" the policeman asked, peering in; his grin drew up as if by poison. "Hard t'see y'in the dark, Doc. How're y'doin'?"

"Fine, officer. Doin' just fine, sir," Doc laughed. His proper speak came earlier in phlegmful baritone's range; wording to the policeman he ascended uptone an octave, cloaking threat with callow sound, blatant in desiring to do naught but please. They behaved as if by stagecraft, for some unimaginable audition. He drew a paper from his wallet and gave it over; the policeman shone his flash over it. "Been over to East Orange, sir. Ever' Friday night, you know. That hospital work never do let up."

"Who y'got with you?" the policeman asked, blinding us with his beam's sharp light. "Patients?"

Doc slapped me shoulderways, arousing pain—his intent, undoubted. "Yes, sir, mister officer. That's a good one. *Patients!*" He laughed a near-psychotic laugh that could have curdled cream. "This here's my cousin Luther," he said, whacking me again. "Had'm gimme a hand over there this evenin', sir. They made him work the smallpox ward."

"Smallpox," he repeated, slowly. "He can just sit right there, then. Those aren't patients in the back. Who're they?"

"Doctor Jake," said Doc, whose ease with plot impressed, "and his—uh—nurse. Once a week he comes in to keep a *eye* on us, sir."

"Make sure y'don't cut off th' wrong legs?"

Doc's grip wheelways, during his latest laughing fit, so tightened that I thought he might snap it in two. "It's a tricky kinda situation," officer. See, they both live in town here but they don't live together, if you get my drift."

"I get it."

"Well, they was celebratin' after they got off their shift, see, and I think they celebrated more'n they intended—"

"Look like they was fuckin' in a swamp," he said. "What's their problem?"

Doc leaned farther out, looking about as if the conspiracy was set to blow. "Blotto."

"That so?" the policeman said, keeping his light level on them.

"As worded, pokerboy," said Jake. "Dim the blinder pronto." My muscles seized, and I'm sure Doc's did as well; the policeman only returned Doc's papers.

"He's had a lotta trouble with the wife, sir—"

"Get outta here 'fore I slap 'em in the drunk tank."

"Yes, sir. Thank you, sir," said Doc, nodding as if thankful for treats bestowed. He repocketed his essential before I could glimpse it. "Have yourself a good evenin', sir."

Without warning the policeman clubbed the sideview; mirror shards chimed onto the concrete as if tossed by the wind. "You'll get a ticket for that," he laughed. "Better get it fixed."

"Thanks again," said Doc, liptight. Aglow with moment's satisfaction, the policeman returned to his car, heels clicking the pavement, gun and club bumping like pendulous tumors against his thickened hips. We slunk past the feeble barricade onto Fortysecond. Once distanced, Doc beat the door with his hand; his voice roared into true range.

"Flatfoot mick motherfucker," he shouted, unmindful of listening ears. "Cost me ten bucks to fix that shit. Sonovabitch bastard."

"That was unreasoned action," I agreed.

"Unreason, *hell*. No reason. No fuckin' reason at all," he continued. "Goddamn mick cops. Ever' goddamn one of 'em on the fuckin' take. All they do is give poor folks bullshit. Gets me steamed."

"Would a report be fileable?" I asked; ombudspeople lend distraction if little else. Doc didn't answer. We rattled over Forty-second's cobbled epidermis, banging across asphalt-bandaged lacerations. Streetlamps' blurred halos hung in the dark, showing as angels' crowns, their wearers held frozen by proximity to earth. In the centerlane ran streetcar rails, like those in Moscow or in the Bronx, our Bronx; none hummed by before we turned north onto Tenth. Doc swerved round a wooden-wheeled cart easing upstreet; passing, I noted horsepower. The beast's splintered hooves, mired full, supported its spine-sprung carcass; the cart it dragged bore sidewalls armored with heavy, battered pans and pots, holding it secure from informal assault. When we paused at a stop I looked above two small shops with French names; two billboards hid the building's flank. One said HOTEL PENNSYLVANIA/PE6-5000; the other:

Opens August 17 at the Capitol Theatre
THE WIZARD OF OZ/*starring*/JUDY GARLAND/RAY BOLGER/
BERT LAHR

and

W. C. FIELDS *as the Wizard.*

When I looked again we'd driven on; it was gone.

"This is city of New York?" Oktobriana said, her voice startling us all. Jake had removed his phones, and studied all with open eye. He nodded, taking his hand from her face. As her sense returned, Jake drew away from her as would a mimosa from fingertouch; resettling, she pressed nearer as he inched off. When she'd sandwiched him between door and self she burrowed into his embrace; his face waxed over with seeming unawareness.

"How you doing, miss?" Doc asked. "*Khorosho?*"

"*Da,*" she said, acknowledging his dreadfully pronounced Russian. "I noted situation after occurrence. Mild concussion without fracture or hemorrhage. No internal trauma. Swelling on left radia infers possible bonecrack—"

"Miss, you're in shock," Doc said. "Where'd you learn to diagnose?" he asked, laughing.

"Moscow," she said. "Any fool could diagnose."

"Doc," I interrupted. "That paper you flashed. That's a flyer?"

"That's it," he said; his struggles to control unwise wording showed plain. "You from Mars, man?" Depocketed once more, he gave it over; unfolding, I read. His grace came on Interior Department letterhead: the paper was much finer than that used for our cash; the Great Seal's engraving appeared drawn by master's hand, such detail it held, unlike our government's standard design of singleline eagle's profile.

> Norman Quarles *is to be allowed unhindered transit between the state lines of* New York *and* New Jersey *from the period* Nov. 1 1938 *to* October 31 1939 *in accordance with his profession as* doctor, *by my order.*

Undertext was the interior secretary's scrawl and the counterslash of Vice President Knox. Such a document recalled to my mind the old internal passports used between the martialized states in the years following the Ebb, but the notes inscribed here sang a different song. I returned it.

"Say you're American," said Doc, avoiding a milk truck double-parked on right; it looked to have been beaten out from tin. "You say you never seen or heard of these? You a missionary kid or something? Grew up somewhere else?"

"I'm irreligious," I said, wondering when and if to tell. At that moment I could viz him pulling up to heave us pavementways, having done with us all, and cruising back into an uninterrupted life. Before I could run truth through unhearing ears, he voiced anew.

"One of the sons of darkness, huh?" he asked; I'd no idea what was meant. "Look, I can't figure this out. I'm going to give you all the medical help I can. But a lot of this jive just doesn't wash, friend. Once I get you fixed up we're going to have to do some serious talking if you want anything else. And I want straight answers, get me?"

"None other," I said.

"Americans, my ass."

Tenth Avenue, unnoticed, became Amsterdam. As scenes unwound before me in unending loop my head's throb redoubled, but each sight fascinated so that I could do no other than to try blinking away the pain as every vision passed. Long low blocks of tenement drabness, unshattered by highthrown stone and glass spears; taxi's lemon exoskeletons amidst hundreds of gray scuttlers parked and mobile; fitfully illumined allnighters hawking crates of produce, restaurants IDed with neon curls, newsstands safe behind paper battlements; olive-hued mailboxes, enameled blue street-signs, black iron lampposts and churches' stained glass; deadhour strollers rambling under jacket, tie and hat, free of sweat's gel, pacing night's walks as if en route to office: all bespoke a different world's thrall, newmade flesh from history's dust. That we could spend many unguided minutes here seemed unimaginable; doubtless the late hour sent optimism into coma. Doc's breath seemed to be coming easier to him now; perhaps he'd calmed enough to talk of other puzzlements.

"How're you familiared with Russian tongue?" I asked. "You've been?"

"After the war," he said.

"Drafted?"

"We all enlisted, man. Thought we could prove ourselves that way. Come out of it with some respect. Shit." His smile showed nothing approximating happiness. "Kept the whole 369th over here doing KP and maintenance whole damn time. Least I was in the hospital unit even though half the time I didn't do nothing but make sure the blood didn't get mixed, once we was allowed to give blood. Even then I think they just used ours on the French." He sighed; lit another cig. "Our commanders kept saying we'll go soon, we'll go soon. Theirs kept saying not yet, not yet. Once Armistice Day came, *then* we finally get shipped out."

"After war's end?"

He nodded. "Siberian Expeditionary Force," he said. "After the Reds took over. Don't know to this day if anyone shooting at us was a Bolshevik or not, one or two times anybody shot. We just camped out in the middle of nothing, drinking potato juice and wishing we was back home. Froze my goddamn ass off; they said what they gave us was winter gear but I don't think so. Lost three toes. Didn't even feel 'em go. One day they packed us up. Sent us back, same as before, except half of us died of exposure there and another third caught the bug and were dead before we reached home port. Swear to this day only reason we went was so they could get rid of as many of us as they could without anybody noticing." His voice trailed away, as if fading from spectrum range. "You used to be in the service?"

"Retired," I said; the way he'd described the campaign wasn't as I'd read of it, but then his would have been a prejudiced view. "How'd it show?"

"Way you carry yourself," he said, turning onto 110th, heading into Harlem. "Even the mud shines on your shoes. I can always spot a military man."

"The uppers are glossed with Everglo—" I began, explaining my polish; caught myself.

"Where were you stationed?" he asked, not noticing, or choosing not to notice.

"All over."

"Oh." He smiled. "So you was in the service and you're going to tell me that's why you don't know what flyers are? How long were you in?"

"Twenty-three," I said. He didn't eye me directly before we reached the next light. Something had faded the signals' dye; they showed as blue and orange.

"In American service?" he asked; I shrugged. "How old are you?"

"Forty-seven."

"I'm forty-nine," he said; from his face's line and sag I'd have added ten. We turned onto Eighth in silence which thereafter remained unbroken; perhaps fatigue outweighed suspicion. Within minutes our evident destination showed; Doc pulled up on the righthand side of the avenue, before a five-story brownstone older than most of those surrounding. "I can park here till morning. This is it."

Through the carwindow came, from basement's direction, man-made sound, blaring pure with percussion's blast, with horn's entwining notes. Opening the cardoor I heard the music swallowed

by unexpected roar; as it crescendoed-I touched foot to sidewalk.
Black shutters curtained the sky; a slender metal tree burst through
the pavement near. An elevated ran atop Eighth; a train screeched
uptown.

"Let me unlock the front," Doc said, walking round the car,
opening the trunklid. "Follow me. Here's your bags, Luther. Jake,
let me give you a hand with Octoberana." To the entrance stoop's
left, from basement to sidewalk, ran an awning's long tunnel,
aimed out of the club from which the music issued; the club's name
was Abyssinia.

"Oktobriana," I corrected.

"Weighs more than she looks," Doc grunted, with Jake bearing
her upward. I lugged the bags. Beyond the entrance's two-
windowed wooden door I vizzed a broad tilefloored hall lined with
plaster columns, rich with marble detail. A chandelier brightened
the gloom. Unlocking his office's door—his name thereupon was
stenciled in gold—with a key of medieval look, he walked across
the hall, unlocked the door facing and went inside.

"Wake up, Wanda," he cried. "Going to need a hand with some
patients I got here."

"Turn off the damn light," the other, louder voice replied.

"Put on your clothes and get out here." He emerged, pulling the
door nearly closed, approached us, entered his office. "Toss the
bags in here for now," he said, turning on two lamps. "Right down
over there." Oktobriana, conscious but groggy, leaned wallways,
kept from tipping by Jake. "Let me look her over first. You two
oughta be able to hold out awhile longer. Never seen anybody
laugh off a dislocation like you act like you're doing," he said to
Jake.

Doc's office was observably split into two large rooms, one to
receive, one to repair. Opening a window, he switched on a ceiling
fan, whirling hot air into eddies and pools roomwide. Jake carried
Oktobriana into the exam room and lay her on a padded table
covered with Japanese paper.

"Who's Wanda?" I asked.

"Me," came the loud contralto heard moments before. Wanda,
of medium height and solid girth, wore cola-colored skin. A mauve

kerchief knotted round her head hid all but a few strands of straightened hair. She strode through the room as across a boxing ring, her pink robe sweeping the floor. "Who wants to know?"

"My wife and associate," Doc said, introducing.

"Nurse," she corrected. Her voice carried an unspecifiable accent. "Bringin' in strays again, Norman?" she asked; her tone lowered, thickened with menace as she eyed Jake and Oktobriana. "We're treating their kind now? Mighty big of you."

"This is Luther," he said. "That's—"

"Oktobriana," said Jake.

"Who's the hokey-pokey man?" she asked, hearing his interruption, giving an updown over his muddy whites. "What's their racket? Bootlegging?"

"That's Jake," he said. "They're just folks fell on hard times, Wanda. Need some fixing up."

"Need an overhaul, they look like. Cat find 'em or you did?"

"Coming in from Jersey. Get me my bag, darlin'." To us: "You two sit out there while I check her out. Read something. Catch up on the news."

Jake and I, stuck with our own devices, took in all about his reception room. We eyed oak furniture of unguessed tonnage, deep-glossed woodwork, low-watt wall sconces, an ancient black dial phone with unknotted cord. My look shifted over time's easier-ignored flotsam: a malachite lamp in nude woman's shape, an ash wall clock, its filigreed hands pendulum driven; an ashtray where cigs might be clutched by deco penguin beaks; a typewriter of MOMA caliber. Desksided was a wastebasket hollowed from recycled elephant's foot, whose descendants passed from their veldt in my memory, leaving zoo-held stragglers to serve their species' sentence. The details were all; to see such items in obvious use, not hidden in owner's vast holdings, under museum glass or vizzed momentslong in sets of films, lent unforeseen awe, the shock of the old.

"He must be moneyed full," said Jake, totaling bounty.

"All's for daily use," I said. "Thriftshop bound. Fifty old dollars'd buy all, I'd hazard. It only lends wealth's impress."

Jake snorted, unconvinced. The particular history armymen

soaked up served as background for strategy's sake; of Khe Sanh, Passchendaele and Blenheim I could describe each assault, each retreat, every bullet shot. But as to when pens first came already inked, when refrigerators began defrosting themselves, when TVCs learned to speak, I held but little notion. I assumed Jake knew history so well as any American; that is, knew that since he was born, things had changed—though in Jake's case I doubt that they had.

"How's his action trustable?" Jake asked, nodding towards the office's shut door. "How low's his line dip?"

"They're doctoring," I said. "Calm yourself."

"Witchdoctoring," said Jake. "What if he terms inadvertent? Or advertent?"

"He won't," I said. "All differs here. Keep that minded, Jake, trust's essentialled. You vizzed the outside—"

"Calcutta," said Jake. "World within world and nothing more. We'll compensate fine."

"But not sole," I said. "He'll have to be backgrounded. I see no other way—"

"Betrayal awaits," he said. "Think twice."

I shook my head. "Five times I've thought," I said. "All's risked inescapably in whatever situation. His suspicions have grown since first meet. We've attracted, that's the reason he's not let us drop."

"Prep yourself to action once he shows untrue," said Jake, wording me to do to Doc what I'd readied to do to him, when and if time came; I nearly laughed, though I knew he gave truth. Still, we had to take trust upon its deformed face. "What's ragged?" he asked, eyeing tabled mags and papers.

"Let's input," I said. "We need all info availabled. How's the arm?"

"Attached," he muttered. Seating ourselves in tufted leather chairs as if to hear chamber music, we gleaned the past's pages. Life's sheets photoed the known—La Guardia, Goering, Einstein—and unknown: Brenda Frazier, Leverett Saltonstall, Jerusalem's Grand Mufti. Enormous space was devoted to collegiate goldfish eating.

"She'd desire," said Jake, flashing Liberty's cover, whereupon the

Big Boy, agin as we'd seen his image only that morning past, looked out at his American buyers. He ripped it free, folded and pocketed it. *Dime Mystery*'s pages held a Sherlock Holmes tale by Conan Doyle, a reprint, it noted. Having never read the stories, only having seen the vids, I'd never heard of "The Sumatran Rat."

"Is radium silk irradiated?" Jake asked.

"Undoubted," I said, not knowing. "Why?"

"Fools," he said, showing me a *Collier's* ad. "They use it in shirts." Selling for three dollars—old dollars—per, they seemed a bargain for the cancers surely obtained. Such folly amazed, but then, as spoken, these were innocents' times. I tossed aside two *Superman* comic books, and didn't even examine what appeared as a sci-fi mag. Inpiled were two papers, the *New York Age* and the *Daily Mirror*.

" 'Back to Africa—Is the Time Right?' " I said, reading aloud the *Age*'s head.

"*Africa?*" said Jake. "Everyone there's dead."

"Not entirely." The article editorialized; Jake interrupted before I might read what it thought about what.

"What's this garble tell?" he asked, showing the head on the *Mirror*: G-MEN CLIP HOMER'S KANSAS SPREE.

"Unknown," I said; seeing who was photoed below, I felt my neck hair rise. "Look there. He's alive now." There in gray fuzz and white blur Hitler showed; not merely alive but having only begun, the one who ultimately made this world into ours, poised at upheaval's age. We were—I was—so overfamiliared with societal evil that the recognition of personal evil shocked as I'd not been in years.

"Hey," cried Wanda. "Digger O'Dell and Dug-up. Come on in."

Sharp alcohol scent cleared my head as we entered the exam room, enabling me to feel my pain more easily. Oktobriana lay bundled beneath a blanket; damp cloth cooled her brow. With fever-bright eyes she followed Jake's step, his careful move.

"Let's have a look at that shoulder, Jake," said Doc, putting arm on him waistround, as if to assist his walk. "You wear a brace?"

Before seating himself Jake reached undercoat, slipped from its folds his chainsaw, handing it across, as if suspecting confiscation awaited. Doc must have brushed its ignition, or safety, or both; as he touched it the blade roared free, doubling in length. He dropped it floorways, where it sliced in deep before Jake reached down and cut it.

"Careful," he said. For the moment the music below stopped. A blue glass jar topful with pennies sat atop folders nearby; such an odd accoutrement for a doctor's office, I thought.

"Goddamn, Jake," said Doc, his face free of all color but skin's. "What else you got under there?" Stripping coat, jacket and vest, keeping shirtsleeved, Jake counted out his ordnance's inventory, laying down his chuks, chain and trunch; shiny razored knucks; his powerdrill and select bits; the Omsk, retrieved the evening past. With smooth hand he drew Skuratov's Shrogin; Doc eyed its digital display.

"This ain't no tommy gun," said Doc, tabling it carefully, to avoid accident. "Why're you packin' so much heat, Jake?" Doc asked, counting Jake's probes, stickers and flicks.

"I'm a security consultant."

"Pretty damn secure," said Doc, blading Jake's primary switch, used as silverware the night before. "Jacket still weighs a ton. What's it made of? Looks like linen—"

"There's a Krylar underlay," Jake noted. Wanda leaned down to remove his shirt.

"These buttons don't hook into anything," she said.

"Velcro. Just pull. Krylar deflects small projectiles."

"Not enough of 'em," said Doc, seeing Jake's torso revealed in high relief, scar's webbing woven from neck to waist. "Get blown up and sewn back together?" he laughed.

"This alone," said Jake, lifting his left leg as if to spray. In the stash there tabled showed neither the tracker nor his pocket-player; somewhere still enclosed jacketways, too, I knew, remained a thirty-meter line in event a climb essentialled. Doc pounced only on those goods holding obvious harm. Kneeling, he unlocked one of several cabinet doors, gleaming with baked-white glaze. Gathering Jake's toys he pushed all within and relocked, pocketing the key. Jake looked on, surprisingly calm. "Those are necessaries," he said.

"I'll give 'em back when you leave," Doc said. "Don't feel too comfortable so close to an armory. Meantime they can just stay right there."

"Are you all right, Jake?" Oktobriana asked, her voice soft and unexpected; though openeyed I thought her under, so deathlike she lay.

"I think he'll be just fine," said Doc. "Seems a pretty tough bird. How're you feelin', miss?"

"Sick," she said. She looked at Jake as one starving.

"Think you just picked up a bug, that's all. Considering what you been through you're coming out ahead. Jake, you say this shoulder was dislocated—"

"Was," said Jake, looking over his blue-black joint, the lasting swell.

"I don't know," said Doc, running hands along Jake's ridges and holes and bumps. "Nothing displaced. No ribs broke. You still oughta be pretty racked up—"

"Diodin lasts twelve hours," Jake said. "By then it'll have settled."

"What is that? I don't know it."

"A painsucker," said Jake. "I'm no pusher, I can't describe. It was in the plane's kit."

"And she told me she had Extamyl. That's the same sort of thing?"

"I told you," she said. "Synthetic morphia derivative restructured to remove addictive potential."

Doc stared on as if he'd OD'ed on the stuff she described. "Let's just bandage you up then," he said. "Wanda, give me an Ace—"

"Sitting there in front of you," she said. He applied it, wrapping Jake's shoulder tight. Oktobriana's look fixed Jake without letup; her gaze held fear, fear that if her eyes shut again but once, upon reopening she would look upon nothing but an absence, a loved one gone, nevermore seen, stealing away all in the flight. Windowways came a sudden shout. "Doc!"

"Yeah," Doc yelled back. "Who's that? Bill?"

"Up awful late, aren't you?"

"Yeah, I'm burning the midnight oil. How you doing, Bill?"

"Sent but not spent," the unseen spoke. "Really hot downstairs."

"I hear 'em."

"Catch you on the fly." Then, again, silence. Doc finished wrapping Jake.

"That'll be all right. Looks like ever' one of you got bit raw by those skeets. I got some medicated lotion, you can rub it on. All right, Luther, let's check you out."

Bearing no body trauma, I kept clothed. Doc alcoholed a cottonball and painted my headwounds with pain. "Turn this way," he said. "Hell, inch or two deeper, you wouldn't have much ear left. Somebody try to bite it off?"

"I was cuffslung," I said. "Bashed and doublebashed. Jake preserved."

"Cuffslung," Wanda repeated. "You mean with handcuffs?"

"Exact."

"What the hell are you all? Convicts or what?" Her voice rose, foreboding more than it had. "Norman, you bringing in gangsters now? To our home?"

"Be quiet, Wanda," Doc said, matching her pitch, swiping one of my cuts so viciously I thought his aim might be to deepen, not cleanse. "They're not gangsters. I thought that at first, but on the one hand they seem too smart to be crooks—"

"We've no criminal orientation," I said, keen to assure.

"—on the other hand they're too damn dumb," he concluded. "Nothing but babes in the woods. Telling me they're Americans—"

"We are," I said.

"Not me," Oktobriana noted.

"Luther never seen a flyer, he says." With a bandagelength he affixed gauze to my head. "Didn't even know what one was."

"Get out of here," said Wanda. "You shittin' me?"

"I'll tell the world," said Doc. "I'm wondering if they might not be spies. What do you think?"

"Spies?"

"Hell, yes, spies. Piss-poor spies at that. Crashing in some kinda plane, hear you tell it. Act like you don't know your ass from a hole in the ground to the point I don't think you do. Don't speak English worth a damn—"

"We word perfect," said Jake. "Your dialect hinders."

"*Listen* to him. Look, there's been a lot of talk lately about spies. Nazi subs coming up off Long Island ever' night. Hanging out down by the waterfront. Yorkville's full of Germans and probably half of 'em are into something. If you all were krauts it wouldn't surprise me—"

"Krauts," I said. "What's meant?"

His face beamed with exasperation. "Germans."

"*Me?*"

"Whitest nigger I ever saw," murmured Wanda, lighting a cigarette with a scratch match pulled from a small paper box; these people smoked like Russians, keen for dragonsbreath.

"But I don't think that holds up either," said Doc. "Too damn crazy to be spies, too. What the hell are you, man? Where're you from? You going to spill the beans or am I just gonna have to boot your asses out on the street?"

Still, we'd snared his interest; but how to explain such a thing, where to begin? "What if I tell and receive no belief?"

"Bound to be a hell of a story."

I could do no other but earplay, testing one approach and then another. Obvious examples seemed safest to employ. "All right," I said. "Jake's guns. His whole works. Their look unfamiliared, true?"

"They was talking about secret weapons on the *March of Time* last week at the picture show," said Wanda. "Don't mean nothing."

"Clothing of such styles as we wear?"

With probing hand he fingered my jacket, collar and tie. "So you don't use dry cleaners. Got something instead of buttons on your shirt. So what?"

Unpocketing my wallet, flipping it over, I demanded: "Examine."

Doc caressed the cover as if stroking his wife, with wonder and fright, and ill-hid tension. "Your billfold's some kind of soft shit." Spreading it, hearing Velcro's snap, he examined its strips, closing and reclosing several times, listening to the pop. He gleaned my personals within.

"This some kind of—" He didn't finish.

"What is it, Norman?" Wanda asked, stepping over. He pulled

and showed my Drydencard, my Citicard, my Amex and Nynex; the national number; my driver and army IDs with holographic safeties ashimmer. They studied my snaps: my sergeants and myself, Johnson foregrounded, in Long Island, all gone now but me, taken just before the Children's Hour; a self-portrait as I stood in Istanbul, Saint Sophia backdropped; the VP and myself before the White House's Berlin-like wall; Katherine, my ex-wife, perched hoodways on the uniform blue Castrolite Dryco provided me with upon my joining the firm, her smile lying that she knew no happier life than with me. From its clasp Doc shook ruble notes, dollar bills and a clang of coins from my wallet. They gazed silently upon them, as if watching sunrise at sea. He flicked a quarter airward; landing, it thumped.

"This shit's not silver."

"Cuprolite zinc alloy," I explained. Doc rubbed it on his pants as if to strike sparks, scratched it with his nails.

"These dates right?" Wanda asked; I nodded, but she didn't see.

"Still old George on 'em, though," he said. "Just like ours. Look here." Unpocketing his own coins, he palmed them into mine: a quarter, a dime, a heavy half, two pennies. The silver sang like bells, hitting tabletop. The dime's symboled head wore a winged cap; a negligeed woman strode the half's obverse. Washington, true, was quartered. Each penny bore an Indian's head and a nineteenth-century date.

"Lincoln?" Doc queried, seeing my bills, as if ignorant of his being. Awaiting further comment, I heard none. They looked at each other, then at me as they returned my holdings.

"You were an officer, your army card says?"

"I was."

"Told me you were in over twenty years. What was your rank when you left?"

Of course; the hologram meant nothing to him. I returned my army ID to their hands. "Slant it lightways," I said. "Viz the doublestar? That demonstrates major general's rank. As of retirement, certainly."

He shook his head as Wanda stared calmly on. "How'd you get to be a general?"

"Promotions," I said. "One automatic upon retirement. Earlier, a lack of applicables—"

"You can't rise above master sergeant in the army," said Doc.

"I enlisted as a second lieutenant."

Again, he vizzed my ID. "What is this thing, anyway?"

"A hologram," I said. "Sort of a photograph."

"You're full of this Buck Rogers shit," he said. "How'd you get here?"

"We flew. Oktobriana understands the principles. I don't know how we got here, otherwise. I warned that belief may come hard."

"Damn hard," said Wanda.

"How can you fly into the past?" Doc asked. "That is, seeing how you're from the future you must do this all the time." I wondered if he was serious.

"Certainly not," I said. "I've no idea what proof testifies—"

"You all do seem kind of confused about pretty simple things."

"So's Herman Brown down the street," said Wanda. "He don't tell people he's from the future."

"She knows how to get you back?" Doc asked, ignoring his wife, his vast back turned towards her. "You are going back, aren't you?"

"Back to Germany," said Wanda.

"Hush!" he shouted. "Let the man speak."

"Variables interfere," I said. "If a fellow of ours isn't uncovered we may be limboed here till—" Till when? Till we were born again? I wished not to wonder just then. "Whenever."

"Say we give you a hand, wherever you're from," Doc said. "We get anything out of it?"

I shook my head. "We've nothing offerable."

"The future, huh?" said Doc. "What kinda help you figure on needing?"

"We need to bed it first," I said. "We need guidance here. We wish to leave before you wish us gone, undoubted—"

"Don't bet on it," said Wanda.

"We don't need none of your lip," said Doc, his forehead's central vein rising as if tourniqueted. "All right. One step out of line and you get the boot. You can stay with us awhile—"

"Oh, Norman—" He lifted his hand as if to slap; didn't.

"Stay awhile and if you need a little help gettin' on your feet, I'll do something."

"Appreciated."

"Main thing you're going to need if you're going to be sticking around, though, is papers. First thing in the morning I'll call a friend of mine, he's good with that sort of hooey. He owes me a favor anyway."

"Should Jake and Oktobriana be papered as well?"

He seemed surprised. "That's not necessary."

"This ain't no mission house," said Wanda. "Anybody wants to eat they going to give me a hand, no matter how bad you're feeling when you wake up in the morning. You're going to help me keep the joint picked up and you're not moving in permanent."

"Don't be so hard-nosed this time of night, Wanda," he said. "I'm beat to the bricks." The rhythm below began again, shook the room's floor. The horns sprayed uncountable notes through the muffling underfoot. The sound attracted; it was so human. "There many Negro generals in your army?" he asked, laughing.

"Sixteen, at present," I said. "Natural selection. Nothing other."

"Maybe where you're from," he said, that head vein of his close to explosion. "Probably even have a Negro President—"

"For two years," I said. "He was shot in Kansas City—"

"Like they're always saying, Wanda," Doc said softly; happiness of unknown origin nearly aureolaed his face. "Better times ahead. See?"

"Shit," she said. "We'll never see 'em. I'm going back to bed." She turned, left the room. Perhaps only my perception of their conversations made so much seem as riddle.

"You just got to laugh it off," Doc said. "She's moody, this late. And she wasn't expecting company. Come on. I'll spread out some sheets on the front room floor so you two can make up pallets. Peewee can sleep on the davenport. I'm guessing you all know each other fairly well." I shrugged. "Good thing tomorrow's Saturday," he continued, replacing his medical tools within a worn leather bag. "Let's cross the hall. Good music playing to go to sleep by, ain't it? The Prez—"

So, perhaps we could trust; perhaps not. Choice wasn't inherent. Onearmed, Jake cradled Oktobriana during transit, his face free of either pain or concern. Into his glassed eyes she directed her glance. Even at my distance her fire flamed full, her unfathomable devotion keen to burn, if not both, then one; if not one, then the other. I lugged the bags, doubtful now as to the essentiality of all that we'd brought.

"You got nightclothes in your bags?" Doc asked.

"Her bags," I said. "We weren't expecting an overnight."

"Some spies. Don't even bring pajamas—"

"I have no frivolous sleepwear," Oktobriana muttered.

"Just keep bundled up good, then," he said. Their apartment resembled old ones I'd seen, though theirs was of purer form: woodwork's edges weren't rounded by the usual palimpsest of pain layer; all original fixtures were properly placed; the walls ran smooth beneath mauve-flowered paper. A large front room, kitchen and hall evidenced; downhall, I estimated, was the bath, their bedroom and possibly more. The three-meter ceiling enlarged the roomspace by inference and impression, lessened the massive furniture's bulk. All windows along Eighth Avenue's wall were open; this room's ceiling fan almost succeeded in cooling air.

"I'll get what you need. Make yourself at home," said Doc. For a moment we stood in crystal stillness; a grinding shatter from without tore away all calm. The elevated ran along Eighth, I recalled, just outside, five floors above.

"We'll adapt," I said, fingering loose optimism's crumbs.

"If need be," said Jake, settling slow into an overstuffed chair, favoring his injured arm, resting his head upon an embroidery draped across chairtop. Oktobriana unbundled, sitting upon the rowboat-sized couch; in silence stripped her shirt and trousers, stretched and yawned, showed underarm puffs, pink nubs of nipple, stomach's flat board, an untrimmed tuft of dark at belly's base. I shifted my look away; saw, looking again, then she looked at none but Jake. Jake tried not to see her; did, did again, and eyeshut, as if to gaze overlong would make him as stone, or worse. Rewrapping within the sheet tucked round her earlier, she lay down, coughing as if she smoked; she didn't.

"How're you feeling?" I asked again, my voice cracking as if with rebirthed glands.

"Tired," she said. "New York is always so hot?"

"Usually," I said, realized that I referred to a different climate. "Often." Finding another chair, one with arms so wide that it could have seated four, I sat alone.

"What's behinding?" Jake asked. "A mainframe?" Turning, I saw only a wooden box, its leering face made of two knobbed eyes, a clear yellow dial of a nose, a broad fabric smirk.

"A radio," I said, studying the dial. "Stromberg-Carlson."

"So oversize?" he said. "Why?"

"Vacuum tubes," said Oktobriana, her eyes closed as she lay down. "Communication media here operates only with use of many vacuum tubes wasting much valuable space in inefficient manner. Is most unavoidable hindrance if need to employ progressive technology is seen."

I thought of our own tech; how to recover it. "Where's the tracker show him, Jake?"

"It's set still to Moscow grid," he said, looking. "The light flickers, the green shows. He's viabled, wherever he is."

Doc returned, bearing a load of bedware; threw sheets upon the carpet, placed covers and pillows on an empty chair.

"I'll let you all do the setting up," he said. "I got to get some shut-eye, myself. Get you some towels in the morning." He spotted the tracker. "What's that?"

"We're following our friend with it," I said.

"I've never seen anything like that," he said.

"Of course. Jake, we'll reset it in the morning. At this hour I'm barely thinking, much less thinking straight."

"Maybe in the morning," Doc said, "you can tell me what the future's going to be like." Morning, yes; it wasn't something you wanted to hear before sleep. "Good night," he said, leaving the room for hall's darkness. In several minutes we'd made our beds. Oktobriana sneezed, groaned and stirred again.

"Is extra pillow there?" she asked. "Such hard springs in these cushions."

We'd no extras. "I'll try to snare one," I said, rising and moving downhall to where light showed underdoor; the sound of waterrush within comforted me that it was bath and not bed.

"Doc?" I asked, tapping the wood. There came the sound of closure's click, and of medicine chest's slam.

"What, Luther?" he asked, whispering as he opened the door; a pinprick at elbow joint yet bled, a round dark dot rising from his skin. "Need something else?"

"Oktobriana needs another pillow if you're spared."

"Right in the closet here. I'll get it." When he tugged a long chain, switching on hall light, I saw he retained his sleeveless under, though his shirt was long removed. When he grasped a pillow topshelved I saw something right-shoulder centered, half hidden by shirt strap.

"You get that under fire, Doc?" I asked. "A warscar?"

"What?"

"On your back."

"Never saw one of these?" he asked, so quietly I barely heard; he turned to show. Upon facing me again, he switched off the light before I might see his eyes, passed me the pillow. "See you in the morning."

"Good night," I said. "Thank you." He slipped behind the bedroom door, shutting it close, leaving me feeling as if accidentally I'd cut into his soul. Returning to the front I saw Jake's suit piled next to where he lay between his covers. Oktobriana, already asleep, had pulled her thin white sheet tight round her; she sweated so that she seemed even more nude then than when she had been. Shy in strange women's presence, anxious to conceal inadvertent reaction, I retained my pants as I turned off the room's lamps and lay down. The floor felt almost soft.

"What's to be done, Luther?" Jake asked.

"Sleep," I said. "We'll earplay. I don't gather all that's up."

"I gather none," he said; fell silent after. The elevated's grumble seemed barely heard after the first two hours, and came almost to comfort. Towards dawn I awoke, finding the room lit with sun's amber glow, summerlight full of haze and wet, banded by the elevated as if by an arbor's ribs. Flies tickled my skin as they reconnoitered.

"Jake—" I heard; gave no sign of my listening. Earlier—how much earlier, I couldn't say—she'd awakened and crept floorways, sliding next to Jake, between his sheets. From across the room I watched, giving ear to inaudible murmurs. When she pressed close, he pulled away; when she wrapped round, he unbound. She slipped and rolled, dove undersheet, rubbed and nuzzled; clung to his shoulders as if her hold on him were all that kept her from sinking. Her energy astonished; still, she drew no reaction. Throughout all Jake remained still, as if to move would be his end. She must have felt to be loving the dead.

"I can't," he said at last. With voyeur's view I saw her cry, doelike, with no sound other than the hush of tears rushing down her cheeks.

"Jake," she said. *"Brazhny."*

She returned to the couch, leaving her bastard behind, his perfect control undisturbed. Before sleep took me again into more bearable state, I recalled inescapably clear what I'd seen; remembered the impression in Doc's back, the mark which reawared me with Alekhine's warning, that all that seemed familiar would show as other as time passed. The notion buckled my mind, the memory terrorized it. Scars etched Doc's back, but this was no scar; a message passed without tattoo's signal. He carried a brand name: an elongated oval keloid-raised from his shoulder blade. The oval's upper curve read NO DEPOSIT; the lower, NO RETURN. Centered within that ring, in the oldstyle script used to the day we absorbed them, their mark: PROPERTY OF THE COCA-COLA CO., ATLANTA, GA.

6

"HUNGRY?" DOC ASKED SHORTLY AFTER WAKING US AT NINE, while we dragged ourselves free from sleep's grave. Jake and I hadn't chowed since Skuratov's treat the night previous plus one, so many years gone by.

"Is a scrubber close?" Jake asked, unfolding his blackened whites. Hearing no reply, he remarked: "Supply detergent and I'll tub it."

Oktobriana rose, her sheet sticking to her as if with glue. "Detergent is not yet invented, Jake," she said.

"We got laundry soap," Doc said, grasping the drift. "Won't you ruin that suit if you soak it? Won't it shrink?"

"It's sized and set," said Jake, standing, keeping his sheet one-handed before him. My suit, of highest corporate style, was of course naturalized, and its wrinkles were such that it appeared to have been plowed under by tanktread nightlong.

Doc nodded, semblancing that he understood. "How're you feeling, miss?" he asked. "You want to take a bath?" Her sheet unwrapped as she stood; Doc averted eyes, seeming not so comfortable with nudity's sight without an examtable near to certify propriety.

"Too early for feel of water on skin," she said, kneeling before one of her cases, reaching forward for the other, her left leg rising for balance. "My name is Oktobriana. Mother's familiar name for me was Chada, if you find that more easy to say."

"I couldn't call you child, miss—"

Wanda padded in; sighted upended Oktobriana and blew. "Put on some clothes, girl!" she shouted. "Don't you see those damn windows are open?" Oktobriana, unnerved, drew a shirt round her top half. Wanda spotted Jake tugging his own sheet round. "Ever' damn one of 'em buck naked. In my house—"

"Where else they going to dress, Wanda—"

"What if some cop looked in and saw you two in here with her? Running around bareass like she was the main course at a buffet flat. That's not how you act around here—"

"All right, Wanda," Doc said, moving hallways. "Jake. Luther. Thisaway."

"Haul ever' one of us down to the precinct house," Wanda continued; noted Oktobriana's deliberations. "They may want to see what they're missing, girl, but I don't. Put on some pants."

At bathroom's threshold we stopped as if bluntaxed; Turkish lavatories weren't so primitive. Jake stared at the toilet as if deciding how to disarm it.

"She's always beefin' this time of morning," said Doc. "What're you looking at, Jake?"

"You know this is flooded?" Jake said, regarding the bowl. Doc clamped a hand onto his mouth, keeping from shooting untoward word.

"See that chain hanging down? Do what you got to do, then when you're finished, give it a good hard yank." Overhead, we sighted the chain's root emerging from a wall-affixed porcelain tank. "This is the tub," Doc continued, explaining. "Want to take a shower, use the top two knobs there."

"Recognized," said Jake, reaching past the curtain, pressing the knobs with his fingers.

"They turn," said Doc. Stepping hallways, he added: "You don't both have to go at once if you don't want to. We got plenty of water."

"Unintended," I said, closing the door and seating myself upon the shut lid. Beneath the tub's freestanding legs showed a lakebed's

sediment, a host of life. Running my shaver cross my face I
wondered what feelings remained from the dawn encounter I'd
eavesdropped; had no desire to inquire, yet. When Jake untubbed I
saw he'd dressed within; his drying suit dripped from his frame, its
ivory restored.

"Alkaline," he noted, with slim fingers touching a waterdrop to
his tongue. "It'll loosen the fabric if used overmuch."

"So don't." As Jake examined his look in the mirror I readied,
and stepped in. Standing beneath gurgling waters, the drizzle
itching rather than washing, or so it felt, I considered the ease with
which one might, if prepped as I was in such sitch, slide into alien
culture. Years past I'd first entered New Guinea incog with my
select team, coming as wanderers that we might meld into the day-
by-day for a time and so work our subterfuge upon the chosen
before our opposition showed, leaving quietly as we'd come once
we finished, trailing behind us changed minds and scraps of consumed belief. All we did at first was appear, needing help; within
hours found locals keen to assist, our strangeness alluring overmuch. Once attracted, success assured. Such, I told myself, didn't
differ here; it was the old case of the advanced circling the primitive
to accomplish broader goals.

As in induced afterimage, I suddenly recalled his Cain's mark,
and felt rather rounded myself.

Feeling near-human again once toweled and redressed, I returned to the front, seeing Oktobriana again sitting close to Jake;
nonetheless, he evidenced no passion. Doc lounged in a nearby
chair; I hadn't seemed to disturb conversation. Wanda appeared at
kitchen door, a white apron shielding most of her Halloween orange
frock's shine.

"Anybody want to come give me a hand?" she asked. "Anybody
want to eat?"

"That means us," said Doc. "Somebody got out of the wrong
side of bed this morning," he said to us, winking.

"Oktobriana and I require conferencing," I said. "We'll assist
shortterm."

"Let's get to it, Jake," he said, rising.

"Jake," I said, catching him in midflight. "Let's reset the coordinates. The green's still on?"

"Still," he said, tossing it, disappearing into cook's void. "Dot's not moved."

"Tiny buttons on side," Oktobriana said, looking after his path. "You know latitude and longitude here?" I nodded. "Punch them in. Moscow grid will be replaced by New York area grid."

"How many are in memory?" I asked.

"All major cities and all Russian cities with populations over five thousand." Clatter's sound rebounded from the near distance. "No, Jake. This way. That's right," we heard Doc say. As the grid reformed, fifty kilometers rounding midtown showed. Repressing, I gained closer view. In Jersey, amidst the lines of nonexistent express lanes, his speck showed blue.

"Hasn't moved," I said. "Unconscious, possibly. Dying, perhaps. Brokenboned or stuck in the mud."

"But living still," she said. "We must see if machine survived fall."

"Maybe Doc can drive us back out there," I said. "What's purposed, though? It's chanced you can effect readjustment?"

"No foreseeable chance, but is worth effort," she said. "Not foreseeable does not mean impossible."

"Can we contact Alekhine somehow?" I asked. "Your transferral's possibility must have seemed an option."

"He did not recommend."

"Still you must have incorporated a contact mode."

"There is method of signaling, yes, but remember that I did not expect to be in city of New York if transferred. As said, Sashenka was stationary at both times of use. Such shift in location while moving from one plane of earth to other was not foreseen."

"What's the signal method, then?" I asked. "If he's—"

"Likely he is not," she said. "I prefer to leave as last-chance attempt."

"That's senseless," I said. "If it's remotely chanced it's worth it. What's the method?"

"These trackers have special method of contact capability without danger of observation. Sanya obtained pair for us before first visit. By resetting tracker I can signal to show arrival using Morse code. Transmit location and message in white flashes on tracker screen."

"What happened to yours?"

"Disappeared immediately before I left Dubna. Made me realize time had come to move. I knew they could find me but hoped they would not see effort as necessary. With mine, certainly, they knew I could see them—"

"So let's transmit to Alek—"

"Without access to mainframe resetting of tracker back to original use is thereafter impossible. Where is mainframe here? As said, this is vacuum-tube existence. Holding only one instrument it seems senseless to rush till we have our device back in hand recovered, yes?"

"If I hadn't left him with the other tracker—"

"If shit was gold we would all be capitalists," she said. "Again, there is no choice. We got get malcontent Skuratov. Retrieve machine. See if it is operable. Try to contact Sanya then. Sanya not to be found, we try to reset device—"

"But can you?" I asked.

"Is worth *effort*," she said. "Men such defeatists. Device I believe can be reenergized by proximity to operating Tesla coil. *Large* coil. Larger perhaps than any in existence here, but uncertain. Problem is if I can infer directives given as programmed by Sanya. If not—" She quieted, her lip twisting beneath her teeth. "So we try to reset device anyway. We succeed or fail. If we fail we are faced with great problems—"

Wanda's roar broke our conversation. "Wha'd you mean I'm baking bread that's already baked? Help me fry this bacon—"

"Have you noted inexplicables in the surroundings?" I asked, thinking again of that movie poster, Doc's brand, unspecifiable feels.

"Being unconscious most of time since arrival makes thorough observation difficult," she said. "There are things I have noticed. What is point?"

"We're not in the past, are we?" I said. "Not truly."

"Certainly we are not in past," she said. "How many times I tell you causality prohibits? You cannot drink vodka already drunk."

"During his first passthrough he certainly realized, then. You mentioned as much." A fly, stricken with lust for my head, repeatedly caressed and stroked. "He surely told more than you've told. Early on you must have clad old theories in new clothes. So where are we?"

"To us it seems past," she said. "To them, and in fact, it is present day."

"Repeat and clarify."

"This is coexistent sphere of existence," she said. "Occupies same space as ours but at different aspect. Neither world has known of other's existence. Perhaps each started as mirror image of other. It seems this one developed at slower rate though following like path. We have theory that at places there are windows between worlds naturally occurring for short time, allowing accidental transferral. That explained many paraphysical aspects in theory. Sanya, therefore, developed method to get between places at will—"

"That's crazed," I said. "It's comic book—"

"True, just the same."

"It's impossible to put two into one."

"Is obviously possible," she said. "Visualize wide meadow with high mesh fence running down middle. Mesh in fence so fine that person standing on one side cannot see other side's presence. Meadow same on both sides but perhaps fence's shade causes slower growth on one half. Makes sense?"

"What occurs within the fenceline?"

"Anything," she said. "We believed that it is area of extreme flux. Passing but halfway through would probably be very hazardous."

"Sticking to this imbecile metaphor," I said, still disbelieving, "how then is access gained?"

She shrugged. "Aim water from hose at fence. Water pours down on other side. We are water."

"In theory we can return—"

"In fact Sanya did return," she said. "All is needed is operable device. New hose, as it were. Fact remains that we must leave here soon as possible. Inherent problems contain great potential for much mischief and harm."

"What?" I said. "We'll marry our great-grandparents by mistake?"

"You don't need umbrella unless rain falls," she said, annoyance rising. "There is nothing to that. Here they would be other people. Silly fantasies may be put aside. Two unavoidable problems of which I am thinking are much more serious and likely."

"And they are—"

"This world would seem to be following path similar to ours but we do not know for certain. We cannot foresee how actions here will cause hurtful changes affecting this world's future."

"Or helpful changes," I said. "That's considered?"

"That was Sanya's idealistic belief," she said. "Before leaving second time he said in fact that he saw it as solution, not problem. I disagree because we do not know what effect our actions have, and we should not have power to change such things. But problem of disease is much more immediate and terribly serious."

"Disease?"

"Simplest disease here may kill us if our immunity does not match, and there is no reason it would. Think of common transfer of plagues from culture to culture in past. Medieval Black Death. Your American Indians wiped out by white-man diseases. Is same principle. Longer we are here, the more we are exposed to whatever might be here."

"He wasn't qualmed by that?"

She shook her head. "Such a fool."

A thump, as from a blunt striking a solid, came from the kitchen. "*Jake!!*"

The possibilities unlimited. I rushed in, fearful of what casualties might have been sustained, Oktobriana-trailing, and my stomach did flip upon entering—not from sight, from smell; frying food's excremental scent permeated air at oxygen's exclusion.

"We got enough help in here," Wanda shouted, her hands fisted. "Look how *he's* helped. Couldn't you just step on the damn thing?"

Embedded wallways, at noselevel, was a cleaver; on the floor below were a roach's halves.

"Got it," said Jake, nonchalant.

"Just swat 'em, Jake. Get the Flit can," said Doc, freeing the blade. "Didn't know who you was trying to get."

"Crazy man," muttered Wanda as she shook a skillet holding baconstrips in a depth of grease over the stove's free flame. "Sticks bacon in the breadbox, shuts the lid, wants to know how he's supposed to watch it cook. Pokes knobs instead of turning 'em. Lays pans on the oven half a foot from the burner and wants to know how long they'll take to heat. He ever been in a kitchen before?"

"Like your eggs fried?" Doc asked. I peered into a stovetopped warmer. Therein eight jaundiced baby crania floated in their brownish gray drowning pool. Their smell muckered twiceover, so early in the morning. "Jake's just used to kitchens in the future, isn't that right, Jake? They've probably got gizmos that roast your food right on the hoof, right?"

Jake nodded. "Napalm—"

"I have such appetite," said Oktobriana. I mouthbreathed, to lessen that overpowering smell, the permanent scent of greasy burn.

"Dishes that wash themselves," Doc went on. "Turnips the size of basketballs—"

"May I have two unshelled eggs?" I asked, knowing that something essentialled.

"You want 'em raw?" Doc asked. "Got ulcers?"

"Terrible ones," I lied. "I'll have them glassed, please—"

"Cook for 'em half the morning in this heat and he's gonna sit there and suck eggs? Shit—"

"Come on, Wanda," said Doc. "Cool off."

"All of you just go ahead and sit down," she said. The kitchen's size impressed, so used was I to the dry shower stalls New York realtors of our day call Ingestion Areas; each of us had overmuch room as we tabled round in the room's center, the broad window facing us, flies' ceaseless whine tingling our ears. While our hosts and Oktobriana ravaged their emplated horrors, I stirred my eggs until drinkable and Jake tore away his toast's casing.

"Don't like crusts, Jake?" Doc asked, cramming down bacon.

"Surface particulate concentration highest thereon," he said, staring down. "What's the flooring?"

"Linoleum," said Wanda. The name unfamiliared; whatever it was, it split and peeled at flooredge, showed dirt's annual accumulation beneath surface gloss. "What do you have? Something else?"

"Mirafloor," said Jake. "A springy industry by-product compressed flat—" Wanda appeared unimpressed. An unavoidable aspect of this time, it seemed, was that as the outer world grew more gray-brown while Depression lingered, the inner shone as if polychromed, one's loss overcompensated by the other. Sitting on an aqua chairpad, vizzing sunlight filtered through the kitchen window's green-and-white awning and chrome yellow curtains, my knees brushing a red-checkered tablecloth holding an odd, slippery feel, drinking from a bloodred tumbler, eyeing others' shiny blue plates, I felt mugged by hue, strangled by a rainbow.

"Called that friend of mine I was talking about this morning," said Doc, forcing yellow oil from his yolks, dipping toast in its sebum. "Doesn't have any blank flyers handy but has something just as good. Said to come up after breakfast. They're just a little ways up the street."

"You talk to Cedric or you talk to Lee?" asked Wanda.

"You know Lee's never up before noon," he said. "This'll even us up till the next time one of his girls gets into trouble—"

"That'll be next week, more than likely. Why don't you men eat like this little girl here?"

"A carboload's nonessentialled," said Jake. "I'm sufficed." Flies circled round before diving into fresh runs across our plates.

"I am not little girl," Oktobriana corrected, clearing her initial plate; Doc reloaded.

"Don't eat like one," said Wanda. "Want me to take the general up there, then?"

"Why don't you," said Doc, in a quiet monotone. "Luther, pull that picture out of your passport before you go. He's going to need to put it in your new one."

"New American passport?"

ʼc's right eyebrow lifted, owl-like. "Venezuelan. It's all he had right now. I give him your height, weight, how old you are. He's going to give you a new name, too, just to keep it all kosher."

"I don't look Venezuelan—"

"Don't look like you're from Norway," said Doc. "They mix a lot more down there than they do up here. You'll pass. You speak any Spanish?"

"Some," I said; Spanish, Turkish, Russian, French. "I still think I'm too dark—"

"*Dark?*" Wanda laughed, showing her old gold. "With those big green eyes? Look like there was more'n one ice-cream man hanging round your mama's woodpile."

Feeling suitably placed, I decided a check necessaried, to distract if nothing more. "Jake," I said. "Movement seen or not seen?"

Unpocketing the tracker, he looked. "None."

"What's that thing?" Wanda asked.

"Keeps us apprised of others' movements," I said. "Or lack thereof. We're eyeing one who holds our exit visa."

"A friend?" she asked.

We grimaced. "Another orphan of time," said Oktobriana. "Is terrible countryman of mine. Tried to take us prisoners. Tried to kill Jake with bomb. On plane he attempted takeover once more so Jake threw him out into swamp below."

"You sure you need to keep in touch?" Doc asked; we nodded. "He's still in Jersey, then?"

"Close to descent point." A fly careened down, attacking; Jake, bored, caught it without seeable movement. Fisting tight, unclamping, he wiped it on his napkin and kept eating.

"Big-game hunter," said Oktobriana, smirking as she cleaned her second plate.

"I can run you over later, probably, once you get that passport," said Doc. "You seem to be making quite a recovery, miss."

"Such exuberant feelings I have," she said. "So unexpected after fever's passing. Head sore but not painful. Expected stiffness fading."

"May I?" I asked Doc, spotting a paper countertopped near.

"Here," he said. "It's this morning's. I read it already. Toss it up on the icebox when you're through." The rag resembled nothing

published in my New York, as had the *Mirror*; June 17, 1939's
Herald-Tribune and Mail carried few photos, superabundant print,
and semirational heads. Glancing across, I read: KING BIDS FARE-
WELL TO NEW YORK, MEETS PRESIDENT LATER TODAY; HEAT WAVE
SEARS EUROPE; LA GUARDIA SWEARS TO FIGHT LEGISLATURE'S
BUDGET CUTS—

"So many flies," said Oktobriana, swatting.

"No more'n any summer," Wanda said. "Beelzebub's hosts.
Bringers of dark. You get used to 'em. Don't they have flies anymore?"

"They've probably killed off all pests and such in the future,
Wanda," said Doc. "No roaches. No rats. No spiders or mice."

AMERICAN JEWISH CONGRESS REQUESTS LIFTING OF REFUGEE
QUOTAS; LONG PLANS RUN ON THIRD-PARTY TICKET IF DEMO NOM-
INATION DENIED; THREE DEAD IN BRONX FIRE; TESLA TO THROW
SWITCH SUNDAY NIGHT, WORLD SCIENTISTS TO ATTEND CERE-
MONY—

"Tesla?" Oktobriana said, espying the last name. "What is ceremony where?"

"The World's Fair," said Doc. "Out in Flushing Meadows. In
Queens."

"Let me see," she said, ripping the paper from my grasp. "He is
to be honored in great festival at this fair. Will throw switch to
begin operation of new device. Peacetime use, I would guess—"

"What's Tesla?" Jake asked.

"Tesla was inventor and scientist," she said. "True genius.
Slavic, it goes without saying, though Yugoslavic. Alternating
current system of electric power enabled with use of Tesla coil.
Allows electricity to be used in all places safely. Many splendid
ideas he had never employed. Brave notions and concepts ignored
even in our day. Too visionary."

"He's been working on death rays lately, I read," said Doc.

"That would infer use of large coils with attached tower," she
said, thoughtful. "Could perhaps prove useful. I have certain
familiarity with his work." A tiny bombardier closed in on her; had
her glass of juice not been sent floorways by the movement it

couldn't have evidenced that her arm ever left the table. One second her hand was open; the next, it had closed.

"Damnation," said Wanda, pressing her cloth napkin linoleumways to suck the spillage before it merged with the floor. "Catching flies only thing you all are good at?"

"Watch me do better than Jake," she laughed, standing to attain wider armroom. Her captive's fellows circled round as if in tribute to the fallen; their mistake. This time I caught the flash as her arm shot; drawing down her hand to eyelevel she unclasped. Four flies lay stunned upon her open palm, perhaps so surprised as we. She shook them awake, sending them skyways again.

"How'd you do that?" Wanda asked.

"I'm not sure—" she mumbled, reseating herself. "Lucky accident, maybe."

Doc lay down his fork and knife, though food remained before him. "Listen," he said, "last night I was so busy taking care of the obvious complaints that I never got the chance to do a couple tests I wanted to do. Nothing to get all riled up about, just want to check a couple things. Would you and Jake come across to the office with me after we finish eating? Won't take ten minutes."

Amateur's cloakings never concealed; no matter how still the face, the eyes of the nonprofessional never carry the lie. Whatever troubled him, troubled deep, no matter his feigned nonchalance. His gropes and plaints hung swordlike in the air.

"All right," she said.

"Luther, you too, once you get back."

"Get back," said Wanda. "Haven't even gone yet. Let's get moving if we're going to. I got things to do besides babysitting and serving as a tour guide for this bunch. Come on." She stood, pushing herself away from the table. "I'll let you all do the dishes."

"Jake," I said, distracting his roomwide search for the washer. "Tracker me while I'm out. I want to tab any stir that shows if he moves."

"If he moves," said Jake, "follow."

"Don't let nobody see that thing while I'm with you," said Wanda.

"Anybody asks, tell 'em it's a Hershey bar," laughed Doc, something still eating him from within.

"Those your only clothes?" Wanda asked me; my two-piece wool with faint pinstripe, medium lapel, no longer held even press's resemblance; most mud trousercuffed had returned to dust. I couldn't imagine it showing overstrange, still.

"Sole and alone," I said.

"Well, just don't get out of eyesight," she said to me. "Stick to me like glue. All right?"

"A follow's essential," said Jake. "I'll prep."

"Stay here, Jake," said Doc. "People they're seein', uh, don't cotton much to, uh——"

"Ofays," said Wanda, shouldering her purse; its skin looked to be drawn from lizards, though I couldn't imagine that it truly was. "Let's get it done with."

Following as specified, I trailed her steps, emerging behind her into clear light and streetrush as we left the house. Abyssinia's bill evidenced beneath the tunnel-like awning. I vizzed the attractions listed: *Friday Lester Young and Charles Parker/Saturday Robert Johnson the Blues Man/Cover fifty cent.*

"They're just a few blocks up," she said. "What're you gawking at?"

"All," I said. "These associates are fellow medicals?"

"Fellow lowlifes," she said. "Lee the Blood's nothing but a pimp. Carries cards says he's an entertainment director. Keeps a three-girl stable working the street but they hold out half the money on him and he's always too drunk to know. He's nothing but a hog in shoes. Crashes rent parties, that's how low he is. Cedric's got the know-how. Runs numbers, keeps hooch pouring through the bars, fences anything a hophead'll drag in. Hooked in with the precinct house somehow. Swear to this day he must be the one funding the man who buys the souls. And, he gets papers to those too sorry to have any of their own." Glancing me updown, she winked. "Queer as a three-dollar bill. He'll be *glad* to help you."

"Does Doc have overmuch contact with underground trade?"

"When necessary," she said. "I'd be glad of it if I was you, considering."

Above us trains rattled, shaking along their run; sunlight leaked onto the street as through a jungle's canopy, its tones showing pure against constant shadow. On streetlevel, traffic streamed: battered cars plain with years of unmuseumed use, looking less insectival as they familiared themselves onto my mind; streetcars, gray topped, red and yellow sided, their windows removed for summer comfort, buzzed down centerlane. We edged past a sidewalk-wide mass of stacked boxes and jumbled furniture, rolled rugs upon which children sans shoes perched.

"Somebody else evicted," Wanda muttered. "Damn landlords never give nobody a chance to make good."

As in our day, a radioed teen added sound onto noise; here his implement was lasereo size, held but two buttons, plugged into a lampbase with a long cord and broadcast a pregame baseball show from the Polo Grounds, wherever those were, to an attentive crowd. All along the sidewalks locals hung, chattering in groups, arguing between pairs, wandering along. Men kneeled above subway grates, dropping down lures of string as if to fish.

"Built the grates," she said. "Never built the subway. Ran out of money. Still going to tear the el down next year, they say. Tore down the one on Sixth Avenue last year."

At one shaded streetcorner an elderly woman sold big pretzels, her cart two wooden crates, her display case a worn wicker basket. "Pretzels," she mouthed, toothless. "Pretzels a penny. Please buy a nice pretzel." Plaid-skirted little girls hopped across chalked pavement; shirtless boys flung pocketknives into a patch of dirt where once a tree had stood. Dozens waved and smiled at Wanda as we passed; she acknowledged all with word or nod. We passed two men in ragged wear curled atop themselves, bunched behind trashcans, dead to all worlds save their own.

"Bet you don't see that in your day," she said. "Damn Depression's never going to end, I don't think."

She was right; in our day, in similar terrain, there'd be twenty piled deep, sleeping as they might until they were awakened by assault or siren or the smell of their own flesh burning away.

"Least it finally caught up with the ones that had all the money," she went on. "They're still better off than us but they're hurting bad. Serves 'em damn right."

We walked before a newer building, a three-story stone with curved chrome trim and silver letters. UNITED STATES BANK, it was; FOUNDED 1933. Wanda spat on its steps.

"Your bank?" I asked.

"Only bank there is," she said, "if you use banks." At the next corner we pushed through an audience; they surrounded a man standing atop a rickety stepladder, flapping his arms as if to attempt ascension, his voice echoing like summer thunder.

"Negro man wants a *fair* deal!" he shouted. I eyed two black policemen standing near. "Wants the same pay as a white man if he does the same work. Wants to go where he wants when he wants like a white man do. Wants respect for being a man!" His crowd assented. Having passed, Wanda paused, turned to listen. "Not a half man, a *whole* man. With whole rights. Have schools worth sending your kids to. Have subways you can sit on and not stand!" An enormous *yes* rose from the crowd. "Have police working for you and not against you!" His small mob's roar tripled twiceover. The two policemen quickly moved.

"All right, break it up—"

"Move along," said the other, pushing aside two white-haired elderlies. "Break it up."

"Look at 'em," said the speaker, descending from his ladder. "We want free speech in this country like the white man has—"

"Get back to Russia," cried the larger of the two guardians, rushing up, clubbing the man pavementways; before he kissed the street his crowd was gone. Wanda lowered her head; turned and moved on.

"What's ongoing?" I asked, following.

"One of those speechifyers," she said. "Most of 'em hang out over on Lenox. They don't like 'em comin' over here too much and they never like 'em when they start talking about cops. But ever' word he said's true."

"He bore no Russian look," I said. Wanda laughed.

"Babes in the woods, all of you."

A few hundred meters more and we reached our evident destination, a small candy store with dirt-blackened windows. Eyeing up- and then downstreet, she entered; a bell attached to the door tinkled as we crossed over. The windows were dew clean in comparison to the shop's inside. Beneath a long smudged glass counter lay Kerr's butterscotch and Oh Henry! bars, their gray paper crinkling around their grisly cores. Several yellowed papers stacked near bore previous month's dates. Countered behind was a sullen young boy, an oversize cloth cap shading most of his head, a toothpick wiggling at mouthcorner.

"They're in?" she asked. The brat nodded without looking, thumbing rearward towards an all-concealing drape. "Better be." Slipping behind the curtain, we faced a smooth wall broken by a single metal door. She knocked three separate knocks. Someone sized us through the door's spyhole before unlocking; the watchman showed, a slender man of café-au-lait tint, wearing a dress vest and trousers cut for look rather than ease. Lowering his pistol, he smiled, gleaming incisored diamond's glint.

"Hi-de-ho, big woman." He sounded theatrically trained. "Come right in."

"Put away that cannon," she said, entering. Within showed an unwindowed office holding no furniture save for filing cabinets, a massive wooden desk and a tall coatrack. Two of those antique phones were desktopped. Hanging above the desk was a framed photo of Teddy Roosevelt; Cedric, I noted, wore similar nose-pinching glasses. Cornered was what, in these days as since discovered, was called a Victrola; on its spinner black wax played Verdi's screams, and I wondered at my musicmate's taste. Atop Cedric's silk shirt lay a broad green-and-purple tie, noosed tight round his slender neck. Hanging on the coatrack was a dark pearl-buttoned jacket and a sky gray derby; dried vomit speckled both.

"Miss Wanda," he said, "I'm just a wreck this morning. Up all night taking care of Rockefeller back there—" Downhall, rearward, I heard stumbling's sound, as occurs after a long bout.

"Dump him in a bag and drop him in the river. Cedric, I didn't come here to get an earful—"

"He and one of his floozies got into a row last night, don't want to know what happened but his knuckles were all skinned up—anyway, they must have been drunk. I know he was. Came home, ripped all his clothes off like he was Josephine Baker and went to the bathroom. I hear this *thud* like a horse keeled over in the heat and I go in and he's passed out between the john and the wall. I greased him all over with Dixie Peach and then took hold and pulled—"

"I don't want to hear about your love life," she said. "Where's this passport Norman was talking about? I got things to do, Cedric—"

"Oh. We'll just gossip when Miss Wanda wants to, I suppose. All right," he said, trotting deskways like a new-groomed pony. "This is our man in need?" He measured me plain; I felt X-rayed. "A military man, I hear. He's staying with you?"

"Quit flittin', Cedric, and get with it."

"Put curdled milk in the coffee this morning?" he asked, arming me with quick hand. "When she gets too big for her britches"—he winked—"shouldn't be long, you just come up here and stay with us as long as you like."

"You've what's wanted?" I asked, preferring not to commit.

"Never heard any complaints." Unlocking his desk drawer, he took out a thin green booklet. "Here you go, you Venezuelan firecracker. Brought a snapshot? Won't work otherwise." Passport handed over, he toreaway my photo without looking it over; swabbed its rear with mucilage brush and thumbed it pageways into the booklet. After flapping it a few times, he decided it had dried. "Sign as I've got you listed. Gave you a new monicker, you'll see."

My readjusted natality was August 7, 1892; my alias was—

"Anselmo Perón y Caracas Valentino?"

"Sounds so south-of-the-border, doesn't it?" he said. "I can almost see the cactus. Sign there, muchacho. A high yellow like you won't have no trouble passing."

A shambler emerged from hall's dark; his form, once muscular, raced towards fat. Lee the Blood showed in less than magnificence, wearing knee-length undershorts dabbed with red hearts; a sleeveless under was tucked under shortsband.

"Wanda," he said, rubbing his face as if to transform its shape. "What're you doing here?"

"Collecting on tramp's debts," said Cedric. "Miss Wanda, you just tell Doc that if he ever wants a *big* favor all he has to do is get Lee to bring in all his girls for an exam"—he paused, eyeing Lee with blood—"and then plug the bitches up."

"Easy, Cedric," she said. Lee leaned nearer, reached around her waist as if looking for a handle with which to hold himself upright, patted one casabalike buttock.

"My fine dinner's not gonna ride with the master?" he asked, sounding yet drunk. "Ain't comin' in on that tab?"

"Keep your hand offa my ass," she said, pushing free. "Jiveass pimp. Think I want to look at your ugly face first thing when you haul yourself outta bed?"

"You have," he said, grinning. "Got killer fizz out back. Come send me."

"Shit. Send your dead ass to the pen. Go feel up somebody wants feelin' up. Come on, Luther, let's go." Lee shrugged, grinned again, bumped back into the hall. Cedric clasped my shoulder as I trailed, his frustration all but smoking.

"Drop in anytime," he said, unsmiling. "Soldier boy."

Once we'd restreeted I looked at Wanda, her face bright with anger; this time, at least, I knew we hadn't been the cause.

"You're connected as well?" I asked.

"Did some work for him, long time ago," she said, disposing of the subject as she would a used tissue. "Anyhow, that passport ought to keep you out of most trouble."

"The name's senseless," I said. "My residence is typed in as Bogotá. That's Colombia—"

"Who'll know?" she asked. "Colombians?"

Jacketing the pass, I bumped hand into the tracker; decided to recheck Skuratov's lack of movement. Covering it with jacket and hand, I flicked it open as Wanda stopped to buy a paper from a newsstand fitted below an el stair; the ascent's three-flight rise was roofed with metal shingling, upheld by delicate iron posts showing rust, needing paint. The moving light showed plain on tracker-screen.

"How's to downtown fastest?" She pointed upward, seemingly unsurprised by my outburst. "He's moving. On rubber, must be—"

"Just hold on a minute," she said; grabbing my arm, whispering earways. "Don't let people see that damn thing. What're you talking about?"

"He's enrouted," I said. "We've got to see where he settles." Judging the tracker, he'd entered lower Manhattan; no chance he was ambulatory alone.

"That thing shows where he's going, right?"

"Someone's taking him. What if he's being airported or inaccessibled? He's got our only ticket and I've got to trail—"

"Mean you want to go downtown?" she sighed, knowing my answer.

"It's essentialled," I said. "If he was footing, no, but at this speed—"

"Well," she said, "sending you down by yourself be like having a baby crawl through a snake pit. Don't suppose we got time to run home first—"

"No," I said. "It'll be a follow only. Safety's assured."

"Let's go then. But look, I'm not going to chase some asshole I don't even know back and forth 'cross town all day long. Once you get used to things you can do your own running." Reaching into her purse she extracted a coin, handed it over; the nickel bore a bison and an Indian, each finely sculpted. "Slide it in the turnstile slot when we go through."

The station at ascent's summit outwardly resembled an overworn Swiss chalet bearing muddy orange gables and tilting cupolas; RIDE ON THE OPEN-AIR ELEVATED was stenciled along its side. The place's innards showed as a museum's period room, its fixtures and look antique even for that day. A uniformed clerk kept watch over all from within a black-brown cubicle, guarded from those without by a window barred with brass rails. Friction of many feet gave the floorboards rolling rises and valleys. A cast-iron stove's sooty pipes shot upward, through the pressed-metal ceiling; round its black pot and stubbed legs, buckets of sand grouped as if for storytime. Blue glass windows inking the light daubed azure wash over all. Passing through the light metal turnstiles, we heaved open the high doors leading to the platform. Forty blocks down tracks vanished in perspective's depths. Cantilevered above, on track's left, were additional tracks; expressline, undoubted, unreachable from where we stood. Wanda spread her paper's wings; I eyed Skuratov's progress, Eighth Avenue's roar ringing unabated through my ears. He was on Canal bearing east. To lose him before finding him would make hash of hope's semblance; I swore he wouldn't get far from our grip.

"Should you contact Doc?" I asked.

"No phone up here," she said. "I'll call once we get where we're going, wherever that is."

Her paper was the *Journal-American*; knowing but a single city daily in my normal life, the multitude here struck me as recklessly superfluous. Studying seeable pages as she held it before her, noting an entry believed pertinent, I grasped a corner of the sheet to attempt to read.

"Want to see it?" she said, releasing the rag's front unit. Its lead concerned Landon and Edward, whose names unfamiliared; upon a quick scan, realized that the President and King of England were meant. More essential to our own moment was an astronomic note, filling lower corner right.

METEOR BELIEVED LANDED IN JERSEY MARSHES
No Martians Reported This Time

No details there inhered; as well, no word of search and seizure, though such seemed certain under circumstance. This tale, obviously, was nothing but a coverfable. How was Skuratov? While green evidenced life, it didn't guarantee consciousness—yet if his mind ranged free as ever, would he not send for us, rather than await our own search to turn him? If he developed a new cadre of minions here with which to work his ploys before we accessed him, there could be no telling the things he might manage to loose down upon us.

"Here's the train," she said, looking north. Its slim bulk widened as it neared, and soon enough its six olive-drab cars clanked to a stop before us. I approached the nearest steps; noticed pale startled faces peering through the carwindows.

"Where you think you're going?" she asked, fastening my arm

with vicious hold, dragging me rearward. "Come on. Down to the
baggage car."

"There were seats aplenty there—"

"It's the law," she said as we shoved in. The rear cars teemed with
mob; we slicked past, butted through those standing, found places
to toe our feet. The jungle-wet air bore the scent of a million
unwashed; tiny fans bolted above us, ceiling-attached, lay still
within their grilles. None but black faces glistened around us, all
drenched by noon's humid sponge. As we rolled ahead half the
standees lurched; none had room enough to fall.

"Why aren't the front cars availabled?" I asked, my face shoved
almost into hers.

"They aren't," she said, clutching a nooselike loop hanging
from the ceiling. "Things must be mighty different in your day,
Mister Major General."

"Multichanged, yes," I said.

"Give anything to know how it is we turn into you," she said. I
had no idea whether they would or not, and so said nothing.
Through an entanglement of arms I looked towards the window,
taking in views down passed streets, quick shots of Harlem's roofs
and spires and steeples. At 110th the line curved as on a roller
coaster, sweeping west at seven-story height. Across the park's June
green bower, midtown showed by daylight, six kilometers away, its
towers' pastels grayed and blurry in the shimmering air. Full
though the sky must have been with particulate and poison, there
was so much more of it to see, and all heaven seen seemed
newmade, creation's dust yet sparkling its vaults.

"Ninety-sixth!" At each stop the conductor shouted station
name. "Ninety-sixth and Columbus Avenue. Watch y'step gettin'
off—"

I rejudged the tracker's tale. "Whoever's with him stopped," I
said.

"Where is he, then?" she asked, fanning herself with her paper as
the crowd slipped away. After we pulled away from Ninety-sixth the
car had nearly emptied; we took space on the varnished-rattan
seats. Pressing appropriate buttons I blew the grid.

"Centre Street north of Canal," I said. "Near Grand. China-town."

"That's not Chinatown," she said. "That's Little Italy. That's where we're going?"

"Unless new movement shows," I said. "It's reachable from here?"

"We can get off first stop above Canal and walk across," she said. "I forget the name but I know it when I hear it. Just be damn sure we're not down there longer than we have to be."

As we rattled down Columbus it became Ninth, and then Hudson. Tenements became lofts became pinnacles, became tenements again, dipping and rising where in my time stood nothing but glass spire and small-balcony condo. As I sat squashed between Wanda and a sleeping man, newsprint edging from betwixt his shoe and sole, I felt sudden wrack, filled with isolation's rage: never had I felt so inconsolably alone. I'd sustained parents' loss, seen battlemates liquefied in midconversation; felt loneliness's breath cool my neck during advance solos in distant lands; scratched away at the unscarred wound left when, without warning or evident reason, my wife vanished one late afternoon. Only the latter pained as much, yet here, surrounded by strangers whose actions never showed plain, in a city disorienting by its vague similarities, in a world whose soul was of alien stuff, the worse worsened. Not even Alice could comfort here.

Not far-distanced stood downtown's needles; we neared.

"You and Doc partnered long?" I asked, desperate for the human touch.

"Since I was eighteen."

"So few years—"

"Norman was sixteen." She smiled. "It was arranged," she said, not explaining further. As we instationed the conductor shouted Desbrosses' name. "This is it." Standing, she centered her balance to keep from tumbling as the train slowed. "Come on."

Descending, following a zigzag north of Canal, we scuttled past radio shops hustling Tesla lamps, restaurants offering pigs' feet at ten cents per plate, grocery windows shuddered with carcasses of rabbit, pig and calf, clothiers peddling knickers, flappers, breeches and BVDs.

"Haven't seen a phone yet," she said. "He'll just have to wonder."

As we waded Broadway's river a Rheingold beer truck nearly swept us out with the tide; its carmine flatbed bore a hundred wood-staved kegs. As hoped, familiarity's narcotic began settling; the more seen, the more all contained a certain expected inevitability that vanished only with examination of details. They carried the charge that shocked without warning: the thumb-and-fingered way a cig was held, the shine of an amber button; the pattern of a pair of socks, the letters on a box of cereal; a pronunciation, a haircut, a gum wrapper twice expected weight for its foil being tin and not silvered plastic. Without the details all might have bored.

"Centre and Grand," I said, pinning his dot. "Exact."

"All right," she said. "Here on out, you stick right by me. Don't be a wiseguy hotfootin' it off by yourself."

Beyond Broadway streets narrowed and darkened; buildings grew heavy with cornice and molding. Where sightlines showed backcourts, long lines evidenced, sagging between windows, clothes pinned upon them flapping like flags. Children's shouts grew overloud; vegetable perfumes freshened the street stink.

"These dagos down here act like they own the damn city, but they definitely do own this part. They mouth off, you ignore 'em. They do anything, let it pass. Don't fight back, don't smart off. Walk fast like we're just passing through and be set to scram. If we're heading where I think we're heading—"

Her thought faded without ending as we continued on. Bakeries rich with yeast's smells, stoops crumb encrusted, showed their loaves piled high in windows, near framed snaps of Mussolini, this quadrant's Big Boy. Further along saints appeared in windows, crucifixes upon chests; the lingua overheard carried flowing phrase rather than harsh bite. Throughout downtown there'd seemed a shortage of non-Caucasians; here, we were sole and only. Elderlies crossed themselves as we paced by; middle-aged women eyed us updown, sending only mutterance and not audible word; keg-shaped men turned vast backs towards us until we drifted past. A ganglet of young men lounged at café's door, near Centre. One wore a sleeveless under to better flash his furry shoulders; a forearm tattoo looked to have been done with hot coat hanger and crayon. As we passed, Wanda stepped lightly when the tattooed boy thrust out his foot.

"Watch where y'goin'," he giggled.

"Lookit that turban," one said; I'd nearly forgotten my bandage, and how it showed. "Must think he's Gandhi."

"Why ain'tcha monkeys in the zoo?" another shouted. "Lookin' for y'organ-grinder?"

"Keep walkin', Kingfish." Something pebblelike struck my back as we turned briskly northways, onto Centre. "Ruby Begonia—"

"Fuckin' niggers," I heard the one who'd tried the trip say.

"That word," I said as we left earshot. "What problematicks them so?"

"Ignore 'em," she said, tightlipped; her pupils dilated as if to draw in all existent light, to defend against the dark. "Got to if you're going to be flatfootin' it down here."

Something unignorable rose above the surrounding town ahead; if it ever stood in our New York I'd never vizzed it. Likely it was long-wiped; in our day this sector was well within the old Loisaida Zone, years cleared by Mister O'Malley's order, its scraps delivered uptown, for the new Bronx buildings. Possibly only the contrast between the low redbrick buildings surrounding the close lent the effect, but no cathedral showed so holy, no castle seemed so secure. Its carved-stone walls stood as bulwarks; over its windows rock curved and swept as if poured and frozen fast. Above its defended roof rose a pillared barrel capped with green copper dome. The tracker pulsed as we drew near, reaching the square's edge.

"He's there," I said, switching off and pocketing. "What is it?"

"They must have thrown your friend in the slammer," she sighed. "That's police headquarters."

Dozens of black beetles lay still round their nest, as if, sprayed unaware, they'd crawled home to die; their uniformed, weaponed drivers showed only too much life, coming and going. Amidst the surroundings, too, lurked threat; hanging from one building's face, crosstreet, was a pistol of four-figure caliber, aimed directly towards the building. A shop, it seemed; a shop selling, to New York's illtempered public, guns.

"Think he turned himself in?" she asked.

"His affinities lean towards those assuring security," I said. "If nabbed he'd likely volunteer all."

"All what?"

"Fables, undoubted," I said. "Dangerous nonetheless. His fancies kill. I'm judging protective mode holds throughout the place?"

"Protective mode," she said. "What the hell you talking about now?"

"Is it secured?" I asked. "If I entered now, what would happen?"

"Go in there without a reason or an invite and you won't come out anytime soon."

"No choice for the moment, then," I said. "Likely he'll linger. Keep an afar eye and action if movement's seen—"

"Then we can go?" she asked. So I wished; turning, we saw, several meters downstreet, three of our verbal abusers, waiting with staring eyes.

"Hey," shouted the tattooed boy. "Didn'tcha hear me say keep walkin'?" One darker than I, to his left, held a bat, palmed it with his free hand, set to slam.

"Turn around," said Wanda. "Head north. Don't run but don't shuffle."

We didn't run; they did. We'd not covered ten steps when I was shoved pavementways, scraping forward.

"Ya *deaf*? Not gonna answer when somebody's talkin' to ya? Huh?" he screamed, grasping my lapels, hauling me upright.

"We goin'," said Wanda, stepping closer, attempting to loose his hold. "Ain't no call to roughhouse." He shoved her aside, not far; enough to annoy. Though smaller than me, he was wiry, and showed but twenty years agrowing. Sweeping his hands from my jacket and pushing him away, I felt my heart shudder; I'd not had a one-to-one in twenty years.

"I'll teach y't'keep th' fuck outta th' neighborhood," he shouted, running at me, seemingly driven mad by our presence. With the position he held there were three defenses; I chose the one that hurt. Swinging up my leg, nearly pulling a groin muscle, I heeled him hipways. As he tumbled, I topsided; he spat in my face. Now I'm no Jake, no Johnson; but seeing his ape's look, feeling the trickle down my chin, I wished nothing less than to have all his blood before me in which I might swim. Enroute to term, however, I froze, repossessed by reason; in the interval his friends, demurring, closed in with fist and boot and shortly had me rolling. The batted one aimed to swing his knockout; he heard the whistle as I did. They were up and off, back into their home's all-forgiving embrace, into love's dark depths. Grounded, fresh blood soaking my old bandage, I heard hard shoes click my way, felt a foot tap my most painful side as if awaring me that all was not yet done.

"Get up," someone said. Opening eyes, I vizzed two policemen, appearing elephantine from ground view. "Nobody gets beat up down here 'less they did somethin'. What'd you do?"

"This man's from South America, officers," Wanda said. "He's visitin'. Not causin' no trouble. I had to come through this way and he was so kind, he offered to walk me 'cause he knew I was scared, yes sir. Then them bad boys, they come up and—"

"Lemme see some identification," said the shorter of the two. "You too, toots." Passing him Cedric's handicraft I drew myself slowly into sitting position. They eyed the passport; lapped it back to me.

"Sorry it happened," said the taller. "Y'gotta be careful in New York."

"No pursuit's attempted?" I asked. "They ran that way. You can snare—"

"Pal," he said. "So you're in the right. Think it matters? Take it easy. Go back to your hotel."

"Where're y'stayin'?" the short, prognathous one asked.

"Says he's at the Hotel Theresa," said Wanda. "Even if he'd been let in a midtown place they don't have any rooms, what with the fair and all—"

"Where's the pursuit?" I repeated, more furious than hurt.

"They live here, right? They're gone now. You'll heal up, bud. So they kicked your ass. Quit bellyachin'."

"What are your numbers?" I asked, doing what I always feared

Jake of doing, of wording without thought; thought seemed unnecessary, under circumstance.

"Numbers?" said the short one, circling back as he started to leave. "Why? Want to file a complaint or something?"

"Exact."

"That how they do things in Venezuela?" he asked. "Lemme give y'a New York complaint." With full strength he clubbed my back; feeling a rib snap I collapsed groundways. "Smart off once more I'll make sure y'miss your boat—"

"He's a foreigner, Mike," said the other. "South American—"

"Nigger's a nigger t'me," said the short one. "Don't care if he's the King of Venezuela." Blessedly, I blanked. Upon awakening from my brief peace I prayed to viz my own world, familiar and dear, where if I was beaten it would be by strangers without ideological reason; therefore understandable. Wanda knelt close, dabbing my brow with sodden cloth.

"Babes in the woods," she whispered, wringing blood from her scarf, mopping me anew.

7

"YOU START PISSIN' BLOOD, WE'LL HAUL YOU OVER TO SYDEN-ham," said Doc, "but I think you'll be all right." With a long wrap he'd mummified my abdomen to keep my ribs from floating free. "Lucky he didn't just kill you."

"For what purpose?"

"For the hell of it. Gimme a finger. I need fresh blood to do that test." Compared to earlier pains his pinprick came as kiss. "There. Didn't hurt a bit, did it?"

"This demonstrates what?" I asked.

"Let me check it out first," he said. "How're you going to get word to this fellow if he's locked up?"

"I doubt he's locked," I said. "Probably has the king's ear in which to shoot lies and nonsense."

"He sounds like bad medicine to me," said Doc, "and I ought to know. You don't think he was arrested for anything? I mean there's a lot they could've gotten you on if they'd wanted to—"

"Unknown," I said. Having bloodied a glass slide with my extract he lowered above it a clear square; pressed the two into one. "His condition's unknown, his plot's unknown. All's to be done is suspect."

"You all seem pretty good at that," said Doc. "What if you can't get ahold of him anytime soon? Thought of that?"

"Certainly," I said. "A slim option adheres that Oktobriana's associate is still viable. He possesses prime essential. If he is, however, he's in Russia."

Doc whistled, laying the slide onto a primitive microscope's rounded glass. "Russia. Damn." My parents gave me such a beginner's model when I was nine, when they still hoped to later afford medical school's unfunded costs. I used it once or twice, never adjusting to blood's sight until later, in different context. "They've tightened up the borders there past few years. They say old Uncle Joe's got something going on but nobody says what. Probably be easier getting in downtown. Sure be a helluva lot closer."

"Three weeks ago he arrived here," I said. "Never returned. I'm doubtful he remains in existence."

"Maybe he's just lying low. Pays to over there, I'd think," said Doc. "You know there'll be Russian scientists in town all through the next week what with those goings-on at the fair. Maybe one of them knows something, ran into him or something."

"Doubtful," I said. "If he's present, he's kept covered. We've no method of safe contact in any event."

Doc cranked his scope's wheels, focusing. "Remember that fellow hollering in the window last night? He works out at the fair. He's a Red, too. He might be able to dig up some dirt over at the Soviet Pavilion. See if anybody admits to hearing anything. Can't hurt to ask."

In some situations it killed to ask. Still, any straw was worth a snatch. "We can contact soon?" I asked.

"He'll be downstairs again tonight. Comes uptown ever' weekend. Rabble-rouses over on Lenox during the weekend, during the day, comes listening to jazz at night. We'll go down there this evening and wait for him. Usually gets there around eight."

"What's his role at the fair?"

Taking a sausage-sized glass hypo, affixing a clean needle to its end, with it puncturing the cap of a squat brown bottle, Doc drew in fluid that he then injected into the blood sample. "He worked on the Futurama," Doc said. "For GM. That's the best exhibit out there. Shows what the country'll be like in 1960. Being from the future, of course, it's bound to be old hat to you. Writes articles predicting things, too. Scientifically, of course; it's fascinating stuff."

"What's foreseen?" I asked.

"You've got to ask? You don't know?" he laughed. "All kinds of things. Superhighways where you can go eighty miles an hour right through town. Ever'one living in these skyscrapers surrounded by parks. Cars and planes and trains'll all run on atom power." I smiled; wished not to say that his world as it evidenced appeared to be growing into an adulthood not unlike ours, and maturing much more quickly. "Machines that control the weather. You know all about it, I'm sure. You were flying an atom-powered plane, weren't you?"

I shook my head. "If so, the swamp would still be burning and half of New York would be irradiated."

He lifted gaze from the eyepiece. "Irradiated? Like with X rays?"

"Worse," I said. "We employ more traditional techniques for transport."

"Guess it's like gambling," said Doc. "Can't be guessing right all the time. I'll admit I've always been a sucker for those world-of-tomorrow stories, though—"

"Let the future show as it comes," I said. "It always disappoints."

"If you all are any example, I suppose it does." His stone face cracked with sudden laughter. "I still don't know how's I believe you all. Guess I'm just waiting for you to make a slip."

"I'm grateful for your help," I said, knowing we'd make no such slip. "We'd be lost without."

"You all seem like good people," said Doc. "Even Jake, considering."

"He's very set in his ways," I said. "Sometimes he frightens without intent—"

"I mean considering that he's white," said Doc, taking the slide from its slot. "You're clean, Luther."

"What's meant—?" I began; didn't finish.

"That fellow, Bill, one I was talking about," said Doc, seeming thoughtful. "He's better than most, but even so . . . whenever I read his articles or he shows me something he says is just around the corner, it always seems to me something's missing. One time I asked him, I said, 'Bill, you mean colored people'll be living like this too?' Cause I started thinking, if they're not, then where're they going to be?"

With the rest, in the valley, under the rocks, between the bricks and lost amidst plenty. "He responds how?"

"He shrugs, he says, 'Of course they will. Ever'body'll live the same way.' Like I say, he *is* a Red so you got to take ever'thing he says like that with a grain of salt." Doc stood, walked over to a wooden chair set atop a wheeled pivot. "Don't think the thought ever really occurred to him. Don't guess I should be surprised. He's still not like most whites though, just the same."

"Doc," I said, "had I been white would the police have still trounced?"

"Yeah, under the circumstances," he said. "You were smarting off, to their mind, and so they'd have beat you up anyway unless you made it clear you had connections somewhere. Point is, if you'd been white nobody down there'd have bugged you to begin with."

"It's unreasoned," I said, stepping down from my seat at table-top, reshirting myself with careful gesture, to lessen stab and ache. He'd replaced my old turban with smaller gauze so I wouldn't show so disabled. "I'd read about it but had no idea—"

"You said it," he laughed. "Tell me something I'm having a hard time with, though. You and Jake. I mean he acts like you're white—"

"Jake responds equally to all."

"It seems so natural, though. In your time whites really get along with the Negro people, or have they just finally got used to 'em?"

"Our day has many hates," I said. "More diffuse. No less pain-ful, much more reasoned. Generalized and nonspecific but for those regarding government or class or alien."

"It just seems unbelievable," said Doc, leaning back; his chair squeaked in pain beneath his weight. "They got new laws or something that make 'em give equal rights?"

All have equal right to suffer. "It's not something that comes up. Money and merit decide—"

"Money," he laughed. "If that was the case, ever'body'd be equal here. Nobody's got any money." With thick fingers he tapped his chairarm, as if awaiting word from someone distant. "Still find it hard to believe. Tell me something, Luther. I don't care how well you say ever'body gets along, somebody's got to slip sometime. When was the first time you remember somebody calling you a nigger?"

Twenty-odd years ago, I thought, on Long Island's smooth beach. "Last night," I said.

"All right, tell me this then. There must have been some time some day some white person must have done something and let you know you was different somehow. There must have been. When was it?"

Delving more deeply than I'd allowed previous, desired previous, I drew rotten meat from the broth's pure surface: remembered my white roommates at Andover disbelieving my preference for Nielsen's Fourth or Tallis's *Spem in Alium* over the blues—not Robert Johnson's blues—they so continually played and too often sang along with, claiming that they had to introduce me to my own culture, guardians of it that they felt themselves; recalled how, as a teen, boarding the elevator in our building on East Eighty-sixth, the way older white tenants simultaneously rising seemed instinctively to draw themselves deeper cornerways, their eyes black as Jake's; recalled Skuratov's specification of negritanski in his reference to me; thought of the Happy Golliwogs we'd seen at Detsky Mir. While armied I'd never experienced such, never in the field; in the field, when I controlled many men, in Long Island, most still were black or Hispanic themselves, excepting Sergeant Johnson. I'd known no comment at Dryco where, granted, I was the only black topender but for Ms. Glastonbury. They'd hired me deliberate, true. But had I not been an army success—

"Uncertain," I said, my paranoia brimming as his interrogation's lead settled. "What about you?"

"Early 1905," he said, after second's thought. "After they sold me." His words passed with so little tone that he might have been describing his travels between bed and breakfast.

"Sold?" I repeated. "I'm unclear."

"I'd barely even *seen* white people before then. See, I grew up on Reynolds's burley tobacco lands down in North Carolina. They'd bought the plantation that owned my folks, back after things got worked out, and, having northern money to spare, used it to buy up more land. Reynolds was better than most companies, like you've probably read. It's true, to a degree. By the time I was growing up we had our own little towns on the land itself. Our own stores run by our own people. Time I reached school age we had all colored teachers. Good teachers. In the summer we kids all had to work in the fields pulling bugs, cutting, but soon as school started that's where we were sent. Went home to nice little houses and small plots of land. The overseers was all colored. Lived the way it seemed right to live—" He stopped; gripped the chairarms as if to throttle nostalgia. Doc knew when rage essentialled to tear apart false dreams. "But they still owned us, body and soul."

"That brand," I said, thinking of his back's unerasable insignia. "They sold you—"

"To the only company still did that." He nodded. "They always did what they wanted to do, up till the end. What we'd heard was that Reynolds was getting too much heat from the foreign markets, for one thing. For another, old man Duke wanted to get better teachers and more students for his university but couldn't till the company switched over to paid labor. They needed money to pay paid labor so they sold us and that made everybody happy. Coca-Cola picked us up dirt cheap. Only place that was still buying by then; most were already phasing it out—"

"This was in 1905," I repeated; perhaps I'd heard wrong. I hadn't.

"That's right. I was fifteen. Reynolds had about eight thousand at the place where I was. Coca-Cola sent up these trains from Atlanta. We got loaded on, packed in shoulder to shoulder like we was in goddamn cattle cars. Able to keep just what we could carry. My train carried about nine hundred, went out at night, unloaded at night once we got down there. They'd built a new plant just outside of town. Damn white crackers with shotguns ever'where you looked. They took us off the train six at a time to control us better. First thing they did was bring out the brandin' iron. Then they took us to where we was going to be living. Cheap barracks across from the factory. Dirt ground. Outhouses. Barbwire ran all around the camp. We was ready to run that first night."

"Did you?"

He shook his head. "They shot you if you tried. See, I don't think they thought they was going to have their hands so full with us. Hell, ever' week there'd be trouble. They tried to keep us working the bottling line sixteen hours a day. Fall behind, you'd be whipped good." He laughed. "*Ever'body* fell behind. After a while it must have sunk in their heads that they were going to have to kill off their investment one by one so they stopped doing that, came up with new ways to deal with troublemakers. I was a trouble-maker. Organized a sit-down one day. Ever'body in my part of the line just stopped, sat down, wouldn't budge. Finally had to send in the state militia to get us out."

"They punished, after?"

"Of course," he said, staring windowways. "After the initial steps they sent Wanda and me down south. This was not long after they'd hitched us—"

"A fixed wed, then," I said.

"Any other kind?" he asked, leaning back, bringing fresh cries from his chair. "I didn't mind. Hell, I was a sixteen-year-old kid and Wanda was a *fine*-lookin' girl back then. They wanted to get rid of her, too. She grew up with 'em and so she was even more trouble to 'em in sneakier ways. They married ever'body they had while they had 'em if they could, see, cause in the future they knew they'd be needing a lot more workers and wanted ones that were homegrown. Just the same they didn't want a bunch of babies growing up like wood-colts. Wanted children of theirs to be brought up by a mother and father, in a Christian home." He cleared his throat of its accumulations; lit up a new one. "Wanda and me was troublemakers, though, and they sent us to Cuba."

"Cuba?" I said. "They had some sort of diplomatic arrangement—"

"Diplomatic?" Doc said. "With another state? Cuba's been the fiftieth state ever since the war with Spain, almost. Still a territory while we was down there, but—"

I didn't inquire as to the forty-ninth; it might have been the Philippines, for all I knew, or even Nicaragua.

"I always heard Havana's something, but it was hell where we were. Bugs, spiders, centipedes. Poison snakes. Poison *frogs*. Hurricanes. Kept the men all chained. I still got a big scar on my ankle. We worked in the cane fields, bringing in the sugar. Woke us at dawn, kept us working till nightfall."

"How long were you there?"

"Not long. Lots of people, they think old Teddy was the greatest man on earth for outlawing slavery but I think he had reasons didn't have anything to do with us. There was a stock market panic that year, a bad one. What I've read since says that J. P. Morgan helped save the country by keeping it funded. Now Europe'd been giving the U.S. all kind of hell for years for still having slaves but I think that's when they knew they could pull their trump card. Lot of Morgan's money was tied up in Europe and I have a hunch they said over there, all right, you can get your money out in time if you tell Teddy he's got to do something. Morgan also probably thought that if the big southern companies suddenly had trouble holding on to their workforce then it'd be easier for big northern companies to swallow 'em up, which is just what they did later on. I got a feeling it all got worked out behind the curtain. Bill and I've done some talking about this sometime, and he feels the same way of course. Anyhow, one day in 1907 old Teddy said he decided the time had come to outlaw slavery and he did. One day we went to bed dirt and woke up earth."

He sat silently for a time, sunlight's strips throwing shadow bars across us. "How'd you return from Cuba?"

"Wasn't easy—" The phone rang in the other room, a loud, sparkling alarm. "Excuse me." Stepping out, he answered before the third ring. I looked more closely over the pennies in his blue glass jar. While a few Indian heads showed within, upon the predominant thousands was the grinning, spectacled face of Theodore Roosevelt. Though my feet were firmly floored, below me I felt only air.

"That was Sydenham," he said, returning. "They confirmed what I sent over."

"Why the pennies, Doc?" I asked.

"Christmas presents for the little ones," he said. "In the neighborhood. There's something else we got to talk about, Luther."

"What?"

"I'd guess that in your time," he said, facing me, his dark eyes agleam, "they got cures for just about every disease."

"Why?"

"Can they cure DS?"

"What's DS?"

"You don't know?" His brow rippled like water into which a stone had been dropped. From a nearby shelf he pulled a thick volume bound, seemingly, in el car's varnished rattan. "Maybe they got rid of it by your time." After a moment he'd found the entry sought. "Read this."

Taking the book, I read from the opening:

> **Dovlatov's Syndrome**, commonly known as DS, Brainbuster, or Siberian Plague, was first described at Irkutsk, Russian Empire, in February 1909. . . . By the close of the following decade it had spread worldwide, its progress assisted by mass movements during and after the Great War. . . . The virus is of influenzal origin, though apparently of a mutated variety. . . . In America, House Speaker Joe Cannon, baseball player Christy Mathewson, author William Dean Howells and film star Charlie Chaplin; in Great Britain, Queen Mother Alexandra; in France, Premier Clemenceau, composer Claude Debussy, poet Guillaume Apollinaire and painter Amedeo Modigliani all succumbed to DS's effects—

Continued reading, coming at last to the conclusion:

> All human beings bear the virus within their bodies, although only in the earliest stages is any similarity in symptoms seen. . . . Neither inoculation nor cure has been discovered. There are no known survivors of Dovlatov's Syndrome.

"Horrific," I said, handing the tome back to him. "We've no disease such as this."

"You all are mighty lucky, then," Doc said. "Sometimes diseases just fade away and no one ever gets 'em anymore. Doesn't happen often but it happens. If it was still around, you'd know about it."

As I stared round the room, my mind dizzied with what I'd just read, I discerned a sudden change in all I saw, as if this existence had been suddenly rinsed in shadow, leaving stain on even the purest surfaces. "Seventy million died?"

"Over twenty years," he said. "Took long enough getting out of Russia but once the war came it started spreading fast. Ever'body that didn't die of it knew somebody that did. About ten years ago it started to just disappear, though it's never gone completely away. I think I've read there's still about three thousand new cases a year."

"What's purposed by this info?" I said, fearful to inquire.

"Like I said, you're clean. So's Jake. That is to say, the virus isn't active in you all and probably won't be—"

"It's in us—"

"You been breathing since you got here, right?" he asked. "You got it. It's in you. In me. It's in ever'body. But if it was going to start up in you I'd say it already would have. Peewee—" he said, eyeshut. "She's got it." The el rumbled by, topside; the stoplight in the street outside switched from blue to orange, and the traffic moved along. "It's progressing faster in her than I've ever seen it, Luther."

"Then how long does she—"

"Not a week," he said. "Probably a lot less. When I saw her catch those flies this morning, that was the giveaway. Nobody moves that fast unless they have it. If I'd have thought, I'd have run the tests last night, but I don't think it would've made any difference. We're all just so used to it. I'm sorry, Luther."

"Apology's nonessentialled for me," I said. "What was her response, hearing?"

"I didn't tell her yet—"

"No?"

"Jake, neither. They got eyes for each other, don't they?"

"Of sorts," I said. "Why didn't you tell?"

"I wanted to be sure. That's why I was waiting till I heard from the hospital. It's certified. I was going to say something, but she's so—" He faltered. "She looks so young. Cat got my tongue. Couldn't say a word."

"Then it's finalized?" I asked. "Death's secured? Such a death?"

"Unless you get back and unless you got a cure for it there once you get back, it's for certain."

Otherwise, then, an army death, bringing nothing with it but waste and pain. Returning with all speed more than essentialled now, not simply to save her—for we had no such disease in our world of which I was aware, and therefore no antidote—but if her departure prematured it would almost certainly make finding Skuratov a moot point, and locating Alekhine seemed evermore doubtful. Jake's unpredicted reactions disconcerted as well; that he knew attraction of his own was obvious, if unspoken. If he knew she would be leaving, so soon after arrival, would he act with reason, or—

"Luther," Doc said, "it's in the Lord's hands." To fall through those hands, as ever, I nearly said. "Listen, there's a patient of mine works weekdays. He's coming round in about ten minutes. Let me get ready for him and I'll be down once I'm finished with him."

"Tonight's source"—unlikely source—"arrives when?"

"Eight, like I said. I'm sorry I couldn't tell her yet. I will—"

"We will," I said. Leaving, I moved across the hall, reentering the unlocked apartment. Jake and Oktobriana couched together, a half meter between. She flipped pages of a gigantic book she had lapped before her, riffling them as if for breeze; watching her eyes flicker to and fro I realized that she was reading. Jake stared on as if waiting for an appropriate pause to introduce himself. Spotting me she suddenly lifted the book and heaved it my way.

"Catch, Luther!" she laughed; twohanded, I snared it before it cracked heretofore missed ribs. So red was her face that I thought she'd been drinking; her gestures came as semaphores.

"Marvelous *Time* magazine world history book of Doc's. Read, Luther. So many remarkable differences."

"Where's Wanda?" I asked.

"In dreams," said Jake. "Drawn into slumber by morning's wear and fear." He'd doubleclasped his hands before him as if uncertain of their action, once loosed.

"Is very fascinating," Oktobriana said, perspiration's beads bejeweling her forehead. "For long time all here seemed to follow same historical path as ours, only later. Nearly eighty years ago divergence begins."

Shortly, I'd found desired entry one: LINCOLN, ABRAHAM. *Sixteenth elected President of the United States, Kentucky-born, railthin, legal eagle of the prairie, orator deluxe, history's victim. En route to inaugural in March 1861, entering secession-crazed Baltimore, southern factionalists ambushed, brutally shot down—*

"No obvious reason for sudden change. Factor conceivably could be setting off of first atomic bombs in our world. Unexpected side effect—"

"Side effect," I said. "A bomb in New Mexico there kills Lincoln here?"

"Interconnectedness makes sense," she said, licking parched lips. "No other theory holds so likely. Like identical twins separated by distance. One hurts, other feels pain."

Senseless, I thought, holding neither weight nor reason; no more senseless than our being here. As Oktobriana tossed off theories like firecrackers I ravaged the history held.

"—in hologrammatic theory that which exists contains within itself duplicative pattern which in rationality—"

Checked the Presidents list for the late nineteenth century: Hamlin, Conkling, Tilden, Blaine, Harrison, Cleveland, McKinley, Teddy Roosevelt.

"—possibilities not limited to existence of two worlds only, of course—"

ROOSEVELT, FRANKLIN D. *Thirtieth elected President of the United States. Patrician-born, polio-stricken, former Empire State governor, 1932 election winner over Depression-disgraced Herbert Hoover. Assassinated month prior to inauguration in Miami by anarchist Joseph Zangara. In popular legend believed to have had secret plan to heal economy, in fact held vague notions of institutional socialism, bolshevized U.S. Successor John N. Garner ignored plans, watched banks fail, saw dust-blown, poverty-shattered midwestern states attempt secession—*

"—resulting changes in any event provide miraculous historical mirror in which we see our face as it might have been."

"Churchill was run over by a cab here in New York in 1931," I said, tossing the book couchward after glancing over his bio. "Roosevelt in '33. They had slavery in America until thirty years ago and still feel the results. Hitler and Stalin are prepped to fire for Europe's control. Some mirror. Some face."

"Such monsters," said Oktobriana. "*Tut gavno, tam gavno.*" As translated: Here shit, there shit.

"Skuratov said you loved the Big Boy beyond reason," I said.

She shook her head, her hairbangs wavering in wild corona. "*Chort.* Krasnaya disinformation of most ludicrous sort. My grandfather died in Stalin's gulag."

"You've a framed portrait," I reminded, "of most ideal form—"

"Sanya's," she said. "Kept because it reminds me of him."

"The Big Boy was Alekhine's fancy?"

Thinking of her vanished comrade settled her, though facial tics remained, rippling her cheeks without rhythm. "He was sheltered scientist," she said. "Held faint knowledge of political realities of past. Brain only holds so much, he said often. Had fool's delusion that Stalin would have given scientific work due proper respect and unguided assistance. I tried many times to send cleansing rain over his muddy head. Told him of Lysenko madness and such. He took my words as smears of past nonhistory. Thought use of Big Boy image in ad campaigns cheapened great leader but still served purpose in infusing previously banned presence throughout new generations. Said many times that our world would be better place if he were still alive. Such brilliance as Sanya had so often contains much stupidity." Her glistening eyes fastened upon Jake. "Strong men I like, sure. Their attraction overwhelms sometimes. But I have no love for monsters."

"You allowed him his dreams?"

"He was deaf to reason without hypothesis. And Sanya and I planned marriage after project completion," she said. "At project's beginning, at least, we planned. One loves beloved's flaws better than perfections, within limits."

"You'd set a wedplan?" Jake asked, his face, momentslong but no longer, showing other than stolid; seeming aglow with unwarranted because evident emotion.

"Certainly. Standard state marriage with suitable music. Afterward long taxi ride to Lenin Hills for taking of pictures."

"What music was programmed for backdrop during the ceremony?" I asked, rambleminded, thinking of the music at my own: Satie, Purcell, Elgar, Prokofiev, Moussorgski—

" 'Can't Buy Me Love,' " she said. "Everyone's favorite. But most dreams become ash as time burns away. By day he left I had accepted his departure in spirit long before. Not since last summer had we made violent love."

Jake's face flushed thrombosis red. With unforeseen lunge Oktobriana leapt pantherlike atop him, mad for flesh's rub. Her foot grazed the table near, sending a pressed-glass cup laden with matches tumbling, spilling them across its top. "Great stone man here distracts me now," she laughed, winding round him; he didn't pull away. Inadvertently, she eyed the matchpile. "Six thousand eight hundred eighty-nine," she said. We looked. There weren't a hundred there.

"Your mind's going," said Jake.

"Count them," she whispered. We did, laying them out in fives until the last.

"Eighty-three," he said.

"Square of eighty-three is six thousand eight hundred eighty-nine," she said, thought clouding her face. "How odd to know square."

"It's reasoned you should, I'd think—"

"I have never memorized tables. Would be pointless waste of brain so long as calculator is near. This is so strange. The number appeared to flash in my head."

Rising, retrieving an unopened box from the kitchen, breaking its seal, I slid it open, rained its contents before her.

"Nine thousand two hundred sixteen," she said, at once. "Ninety-six matches." Bringing her hands upward she rubbed her eyes, looked again. "How peculiar. There is factor operating here that I do not understand. Perhaps because I am so tired. Sleep came but at moments last night," she said, lying down, placing her head in Jake's lap. "Suffering from unexpected jet lag or equivalent, possibly. Jake, rub neck please. Such lingering stiffness."

With good hand he drew his slender fingers across her nape, probing and stroking, continuing slow massage for several silent minutes. Periodically her legs jerked as if in hypnogogic phase, before sleep's sweet coma envelops. Our own blips must flash on his screen, I thought. A safe extraction seemed impossible; her implant would be mote small and no unguided digging might haul it forth. At any instant the local team, guided by his word, might show, coming at his urging to mop us away. Through the windows I looked to see those black bugs flitting up; nothing. Not until tonight, I thought, considering. Takeout was strictly a nightgame, in my experience, and so seemed likely here.

"Jake," I said, lowvoiced. As I watched her eyes speed backforth beneath her shut lids, her small fists knotted as if for battle, I realized why Doc's tongue had so stilled. "Come kitchenways with me. Something essential needs passing." Easing himself up, allowing her descent without overt disturbance, he extricated and followed as I led into the sunbright kitchen, sweat pooling at my beltline. He eyed me without blink; folded his arms before him as if certain of answer, no matter the question.

"You've developed an intriguing relationship," I said to him, curious to gather what feelings he had, if any, before I related. "It eased capture—"

"Capture sans escape," he said. "To little purpose, under circumstance. Keep minded there exists but a one-mind intrigue."

"She's quite attracted, Jake—"

"In untenabled way," he said, his suit yellowed by sun pouring through the drapes' filter, "for unlogicaled reason. Passing fancy, a bunch of forget-me-nots waiting to wither."

"Perhaps. Perhaps deeper than admitted. Where's your stand, then? She's physically bountied. Intelligent beyond grasp. Articulate, multi-able. Mad as a cat for you. You say no?"

He nodded. "Untenabled."

"You've let the answer hang, Jake. Where's your stand?"

His mouthcorners drew as if by pickle's touch. As he stood,

shifting from foot to foot, he idly frisked himself for his missing toys.

"Well?"

"She tears my dreams apart," he said at last. "It's not me she sees, Luther. It's whatsisname on the backbound. The Big Boy. A deliveryman could have served as such an object—"

"It's you."

"*Untenabled!*" he repeated, his voice deepening as it rose; not since Thursday night had I seen such rising within his face.

"Why?" I asked, nearly so loud. "What's foreseen?"

"Hurt," he said, shifting again to barely heard mutterance. "The wrong kind."

He spoke true; I had to tell how true. Leaving his words where he dropped them he moved as if to exit. I motioned him to return.

"She's dying, Jake," I said. As I told of all I'd read, all that Doc added, he evidenced no shift in feature, gave no hint that what was heard disturbed. As mentioned, Jake was not devoid of comprehension; he quickly gathered all ramifications. Upon concluding I paused, baffled by what might be passing through his mind. "Response? Reaction?"

With thumb and finger he stroked his chin, pressed upper teeth into his lower lip, looked wallways as he spoke. "As foreseen," he said.

The front door's slam shot us ready and full; only as we looked, and saw Doc walking through, did we loose our tenses.

"Least somebody here's awake," he said, quietly, so as not to wake. "Looked like it was siesta time around here."

"We were dialoguing," said Jake, walking past into the front. "Excuse."

"You tell her?" Doc whispered, nearing. Fly's whine settled in my ear; I swatted it away, grateful not to have snared it.

"Told Jake," I said.

"I hear you," Doc said, sighing.

"I was offguarded," I said. "Once recovered I'll have no trouble. Mayhap we can figure something—"

From beneath his arm he slipped me what I'd seen as a sci-fi mag the night past; what evidenced at prolonged view as *Popular*

Mechanics. "Bill wrote the cover article. You can get an idea what I mean."

THE WORLD OF 1960, the banner printed thereupon read, overlaying a garish rendition of unlikely cityscape limned in primaries, drawn with blockline sketch. The painting's centerpiece showed a cluster of concrete roads rolling between trimmed trees; no traffic evidenced upon the roads but one or two buglike vehicles. Around the skyscrapers' tops, flylike, buzzed copters and blimps.

"Look through there. See how accurate his predictions are."

I thumbed the pages, keen to know what the future would bring my father, or the man who might possibly be my father in this world. In 1960 he would ride atom-powered one-man helicopters to the office, where he worked twenty hours a week; his home's furniture could be washed with blasts from a water hose; the weather within the dome covering his city could be adjusted as desired. Daily applications of pesticides would preserve his food forever; to clean his suit he would only have to walk in the rain. Only the highest art was transmitted through television's unyielding stare. As ever, a combination of laughter and tears proved the only response.

"Did a pretty good job, don't you think?" Doc asked.

"Not at all."

"He must have gotten some things right—"

"Nothing."

"Well," said Doc. "Still, the changes must be unimaginable."

"Your world is more similar to ours than guessed," I said. "We're more accomplished at what we do. That's all."

"I'd think they'd have at least outlawed war by your time," he said. "Way they're always talking about it, though you couldn't hardly think so these days. Were you in a peacekeeping army?"

"Hardly," I said, "and I knew fourteen separate police actions."

"Doesn't ever'one live in better houses and apartments?" he asked. "Like those towers on the cover there—"

"Such as these pictured?" I asked. "You know what comes from such projects?" He shook his head; I motioned towards Jake, sitting next to sleeping Oktobriana, in the front room.

"But look at you," he said. "No one grows old—"

"Most don't live long enough." Doc showed a pensive look, went to the refrigerator—icebox—and took out a bottle of milk, popping off its paper top.

"I don't know, Luther," he said, pouring a glassful. "You're probably just used to it all. See miracles ever' day, don't even realize it."

Miracles, yes, all God's wonders. The poison ocean rising higher each year, the thin air ashine with the sun's cancerous rays, the earth sodden with the blood of the billions killed upon it. The sound of orphans at play in the littered, rotting streets, born alone to die alone. The love that lasts and lasts and then fades as you look on. There were too many miracles in my modern age. "In Wanda's paper was mention of previous Martian reports," I said. "Was a joke inferred?"

"Oh," Doc laughed. "Last Halloween Orson Welles did this radio play about Martians invading the earth. Made it sound like a news broadcast. Scared the shit out of a lot of fools over in Jersey. That's probably what they was talking about."

"Undoubted."

"I guess in your time you talk to Martians regularly," said Doc, delusion again clouding his brain. "What're they like?" he asked, eyes shining with the hope of the hopeless.

"Mars is a lifelorn planet," I said. "Beautiful in physical form as photos evidence but free of sentient nature."

"Sentient?" he repeated, sounding the phrase. "Nobody lives there?" I shook my head. He looked to have discovered that his Christmas presents were lifted along with the tree and all its jewels. I hadn't wished to grinch him so. "There life anywhere else?"

"Only here," I said—and there, certainly, in our world, among our doppelgängers. "Therefore earthlife seems all the more—" Horrible? Doomed? Superfluous?

"Precious," Doc reflected. "That's so."

That, too. Oktobriana's slipped away as we watched.

8

"Interaction's feasibled here?" I asked, discerning through blue smoke none but pale faces gathered stage-near. Our people, dark but for Jake, loaded the rear, housed themselves barside, at intervals drifted through the smog to reappear up front, delivering drinks, rising from the white dough like raisins in batter.

"Feasibled," Doc repeated. "Bastards always take the best seats. But money talks, man. Try getting into one of their joints sometime, see how far you get."

Abyssinia contained as main room a coffin-shaped space with decapitatory ceiling; the illumination therein but grudgingly allowed sight. No coordinated decor systems showed: unframed posters covered walls, booth seats showed several years' slashes; not even the barstools matched. Two African masks of evident years and simple beauty hung above the bar, and I wondered from whose grandparents they had been inherited.

"Still alive," Jake said, hushvoiced.

"So the tracker reads—"

"Not Skurry," he corrected. "Him." His eyes fastened upon one of the newer posters, one announcing a concert past: FROM SPIRITUALS TO SWING/CARNEGIE HALL DEC 23 1938. In the midst of that night's performers, this night's: ROBERT JOHNSON. "You went?" he asked Doc, who smiled.

153

"Wouldn't have minded," he said. "But Carnegie Hall's whites only. They tried to get it fixed for that one thing and they couldn't even do that."

Jake, not noticing Doc's tone, stared stageways, blanked as if already lost within music.

"There's so many here," I said, looking over Caucasians' fine-haired heads, slicked and dyed and balding. "I'd think they'd barely hear rumor of such through the static."

"Depends on who's playing," said Doc. "They always pour in to pay their blues-dues when these boys come up from the Delta. Ever'day I was growing up I heard the blues. Played pretty, played rough. Almost hear the blues in the air down there." He laughed. "Depressin' shit, Luther. Give me Basie any day of the week."

Jake's lack of attention to all but the empty stage concerned, though for the mo there could be no removing his stare from where it fixed. His anticipation seemed more powerful even than that of a child awaiting Christmas, when the child has already inferred that the gift most desired is certain to be delivered.

"These people ride up here in their taxis, in their big fine cars, slum around up here all night long, drinking. Ever watch white people drink? I don't mean no offense, Jake—" Jake, unlistening, bore none. "They sip. They keep sipping till the whole bottle's gone. Then they upchuck all over the goddamn floor. Better that than when they start singing along, though."

"They're lyric-familiar?"

"Some of 'em. Man, you never heard anything so pitiful."

"What brings them in?"

"I can't tell how these people's minds work," he said, edging barways. "Ask Jake. Hey, Jess, down this way," he shouted to the bartender. Jess stepped down, drying a mug with three quick twists of rag, his hands twicesized over mine; his face was networked with scars whose web resembled a railroad yard. Between chipped teeth he flattened a green cigar's unlit stub.

"A sidecar, Doc?" he asked, unracking a glass. "What your guests want?"

"Give 'em beer. Any preference?" We preferred none; estimated it best to follow leads. "Trommer's White Label'll do." With metal tool Jess uncapped two long-necked brown bottles, poured one into a glass, then asked Jake: "Want yours in a teacup?" One of the inward-bent caps lay bartopped. Jake, looking up, retrieved it, poised it upon his thumbs, lay two fingers atop. With quick motion he thumbed the cap inside out, splitting its cork liner; flicked it barways.

"A glass," he said. Jess poured.

"Bill come around yet?" Doc asked.

Jess shook his head, passing Jake's filled glass gently towards him. "Motherfucker's usually first one here come Saturday night. Haven't seen hide or hair of him. His momma drug his ass to temple, maybe."

"Maybe." Maybe not. The wooden wall clock's skeletal hands showed eight-forty; Doc expected an eight o'clock curtain, but then so had the club's audience. They could wait; our minutes passed into minutes lost. Thirst burned my throat; beer it might have been, but I drank, at once hearthappy I had. If the best bread was liquid it would have borne such a taste, sweet with yeast, its head dense enough to slice, not at all resembling our day's bitter water.

"You've heard of Robert Johnson before, Jake?" Doc asked, gesturing towards the awaiting stage. "He's no Cab Calloway. Don't see how he's so well known in your day."

"He's not," said Jake. "Only the most aware see the glory. Long years past I first filled ear with his song. During a weekend at the Old Man's old house. Those hearing as intended to hear know—" Jake paused, waved his hands before him as if seeking unseen prey. "It makes it easier, somehow. No explanation holds." Removing his pocket-player, he set it, planning to tape.

Doc laughed. "Way you all talk sometimes breaks me up. Hell, Jake, you must know ever'thing he did by heart."

"Knew it already," said Jake, seeming exhausted by his speech's worded emotions. "Didn't realize."

A dapper man stepped onstage, held up his hands as if to slow a charge.

"Ladies and gentlemen," he said, "there's a slight delay but don't worry. Mister Johnson'll be out to play for you shortly. Please be patient with us."

"Who's he?" I asked.

"That's Vernon," said Doc. "Wanda's second cousin. He runs the club. We all own the building. Went in together ten years ago, just before the Crash. Laid down cash money. Even if it gets ten times worse'n it is, and they're always saying it might, nobody's gonna toss my ass into the street. Now if one of my tenants doesn't come across after a while, they'll get the deep six, but—"

"You never threw any of those deadbeats out in your life," laughed Jess. "Makes Wanda do it."

Doc ignored, continued. "I handle the apartments. Vernon runs the club. Break about even at worst and most of the time we do better than that. If the building's full and there's a good run of performers down here, well then we're eating high on the hog—"

"We hope you're enjoying Harlem as much as we enjoy having you," Vernon insisted, straight-faced. Jess turned his head away, held a laugh.

"Enjoy havin' 'em stuck on the end of my blade—"

"Grin and bear it, Jess," said Doc. "Come on."

"Mister Johnson will be out any moment now," said Vernon.

"He'd better be," one especially ivory member of the audience shouted back. "These damned shows never start on time." His mate, a young woman, wore her coiffed blondness curled beneath her veiled hat; with white-gloved hand she swung a half-meter-length cigarette holder as if to brand. When she voiced, her words rebounded off the silence that always settles at inopportune moment, so that embarrassment resulting may be total.

"We coulda stayed at the Rainbow Room," she whined, her tone rich with nose. "Oh, no. Moneybags here has to haul us up to Harlem for some damned coon show—"

As Vernon stepped away her voice faded with audience's rising murmur; additional commentary went gratefully unheard, at least by us.

"Oughta smoke the bitch," said Jess, lowvoiced.

"Beats the devil," said Doc. "They haul themselves up here and once they get settled they don't do nothing but beef. It's too crowded. Too hot. Food's no good. Gimme a clean glass—"

"What they expect?" Jess said. "You're right, though. They haul up a lotta green."

"They do."

"They can cry all they want long as they stick around long enough to spend it."

"What was I saying? Oh, yeah. Anyway, see, Wanda and me, we lived in shitholes first ten years we lived up here," Doc continued. "Down in San Juan Hill. West Sixty-second. When I got out of the army they'd just put Prohibition into law. Best damn thing ever happened to us. See, Wanda knew Vernon of course, he'd come up a few years earlier, and Cedric'd been in my regiment—"

"Cedric?" I said. "He's your age?"

Doc sighed. "Nobody seems to look my age but me. Yeah, he is. Anyway, we all started doing business together, see. Lee got mixed up into it later, after I got out of that end of things. Early on, though, Vernon set up a couple alky cookers, ran off batches of bathtub hooch. Cedric always had an eye for organization and the way he set things up we was able to keep the mob from cutting into our action too deep. Made arrangements, you know. That sort of thing. Time went on, we expanded. This place was a speak when we first opened 'er up. Good thing was all Cedric or Vernon had to do was pay off the precinct house and they wouldn't touch us. We did all right—"

"Through illegalities."

He stared at me as he hadn't since the first hour here. "Get off your high horse, man. What was I going to do? Till I took those medical courses I couldn't get a job running an elevator downtown. And where was I going to get money to start anything up with? Only colored banks there were all gone by the end of '33 and the U.S. Bank wouldn't give me paper to wipe a baby's ass. I wanted to *get* better'n I'd *got*, Luther. And I have. If things don't work one way you go another way. That's all." Looking clockways he saw the time; nine-fifteen. "Shit."

"Think he'll still appear?" I asked.

"Might know this'd be the one night he wouldn't—"

"Doc," Jess said, staring windowways, mopping the bar with an imprinted cloth. "You expectin' company?"

"Why?" Doc asked, swiveling round. Beyond the mirror-read neon sign hanging in the window, within the awning's shadow, revolving red light swirled, flashed off. "Oh, hell—"

"For us?" I asked.

"More than likely—" The door swung open; in strolled a gentleman twirling a walking stick, craning his view behind him to see if he was the object of professional desire.

"Who called the G-men?" he asked.

"What you mean, Theodore?" Jess said. "Who's out there?"

"Two white men in dark suits," he said. "Seem to be operating in official capacity. Also two gentlemen of color from the local department. All of them just hopped out of the squad car and went upstairs. Give me a highball, Jess."

"Let's get out of here," said Doc, standing. "If they've gone to the apartment—" Jake already headed towards the front. "No, Jake. Out back. Follow me."

With fast-mustered casualness we moved towards the rear through the club, ducking past a curtain overhanging stage right, and entered pitchblack.

"He's let the lights burn out again," Doc mumbled. Light eking from an open door midway downhall helped us guide our steps. Inside the lit room I vizzed Vernon confronting a tall, lean man standing in a corner as if for punishment, his face turned from view. Upon the dressing table lay a battered wooden guitar.

"It's copacetic," Vernon said to him. "Ever'body's shy sometimes. You're gonna do fine—"

"Not in front of these people," the man said, scratching his face with long, slender fingers.

"Once you get goin' it won't matter. Come on, Bob—"

We continued on; I had to pull Jake along. "Luther," he said, "that was *him*—"

"He'll be playing again, Jake," I said, in foolish attempt to assure. "We've got to move. This crew must be appearing per Mal's request. No estimating what's been told. Prep yourself for anything."

"Chances missed never return," said Jake, his voice lower than usual. "My tools'll help."

"We'll obtain," I said, "if possible." Ahead, at darkness's end, glowed a red exit sign, marking our path out. Doc paused before opening the door, his bloodlit form stalling us.

"Keep quiet," he said. "This'll put us out in the courtyard just below the kitchen window. If it's open maybe we can hear what's going on. Figure something out." With gentle hand Doc opened the door; we lightstepped into the concrete garden. Kitchenglow, yellowed by drawn drapes, shone overhead; as the awning was rolled up, we could have known full view were we three meters high. To kitchen's right showed blank stones and two blacked-out windows.

"Those lead where?" I asked.

"Back room in my office," Doc whispered. "Looks like they haven't gone in there yet."

"Then we should," said Jake. "My equipment's needed. What's eavesdroppable?" We pulled silence round us, the better to hear; two men, perhaps three, spoke in turn; from each we gleaned murmurs and bits of word.

". . . know somebody else . . . make it a lot . . . in time—"

The el ground all sound underwheel, rolling uptown. Jake scuttled crosscourt, reaching the windows without sound; we followed, silent though not as silent. "These locked?" he asked, drawing from his jacket lining a thin, flexible bar.

"Yeah," said Doc. Jake slid the bar between the sashes, jiggled and snapped; quietly raised the lower windowpane, hopped up and pulled himself inward, lifting himself with toe-edge against brick.

"Thought so," he said, reaching down for us once he'd landed within. Doc lodged solid midway through, as if to rest; with considerable effort we squeezed him through, feeling as if we were trying to get the last inch of toothpaste. In yanking me up they nearly dislocated my own shoulder; my ribs felt for a moment to be pulling apart once more, but didn't.

"Don't turn on the lights," Doc whispered, as if we knew where they were to turn on. "Put your hand on my shoulders. Watch your step. Follow me." Through dark we glided, traveling tiptoed so as not to cause the floorboards to weep of our presence. Alcohol's sharp perfume awared me that we must have entered the exam room. I heard jingling metal's clink.

"Jake," said Doc. "The key. Turn it to the left. That one where your hand is."

Jake unlocked and opened the door, withdrawing and jacketing whatever lay topside. Our breathing settled: I heard another sound, rising from below, alternately hard, then soft; as if snared from the heavens it faded and returned, the signal everpresent if rarely heard or caught proper. Robert Johnson sang.

"Darktown Strutters' Ball," someone kept yelling below, but his plaints were trampled beneath the singer's plea. Jake kept still, his ears picking up all.

"I'm cryin' please, please let us be friends—"

"Alive," said Jake, unmoving, stilled as if by amber's wrap, drawing new life from each word.

"Come on, Jake—"

"An' when you hear me howlin' in my pathway, rider—"

"Hush."

"Some a that 'Darktown Strutters' Ball—' "

"Please open your door 'n' lemme in—"

Fresh sound distracted all; the reception office's door crashed open. Sudden light blinded before Doc and I took a single step; Jake, unseen to any, was already gone, as if swept up by angel's order.

"I got the drop on you, boys. Stick 'em up." We lifted arms as if to give praise. The policeman showed nearly so lightskinned as I, and as tall, but bore twice the weight. He leveled his peacemaker our way, a .38 by its look, though judging caliber at distance is never easy, especially with such a collectible as his. At closer view, I noted the barrel bore an evident silencer. "Keep 'em up."

"You're making a mistake," said Doc, in normal, though rage-filled, voice. "This is my office—"

"Keep your trap shut," the policeman said, stepping forward, aiming direct. Catching eye of the open cabinet, spotting Jake's belongings, he froze. "Holy shit—" Keeping his gun, and his look, on us, he shouted across the hall to one unseen. "*Nate!!* Get over here. I'm gonna need a hand with these two."

"I'm telling you this is my office—" The policeman took quick glance at a certificate hanging on the wall. "How long you been at this precinct, son—"

"I work Central Harlem, usually," he said, "and I ain't your son. They didn't want to use anybody on this one you might be too used to dealin' with. Doctor, huh? Dillinger's doctor? Plannin' to knock off the treasury with this shit or what?"

My prolonged hosannas strained my split ribs into spasms; involuntarily, my elbows began to slump. The policeman directed his barrel between my eyes.

"Keep 'em up or I'll blow your head off."

"Who you got, Edgar?" his associate asked, entering; Senegalese dark, he was the size of a freezer unit.

"Old guy says he's a doctor. If this one's the Venezuelan he'll have a passport. Frisk 'em down and pull their flyers. I got 'em covered."

Nate beat us updown as he searched for pocketed harm, patting blindly away, pulling my passport and yanking Doc's papers; he didn't take my wallet.

"Would you get a load of this shit?" Edgar asked, dragging forth evidence once Nate had the drop on us. "You ever see a gun look like this?" he asked, fondling the Shrogin.

"Popgun, looks like. What is it?"

"Popgun, hell. Didn't know better I'd swear it's a machine gun."

"Where's the drum? Keep 'em up," said Nate, aiming at us both.

"Uses a belt, maybe. Must be foreign. We'll haul it all down, let the feds figure it out—"

"What about that pistol, man?" Nate asked. "Evil-looking piece. Stick it somewhere, pick it up later. Those assholes won't know."

"Shit. Take a look at the bullets in the chamber and tell me where I can buy some more. Okay, you two. Let's step across the hall and see your girlfriends. They probably miss you, we been talkin' to 'em awhile, tryin' to anyway. They're playin' hard to get."

"You better not've done anything to my wife—" Doc began;

Edgar drew a sap from his pocket, struck Doc across the side of the head with it. He stumbled back, blood darkening his graying hair. I caught him before he fell.

"Wouldn't touch your ugly wife, man," said Edgar. "It's little Red they're after. Now move it."

With single arm I assisted Doc until his balance returned, both of us prodded forward by gun's sharp poke. Jake wouldn't have run, that was certain; dependent on what he'd had time to recover before our untimely interruption would decide the method of his action, and the timing. It couldn't be soon enough. That, once moving, he would apply total effort was as certain; that thought comforted and terrified.

"It's AO, Doc," I said, helping him along; his head's blood dripped down his face like tears, splashed onto my shirtsleeve.

"Shit," was all he said. Reaching the apartment and entering, we saw Wanda and Oktobriana in the kitchen, under guard of the two white men; they were young, suited and tied. One had brown hair, the other blond; otherwise they might have been brothers.

"Norman," Wanda said, "what'd they do to you?"

"Same thing we going to do to you, you don't shut up," said Nate. "How're you boys doin' here with the ladies?"

"They're being very uncooperative," said the blond. "We've received none of the answers we'd hoped to receive. Stronger measures may be needed."

"Where'd you get that? Whose is it?" asked the other, seeing Edgar lay Jake's goods atop the sideboard's ledge.

"In his office. Think they were tryin' to get it. Must've come in the front after we did and before I went back out there."

I eyed the space, judging position and distance. Doc and I stood stove-near, covered by Edgar and the brownhaired fed. Wanda, across the room, poised near the icebox, her head level with its top-positioned drum. Nate and the blond covered the door leading into the living room. On the kitchen table, in room's center, sat Oktobriana, wearing a baggy red jumpsuit she'd donned at evening's arrival; though I knew she'd noted Jake's absence immediate, she made no remark. The window's drapes were drawn shut; night-breeze billowed their hems. Only streetsound came from without, and the regular roar of the el as it passed.

"You got their papers?" asked the blond. "Let's see." Edgar handed them over. The brownhaired one walked across the room and brushed Oktobriana's hair from her face; her eyes burned as she stared at him. Edgar and Nate eyed the agent's movements with evident suspicion. With whitened hands she gripped the table edges.

"Ready to talk yet?" brownhair asked her, grinning. "Where'd you get this janitor suit? You some kind of dyke?" She remained still, her eyes fixed upon the window.

"I'm no expert but this passport seems forged to me," said the blond. "We can check with the consulate later. What were you doing down by police headquarters this morning?"

"I told you all like I told them at the time," said Wanda. "This man helped me out by walking me through a bad neighborhood and he got beat up for his troubles."

"Gonna get beat up for more'n that if he don't talk—" said Nate.

"There'll be none of that in a federal case," said the blond. "You weren't looking for anyone there, were you? Someone you thought might be inside?"

"Were you carrying any of these weapons at the time?" asked brownhair, his attentions towards Oktobriana momentarily distracted. "Do you have Venezuelan licenses or permits for these, or are they yours?"

"No answers until I'm lawyered," I said. The feds stared; Nate and Edgar laughed long and loud.

"Nigger wants a lawyer," said Nate. "You hear that shit?"

"Wants one to hold his hand while he gets the hot seat—" said Edgar.

"You'll receive a fair trial in the United States Colored Court," said the blond. "Did you come into the country with the young lady?"

"Specify charges for this fair trial," I said. Doc held himself upright by gripping the stove; if he slumped, I tugged him up.

"At the proper time you'll be notified of all charges against you," said the blond. "Who else was with you and how did you arrive? Your assistance will make things much easier for all of us."

Their questions ran with circular reason; though at first I'd been sure that Skuratov's hand behinded this assault, the more they talked the more I doubted.

"As an apparent Russian national, miss, you'll understand why we wonder that you have no visa—"

"Is that your picture of Stalin? What sort of books are those in your grips?"

"Are *you* a Russian national?" the blond asked me, possibly remembering Pushkin. "Are you a member of the American Communist Party?"

"Shit," Edgar said, interrupting. "You assholes aren't going to get anywhere this way."

"This is a federal case," said the blond; we watched the burgeoning debate. "Your jurisdiction, such as it is, enables us to move freely throughout the neighborhood but—"

"Meanin' if we drive you all won't get the shit kicked out of you out in the alley," said Nate.

"You want answers?" Edgar said. "Up here you don't get the right answers unless you ask the right questions."

"Mister Hoover disapproves of methods used by your patrols," said the brownhaired one, moving again to Oktobriana, with light finger stroking her beneath the chin. "They're unprofessional—"

"Mister Hoover disapproves of havin' a colored police force, too, but that don't make much difference when push comes to shove," said Edgar. "You decide on who to make an example first. Of the four, who're the ones to keep?"

"The Russian girl's essential," said the brownhaired.

"We think the Venezuelan might have been the pilot," said the blond. "We're not sure yet what role the older couple play although she was with him this morning—"

"Should've figured," said Edgar. "All right, then. Just gotta show 'em you mean business." So saying, turning his pistol Doc's way, he fired twice at point-blank, his silencer holding sound to no more than brief pings. Doc's knees buckled under him as his white shirt reddened; sagging forward, he tipped floorways with a thud. The el

rolled by as Wanda screamed, rushing over; none stopped her. By
the pink foam bubbling from his lipcorners I could tell that his
lungs were hit; by the darkness of the blood issuing forth, it
evidenced that his aorta went as well. He looked upward as Wanda
held him, as if baffled.

"Norman," she pleaded, "don't go. Don't go. Don't. Don't go,
God, don't go—"

"God," Doc whispered. "God damn. God God damn. Damn.
Damn God—"

"That's what you need to do, you want results," said Edgar.
None of us moved; Oktobriana's lip showed deeper red where she'd
just bitten it. Doc lay on the floor; his heart beat until it had
pumped itself dry. His eyes glossed; his foamy lips closed. What
ran inside now pooled round our feet.

"Feel like talking now?" the brownhaired one said to
Oktobriana, his fingers still playing about her chin. She kept her
head level, her eyes fixed ahead. "No?"

"I think we should bring them in," said the blond. "There're a
number of things we need to go over—"

"There'd be questions we'd have to answer, too. I think we
should get everything straightened out here. What's your name?
Nate? Hold her for me, will you? Just put your arm round her
neck."

"What are you going to do?" his companion asked. Nate stood
there, uncertain himself of what was planned.

"Must be federal procedure," said Edgar, looking disgusted.

Nate held her neckround, in choke position, his gun aimed at
her temple with his other hand. Wanda held Doc's face against hers
as if to breathe life into him again. Jake's collection lay where Edgar
dropped it, across the room; the blond, standing near, was giving
closer attention to his associate's actions than to protecting the
weaponry. If I lunged at the proper time, perhaps I might retrieve
something with which some damage might be done before I was
sent away.

"No procedure I'm familiar with," said the blond, stepping
forward. "There'll be no violence here."

"Course not," said the brownhaired one, taking his fingers from her chin, fixing them on her jumpsuit's closure strip, pulling it open. "You haven't been in the New York office that long. There're benefits to the job—"

"Don't help 'em, Nate," said Edgar. "Take your hand off that woman—"

The brownhaired one raised his own pistol with his right hand, leveled it first at Edgar, then Nate. "Follow the instructions of a federal agent," he said. "We can say anything we want about what had to be done with you two and it'll pass muster. Now just do what I say—"

"I'll file a report," said the blond.

"No, you won't," said the brownhaired, looking up. It was all the distraction needed. Sending her feet elevating express, Oktobriana clapped her ankles to his face, the strength of her lower limbs further increased by DS's effects. The crack heard, the caving-in seen, awared all that she'd broken the fed's jaw on both sides. Stumbling backward toward the window, his arms outstretched, he struggled to vocalize, to sound his pain loud.

"*Shit*—!" Nate said, his hold loosening. At window's edge the fellow stopped, his back to the glass above, his legs meeting the open air beyond the curtains, just above the knees. The el rattled uptown, its echo rebounding off rattling dishware. "Look out for the window—"

"*Jake!!*" I screamed, my voice lost. "Don't—"

He'd readied, standing atop crates new-piled below the window. Through the drapes he thrust his saw, doubling its length as he activated it, raising it between the brownhaired one's legs. Sounds of shredded cloth mixed with harsher grind as a puff of bone dust rose; as he lifted his tool higher, working it through, all that lay in the man's lower half dropped further south, squishing floorways as if to the offal drain. Without sound or comprehension he pitched forward, his split complete. Oktobriana, meantime, advantaged with sharpened reflex; grasping Nate's gun barrel, pushing it beneath his drop-mouthed chin, she crushed his hand round the trigger. He flew back as he fired, his skulltop sending his shotaway cap into the air. Jake bounded inside as Wanda, cognizant again, began crawling towards the living room, offbalancing Edgar,

who froze where he stood; I dived after her. Hefting his saw Jake
heaved it towards Edgar, catching him fullface, pinning him to the
kitchen's lacquered-wood cabinet like a museum butterfly.
Oktobriana rolled off the table, sliding into the bloodpool below,
allowing Jake to leap forward as the blond made for the living room;
with light spring he thrust up from tabletop, leveled his flight,
tackled the last living and brought him down as I collapsed onto
Wanda, keeping her floored; her screams unceased. Taking his
head between his hands Jake did the twist, leaving the blond
sprawled stomachways but staring openeyed, towards the ceiling.
From below, through the carpet's muffle, I heard cheerful song;
Johnson, for a short time, brought joy to all who heard. If any'd
heard what resounded above, I prayed they'd ignore. Not thirty
seconds had passed.

> "Hot tamales and the red hots—
> "Yeah, she gottem for sale.
> "Got a gal that's long 'n' tall.
> "Sh'sleeps in th'kitchen with her feet in the hall—"

Jake eyed the leavings of his craft, his breath coming in gasps as if
his talent overwhelmed even his expectations. "Modern times," he
said. "Postmodern reaction. Forgive, Luther."

Wanda's shoulders heaved as she struggled to crawl away from
me, away from the kitchen; I held her tight, keeping my hand
sealed across her mouth to lessen decibels. "All right," I repeated in
idiot's litany. "All right. It's all right. It's all right. It's—" Her tears
soaked my hand; when she began to vomit I pulled away, allowing her to do as she needed. Looking into the kitchen, seeing Oktobriana redonning her jumpsuit while standing in slaughterhouse's
midst, I felt my own stomach churn, and so quickly shifted gaze to
the living room again, where the sole victim showed as bloodless.
Jake examined his suit; as expected, it showed snow pure but for
where he'd been spattered by his own juice the morning before.
Oktobriana made her way into the front, nearly slipping, leaving
red footprints on the carpet. Drip's sound came from the kitchen;
the charnel's smell already overwhelmed, and in the hot weather I
hated to think how far its waft might drift, how soon.

"What caused the delay?" I asked Jake. "Doc's dead—"

"Known," he said. "That downwent as I prepped to enter, Luther. No chance I could have leapt up holding that saw without putting the boxes in place first. I'm no superman—"

Oktobriana gripped him, squeezing until his eyes popped. "You're all right, Jake," she said, her eyes suddenly wet with silent tears. "Doc—"

"We can't leave him placed like that," I said. "Jake. Assist me."

As unhappy pallbearers we retrieved Doc's frame; with difficulty—he must have weighed two-sixty, even without blood—we hauled him into the front, lay him on the sofa.

"We got to get out of here," said Wanda, surprising us with hoarse voice's cry as she pulled herself upward. "Get the car keys. They're in Norman's left front pocket. Go on, get 'em."

Moving across to where he rested, Oktobriana reached into his pocket, fumbled; seemed surprised by something, though I couldn't imagine what. "These?" she asked, tossing them across to Wanda. Bringing up her hand, she peeled Doc's mustache away, dropped it on the table like a dead caterpillar. None of us said anything.

"Can't they trail us with number and record?" Jake asked.

"Change the plates," Wanda said, her voice frighteningly calm. She showed none of shock's evident marks, though mayhap they simply lay waiting to later emerge in full. "That's all we got to do besides getting away from here fast. Must be a thousand black Terraplanes in the city and long as we don't be too visible they're not going to find us right off."

"Who has extra plates?" I asked.

"Cedric," she said. "Hand me the phone. I'll talk to him. Hurry up, Luther. Give it a half hour more, they'll be sending out a paddy wagon and round us all up." Taking the receiver, brushing away its long black cord, she dialed the number. "Cover him up," she added, barely heard. Using one of the sheets he'd brought in for us the evening past, Oktobriana and I, each taking an end, billowed it over our friend and let it float down around him. The sheet's white showed at once its own fresh red wound.

"Such a kind good friend," said Oktobriana. "Hold me, Jake."

Without seeming thought he encircled her with his arms; before he clasped her waist I noted how his hand shook. As I stood there, awash with feelings I couldn't afford to let surface, I wondered that if our presence could have such dire result for the few with whom we'd had direct contact, what then would occur over time? What would Doc have done, had we not arrived? What would one knowing Doc, or receiving cure from Doc, have done? Ripples from our ill-thrown stone might stretch oceanwide by end's turn. The responsibility overwhelmed; I kept my reason where it belonged, and lay such thought aside for the moment.

"Cedric?" she asked. "Wanda. I need your help, baby. Norman's dead. Cops shot 'im. That's right. No, no, they're taken care of already." She paused. "We need to make a run for it. No, now. That's all right. I got an idea where to go. What we need is new plates. For the car, right. How much you want for 'em?" She said nothing as she listened. "I don't think so, Cedric, just tell me how much. All right then, I'll bring what I got and you can take what's fair. Can we come on over?" Wanda shook her head. "Don't come down here, no. Don't even act like you ever been here before. I mean it. You don't *want* to know. All right. We'll be right up." She hung up. "Let me get my money out," she said.

"He has spares?"

"He's usually got whatever you need. Cedric's a good one to know." Kneeling on all fours, leaning down as if to drink, she reached beneath the sofa and extracted from its guts a small metal box. Before she could rise, Doc's hand slipped from beneath its sheet; a delayed motor reaction, perhaps. When it brushed her neck she knew whose hand it was; said nothing, but shuddered as would a struck tuning fork. Reaching up, not looking, she replaced his hand beneath its cover. With one of Doc's keys she unlocked the box, and withdrew a thick green roll bound tight with a rubber band. She shoved it down her blousefront, between her breasts.

"Take a gander out front," she said. "Don't let nobody see you. Any other cops in sight?"

"Clear," I said, looking.

"Car's parked over on One Thirty-third. Just leave all this shit. Let's go."

As we followed, leaving Oktobriana's cases, her papers and books, Alekhine's portrait of the Big Boy; leaving the kitchen's grotesque additions; leaving Doc, it struck me that, with little thought and no obvious regret, Wanda left behind her life. I gathered she'd had to several times before, somehow; whether or not she ever grew used to it, I couldn't say. Walking upstreet, ignoring all who passed, we reached the car within minutes. Applause resounded from within Abyssinia.

"Can you drive?" I asked as Wanda positioned herself wheelways.

"Can *you*?" The car groaned as she ignited, unwilling to start; once it gave in we pulled away, edging slowly through two teams of young boys playing streetball with sawed-off broomsticks. Circling the block we turned onto Eighth, passing their building once more and all that lay within, and headed towards Cedric's below the overhanging el, pausing at each blue light, moving at each orange, searching each intersection for policeman's signs. Wanda aimed left onto the street below the candy shop and swung into the drive of what appeared to be an abandoned brick barn just behind; above the high-arched entranceway, at keystone position, was a stone horse's head. Beeping the horn twice, pausing between each blast, she gave word of arrival; the metal-shuttered door lifted, allowing our entrance. Standing brightlit in headlight's beam, leaning against the garage's far wall, was Cedric, his tie and vest removed for evening comfort. The door lowered once we entered.

"His deliveries come in this way," she said, cutting the engine as Cedric approached. I noted that sometime during the day Doc had put a new sideview on his driver's door. "You got 'em?" she asked, sticking her head out the window. -

"Oh, Wanda, I'm so sorry," he said. "Do you know the ones who did it—"

"I told you they were taken care of," she said. "I know you're sorry, Cedric. There's just not enough time to think about it yet. Where you got 'em and how much you want for 'em?"

"Here's one," he said, drawing from behind his back a gleaming tag, *New York World's Fair 1939* plain upon its face.

"Where's the other?" she asked. We stepped from the car, all but Oktobriana. Cedric eyed Jake but gave him little heed. "What's the price? We ain't got all night, Cedric—"

"The other one's in my office over there," he said, handing her the one carried, pointing with single finger towards the side rear, barely visible in the dark beyond the lampglow.

"So how much?"

"Nothing," he said. "I just need Valentino here to come with me to help get it. That's all."

Wanda looked at me; looked at Cedric. The fee was obvious; that we needed both plates was of unavoidable import. She moved as if to mash him.

"You little son of a—"

"Wanda," I said; she settled. "Jake, replace the first plate. Where's the other, Cedric?"

"You're not going to—"

"There's no choice, Wanda," I said. "Is there?"

"Oughta club him and just take it—"

"There's been enough of that for one night," I said. "Come on, Cedric. You say it's over here? Every moment counts—"

"I know," he said. "It's over here. I'm scared of the dark." He almost ran to his office; I followed, hearing no more comment from Wanda, expecting none from Jake. We entered a closet-sized room just off the garage where, possibly, deliveries might be checked against orders. In the gloom I saw but shadows even after eyes adjusted, but felt all: unhitching, he drew my trousers down to kneelevel as he dropped down upon his own, as if positioning to pray. Standing inspection-still, eyes shut so as not to break privacy, I discerned but few true differences: the grip behind was harder, the lips more gladly enveloped, his nails were longer and sharper than Katherine's. Yet, the distinction evidenced in deeper form; in heart I felt nothing, and so nothing showed plain. Cedric seemed not to mind; continued until he finished, or grew bored, or realized his efforts brought naught.

"Thank you, Cedric," I said, taking the other plate once I'd rezipped.

"Good luck," he said, "soldier boy." Stepping away quickly, as did I, we left without further word. Reentering the garage proper I handed the second plate to Jake, who took it without remark, as I knew he would. The garage door creaked as it rose again, permitting us escape with but mannerly protest; we slid into darkness.

9

WANDA RACED US THROUGH THE STREETS, BLIND TO ALL BUT THE road ahead, obeying all signals, marking all moves, running without word. We left Harlem, rolling into the park at 110th, creeping over its crumbling roadway, past fields of unmown grass, straggling brush and unpruned forest. Scattered across a moonlit slope, meadowed rather than treed, I saw what at first evidenced as a host of boulders, dropped as if glacier-left; realized upon second look that the rocks were but sleepers, taking rest as they could on their city on a hill.

"Where do we aim?" Jake asked, holding on to Oktobriana still, his shake not yet settled. Full-frame shivers rattled her own body at five-minute intervals; even in darkness, from front-seat vantage, I saw her trembles, and wondered whether the effect came from evening's events, or from her disease. Wanda drove as if struck deaf and dumb; her hands' cords knotted as she gripped them more tightly upon the wheel. At the moment it seemed she acted only sequentially, not concurrently; she drove, and did no other.

"None trail," said Jake, neckcraning to gain rear-window vista. "None obvious, I should say. How undercover works here remains unknown."

"Shoulders, Jake," said Oktobriana. "So sore and tender. Rub them, please."

"Wanda—" I began to say; was hushed by her shout.

"You couldn't just walk in the front door like normal people," she said, all emotion suddenly loosed. "You done that, we might have been able to get out of it some other way. We hadn't told 'em a damn thing. They were just asking those damn stupid questions till they caught you all and then they knew something was up. Don't even know why you couldn't have just waited till they left."

"We were ignorant of intent or design," I said, attempting defense. "Or action as it went in our absence."

"Ignorant's right," she said. "Done it like anybody else, nobody would've got hurt. Act like civilized human beings—"

"Doc would be with us now had we knocked?" I asked.

Wanda, sinking, clutched for any patch of reason; found none. "Her running around this morning like she was just asking for it—"

"She wasn't this *evening!*" I shouted, estimating Jake's usual objections to oral vehemence might pass in this instance; for a moment I thought he hadn't even heard. "Nor this morning, for that matter—"

"Such statements are unfair," said Jake, very quietly. "Action such as encountered demands one reaction. They acted. I reacted. That's all."

"Did you have to go after 'em like you did?" she asked, her eyes remaining on the curving road ahead; midtown's tower lights showed through trees' canopy. "Hogs stand a better chance in the slaughterhouse."

"Hogs deserve better," Jake said. "It was my sole implement at hand. I'd have preferred a more minimal touch but hadn't choice—"

"What kinda world is it you live in?" she asked, her face drawn as if to rein in tears. "Talk about people bein' sawed up like you was making a grocery list. Acting like someone's always out to get you, so you got to get them first. I mean I can understand a mood like that but you all take it so damn far. Norman was the same damn way. No wonder you all got along so good. He was always looking over his shoulder, seeing who was closing in. Crazy man—"

"Not so crazy," Jake said. "Someone closed in."

"He'd be here now if you all hadn't come here!" she snapped.

"We'd be driving on out for the weekend. Or we'd be home. But we wouldn't be where we are." After a long moment, she settled, rubbing her eyes.

"We'd not expected such a detour," I said. Nostalgia's wave suddenly washed over me, nostalgia for a home that seemed evermore distant, never again seen true; seen only in this off-register reproduction.

"Russki krai," Oktobriana said, unexpectedly slipping into mother tongue. "Otchi dom." Russian soil, native home; nostalgia. "Smert. All smert."

"Let's make the best of it," she said, "since we don't have much choice."

"None," I corrected. We emerged from the park at Columbus Circle, seeing no ungainly tower, no wall dividing midtown from the Upper West; where, on the south curve, stood our day's concrete Lollipop House, showed here what appeared as a several-story Victorian mansion. A sign atop its mansard advertised chewing gum of unknown make. Central Park South's thirty-story wall defended midtown from the jungle here as in our time; here only half the wall seemed whole. Several buildings showed only as framework against the night sky, left unfinished, I supposed, when the money ran out. Rounding the circle into Broadway, past bright wide windows holding the latest model Hupmobiles, Pontiacs and Studebakers, we drifted by a Terraplane dealership, seeing our transport in newborn form. Many slept sidewalked, below the shining displays.

"Doc was wonderful kind man," said Oktobriana. "Much goodness in him. Great knowledge of humanity. Knowledge given. Heaven above. In heaven above. If soul survives. Likely so. Floating forever between worlds. Heaven is in fence. Also hell."

"What fence?" Wanda asked, uncomprehending. Remembering the metaphor, I could leap along with her logic, and so followed. That if such were literal it seemed so good a place for him to be as any. Recalling Doc's words, I realized that she had entered a stage where her thoughts passed more quickly than she could give them accurate word in logical sequence. As Oktobriana became less conversationalist than *yurodiva*—an untranslatable, roughly meaning a seeming fool who speaks of saintly matters, always true—her endless commentary became first annoying, then oppressive, and then at last, as with all, we grew used to it. She spoke of all seen as we passed into Times Square, in our time the home of all the misbegotten and wild; here it showed as what I'd heard it had been in my parents' childhood, a rainbow-lit stage upon which uncounted millions performed. Displays twicesized over any of ours shilled in neon ribbon for Four Roses, Seagram's, Chevrolet. One to our rear insisted in tall yellow letters that a bag of Planter's peanuts a day would give us more pep; how pep was applied, I couldn't say. On far left a mouthpuckered head several meters high puffed smoke rings, hawking Camels. A trapezoidal building, vaguely Italianate in look, stood at the Y formed by Broadway and Seventh's intersection; around its facade, just above ground floor, a letterscroll ran, flashing news and weather through the blink of a thousand small bulbs. At Forty-fourth and Broadway men singlefiled blockround like Russian shoppers; here they waited to receive, one to each, a breadloaf passed out from a parked Salvation Army truck.

"Sunday papers are out now," said Wanda, edging into the far right lane, careful not to bump any of a multitude of taxis, cars and streetcars. Seeing a sign, I wondered what an Automat was; there was no driveway leading in. "I'll stop and pick 'em up. You all can see what's going on in the world."

"News of our action'll show when?" I asked. "By dawn?"

"If it'd just been the cops and Norman no paper but the *Age* would've covered it," she said. "Since you all got two G-men as well it'll be front page on ever' paper in the country by tomorrow night and Monday. Not till then, though."

After curbsiding the car near Forty-second, by one of the larger newsstands seen, she got out.

"I'm burning hot," Oktobriana said; her metabolism was increasing everfaster, and even as she sat outwardly still her interior consumed itself with terrifying speed. "Climate seems so tropical here all the time. Unlike Russia where we have no jungles. Here we have forest of light." She murmured some uncatchable phrase as she stared at the lightscroll, just to our left. CLOUDY, RAIN TOMOR-

ROW, I read. UNEMPLOYMENT RATE NEXT YEAR TO HIT FIFTY
PERCENT, SAYS LONG.

"Pardon?"

"Number of times bulbs will light in hour," she said, explaining
her lost remark. Several times she attempted to toss back her bangs
from her face; failed, finally handswept them away. "So tired and
aching. Like stretched on rack. Like running without cease for
weeks. Four thousand five hundred eighty-nine kilometers. Seeming tendonitis in joints. Artoscopic treatment. Mentally I feel
twice the normal person," she said. "What is wrong with me?"

This was no place to tell; growing anxious, I looked for Wanda.
She still stood at the stand, waiting on line. Oktobriana's thoughts
passed and faded at everincreasing rate.

"With appropriate machínery all lights could run with single
machine's touch," she said; Jake kept an arm around her to keep her
from bouncing off the seat. "Tesla could do such. Must have vast
plan. Great business support must help him here. Temperament
more suited to commerce. No fear of round surface. 'New York—
New York,'" she started singing, badly. "'Want to wake up in city
full of creeps.'" Her laugh came as a hyperventilating bray. "Par-
ody version American defector astrophysicist taught me one time.
Before leaving country he moved to Vermont. Hated city. Moved
where Solzhenitsyn lived behind chicken wire. Like fence. Not
like Tolstoy. Not like fence of gulag. Not—"

Through my carwindow Wanda heaved in her buy, lapping me
full with multisectioned Sunday rags: the Times, the News, the
Herald-Tribune and Mail, the Mirror. Info of any unrelated nature
wasn't my desire just then; I'd long reached overload. Before
flooring them between my feet I noted the News's head: WHERE IS
STALIN? In regards to what or whom? I wondered; his attitude
would be surely similar towards all. The pact with Hitler wouldn't
be penned until August, unless it had been already signed, or
unless it wasn't going to be signed. To see the future's possibilities
without being able to guess which would eventually come to
actuality was much more troubling than having no idea what the
next day might hold; it was like watching a car speed towards crash,
knowing one of four within would be killed, but not which one.

"We're going to go out in the country," said Wanda. "Get things sorted out."

"Won't we have to transit checkpoints?" I asked. "We've been APBed by now, surely—"

"We're not going to Jersey," she said. "There's a place on Long Island I know." Waiting until traffic broke enough to allow us exit, she at length pulled back into its flow; we crossed several lanes and bore left onto Forty-second.

"That's safe?" Jake asked.

"Safer than here," she said. I didn't want to go, but there was no choice. When my feet last touched Long Island I'd stepped onto its soil from chopper's safety, laying sole on unmined ground; it was during my first operation following my promotion to first lieutenant. My sergeants and my men belonged to the Suffolk Unit Reconnaissance Forces, and had been ordered out one June day to assist in an assault on Southampton, Amagansett and Wainscott having been slammed the week previous to little effect. Johnson, my Johnson, was with me as my master sergeant. There've been few afternoons more beautiful, few skies showing more unclouded blue. Reflected sealight made even the bleakest ruins glow with old master's touch. The weather was so perfect that there didn't seem to be any. A day so lovely gave me the shudders, everafter.

Passing an unsecured, unlit Grand Central, Chrysler's stone and marble shaft and several blocks of seemingly abandoned tenements, we turned left onto First. Abattoirs and meat-packing plants stood where the UN rose in our time, blood's inescapable tang not yet supplanted by political deodorant. Reaching the Queensboro Bridge at Fifty-ninth, sweeping onto it across its cobbled approach, I found myself, for the first time, being driven across it rather than flown over as we aimed into the eastern region. White light of unknown source shone across northern Queens's distant horizon.

"Where on Long Island?" I asked, the names forever impressed in my mind: Mineola, Farmingdale, Stony Brook; Shirley, Riverhead, Southampton; all the others where so many had fallen.

"North shore," she said. "Takes about an hour and a half to get there. It's what Norman and me called our summer place. We discovered it one afternoon driving around about seven years ago.

We went out there ever' couple Sundays all through the summer ever' year. Place's falling apart but it's livable long as it's not too cool, and it's right next to the beach, almost. Real empty out there. We'd've probably headed out there tonight, in fact, if our plans hadn't changed—"

On the bridge's far side the setting's look suggested that the Depression was in its twentieth year and not its tenth—as in our own time so many places remain as they were left following our own economic readjustment thirty years after it came, changing all everafter. The small frame houses huddled next to one another, five-story courts, small, unpeopled restaurants with signs lacking one or more letters, blocklong factories with boarded windows; all showed neglect's touch plain, even those whose owners continued to attempt upkeep. The limitless gray blocks seemed gradually to be wearing away, eroding with each passing year until, one windy afternoon, the east would send forth into the sky its own clouds, from its own dust bowl. We continued east on Northern Parkway; I noticed a sign arrowing Holmes Field's direction, due north. At the crest of an overpass we sighted the source of the horizon's icy glow.

"The fair?" I asked; Jake and Oktobriana looked on as if at their first Christmas tree. Wanda eyed the scene no more than a second.

"Yep."

From the midst of blackness rose a shiny white world dotted at places with pastel traceries, its elliptical acreage centered with that inescapable needle and sphere. Unmoving searchlights lit the thin bone and fat ball; affixed to the spire's highest surface, just below the point, was a circular metal framework of unguessable purpose; on none of the reproduced logos had it shown.

"Have they a name?" asked Jake.

"The Trylon and Perisphere," said Wanda.

"Why?"

"Sounds modern," she said. "Doesn't it?"

Smaller buildings scattered about held their own peaks and caps; buildings in boat's shape, or with cash registers planted topside, emerged from the surrounding glow. Towards one end of the plot, beyond a lake, another highrise rose over the skyline, a metal framework resembling an enormous utility tower. Parachutes seemed to be dropping from its broad summit, as if sightseers were so appalled by their surroundings that they couldn't wait for the elevator.

"In afternoon paper was picture," said Oktobriana, her hair blowing back in the window's wind; her cheeks twitching without cease. "Central structure has remarkable similarity to needed device."

"Device," I repeated. "How so? What similarity?"

But Oktobriana added nothing to her previous remarks, and fell disturbingly silent. As I looked on I saw what appeared as a great shadow suddenly darken part of the fair's illumination; looking above, I saw but vaguely an enormous dirigible, moving at gentle pace across the sky, its silver belly reflecting the lights below as at groundlevel it darkened them; on its rear fins, I saw swastikas.

"That blimp," I said. "What is it?"

Wanda peered up from windshield view long enough to note; returned view quickly to the road. "The *Hindenburg*," she said. "Coming out of Lakehurst, I'd bet. Heading back to Germany. They was saying it wouldn't be back for a while."

We outdistanced the still-surviving zeppelin soon enough, passing through the tag end of Queens, entering the country. Fair became factory, became farmhouse and field. The moon cast its own shadows over marsh and timberlot. The road narrowed; narrowed again. All before us glowed in negative light as we roared ahead; sidegrowing brush raked our car's sides as if to hold us back. After a time no other cars showed during our flight.

"Much longer?" I asked, feeling that unsatisfied anticipation always suffered when the ETA of one's destination remains unknown; when each minute triples in experienced duration. That we rode a federal highway astonished; its sole improvement over mudtrail was the broken pavement. On odd occasions signs appeared, showing amidst the wild familiar names, names I connected with disconcerting ruin and unforgivable waste; names from the old days, out here.

"Twenty minutes, maybe," she said. "Never can remember the name of the damn road it's on but I recognize it when I see it.

Don't know if it even has a name, thinking about it. We'll be fine though, once we get out there."

"For how long?"

"Long enough," she said. "We will have to decide what to do at some point—"

"We?" I said. "Why include yourself?"

"I'm in this shit neck-deep just like you are, Luther. Accessory to first-degree murder of two colored policemen and two white feds. They got us all on that right now. They can get me on harboring fugitives, transporting fugitives, conspiracy, well, you name it and I think we've done it."

"What options show?"

"For me?" she asked. "None. I go back, say what happened. I get booked. Won't take long to take care of me. Excuses don't hold with Colored Court judges. Then—"

"What options show for us?"

"Less than none," she said. "It'll be the hot seat for you all inside a month, 'less you're lynched first. They lynched some poor bastard in Riverside Park just a month or so ago."

"But the longer you're with us the deeper—"

"Doesn't matter at this point. Can't go anywhere else. Try to get to Canada they'll pick me up at the border. Everything I hear makes me think it's not that much different up there, they're just not such assholes about it. I don't know—"

"All's meant for purpose," I said, offering the feeblest lie I knew; wishing to comfort, all the same.

"Shit. Finally had a real simple life going. Not the happiest life but I could deal with everything in it. Then you all come along. Now look." She spoke more with resignation than with anger, which relieved.

"We didn't intend interference," I said.

"I know. Good intentions. No use crying over spilt milk."

At last, slowing, she wheeled us onto a more primitive road that ran off to our left; its grade was so ill-lain that each bump threatened to throw us into the surrounding woods. No lights lightened its length other than our own.

"Here we are," she said as the house rose into view; as seen through night's cloak it showed as an oldstyle residence, the type in which dozens might hide. It was a two-story stone, long and rambling, with high brick chimneys. Trees surrounded three sides; the fourth side was open to the sea. Approaching a small building behind the house, I heard drumbeats, the pound of cannon: breakers. Across the rear meadow I thought I discerned the ocean's moon-shimmered plain. We pulled into a ramshackle garage, parked and emerged. Wanda pulled the garage door shut with a length of heavy rope.

"What was this?" Jake asked as we headed up the walk, our feet crunching the pebbles below. Insects surfeited our ears with their buzz.

"Somebody's house," she said. "Big old places like this stand all along the shore out here. Few of 'em are still occupied but most have either been repossessed or the owners can't afford to keep 'em up anymore, so they just let 'em sit out here and rot."

"None patrol?" I asked.

"Never saw a guard or policeman whole time we been coming out. Wouldn't be a cop left in the city if they had to keep an eye on all these places." We stepped onto a roofed, wide-planked porch that ran houseround, careful of our tread so as to avoid gaps and weak spots. "Door's never locked, either," she said, slamming it open with her shoulder. "Never have to worry about burglars in the country. Come on in."

We walked into a two-story foyer; within its space my apartment could fit twiceover. Curving upward from floor to second story was a long stairway, its banister and railing leaning outward as if sprung by the passage of millions; in night's black-and-white light the scene looked as a set down which Astaire might dance. Seabreeze wafting through shattered windows cooled the house, brought tidesound. Above room's warped woodwork showed mold-splattered walls. What furniture remained hid beneath ghost-drawn sheets. Mouse's rustle sounded among the debris.

"Looks better in the daylight," she said, crossing the plaster-littered floor, gliding in and out of shadow. "Norman and me, we always slept on that big old couch in the front room. You lovebirds take that, why don't you?" She fell silent for a moment, her face unseen in the dark. "I'll slide a couple chairs together over in the library. There's a trundle out on the sun porch you can sleep on, Luther. We better all get some shut-eye. Sun'll wake us when it comes up and if we don't get a little rest we're all going to be even more worthless in the morning than we already are."

I tossed the papers floorways, immediately regretful as I choked in the ensuing dustcloud. All departed to their respective spots; Oktobriana had fallen into quiet ever since we'd seen the fair; whether there was something to which she turned her thought, or whether it had become too hard for her to speak and simultaneously connect what she heard herself say with what she was thinking, I had no idea. Seasound beat loud throughout the screened, openair porch, sending a soothing rhythm.

"Jake," I shouted into the front room. "He's moved?"

A pause. "He's not." I heard him snap the tracker's cover shut as he pocketed it. By trundle, evidently, Wanda referred to a small metal bed standing in midfloor, surrounded by breeze. Tugging down the dusty, clammy sheet, finding a mattress mildewed but sleepable, I sat at bedside, moonlight making all in the near-empty room visible. A Bible lay floored, nearby; picking it up, I made a quick flip through its damp pages, looking for a quieting passage, finding instead: *For the sons of light came unto battle with the lot of the sons of darkness, which are known as the Army of Belial, and against the troop of Edom, and Moab—* This wasn't the Bible I remembered as a child. In the contents I read the names of the books of the now-discredited New Testament: Matthew, Mark, Luke, John, Thomas, the Acts of the Apostles, the Gospel of Truth, the Hymn of Light. The front page announced it to be the Holy Bible of the Albigensian Church, Redeemed. Unwrapping another gift, I'd found only another body. Having had overmuch surprise when least expected, or desired, I reclined, feeling the pain in my head, my ribs, my heart; feeling pain wherever Doc stepped. No sooner had I lain than I slept.

Dawn nuzzled me awake with groping light; I remained bedded, feeling that to rise too soon would only hurl reality onto my head again too hard, too early on. Hurling was already in progress, I gathered; Oktobriana moaned in pain, pain of disease and pain of knowing of the disease. Shortly I heard crying's sound, deep and choked, as Jake told her.

Freshening as best we could once we'd risen, meeting in the living room, Jake and I sat listening to Oktobriana while Wanda walked out onto the sun porch. Possibly in response to the pain she now felt, she seemed to have so focused her mind on the ramifications and pertinents of her situation—now that she knew what it was—and so kept such grip over her body with her mind that her multitudinous thoughts now came worded clear, with patterned logic. Her English, too, had become perfectly worded with classic phrase, if at times overrich with science's jargon and distance. As she lay on the couch, her arms wrapped round her drawn-up knees, she spoke as if to herself.

"The agent, then, would seem to be a highly mutatable retrovirus of unknown origin. The site of first appearance is fascinating in that were there to have occurred here an incident matching the noted Tunguska astronomic strike of 1908—that was in Siberia—then it would be impossible to disprove the likelihood of a relationship—"

"But have you inkling as to cure?" I asked.

"None will be found here for years," she said, the tendons on her neck bulging as if attempting to rip themselves free. "Even with expanded mental capabilities I can do little more than guess without access to a computer with which I might estimate all known variables. Millions of possibilities would have to be checked with an unknown disease so peculiar as this one. There're too many maybes. Why the virus manifests itself so virulently. Why the incubation period can be so extreme. How neurological functions can be so intensified." She paused, catching her breath; blue bruises showed at her wrists. "Why I have it and you don't. The disease would seem to be so widespread among the population that simple breathing might be the method of transmission. Yet in such a case there should be unavoidable immunity in some. What has made you so fortunate and me so unlucky?"

"Unless we've something worse that hasn't shown yet," I said. "Unless we've caught it since Doc did his tests."

"I doubt that there is anything worse," she said. "And while it is certainly possible that the virus has shown in your blood since the tests were made, I would suspect that your reaction might not be so much more different from mine. Possibly unknown preventative or enabling factors are at work here." As she brushed her head with her hand, long strands of hair fell out; pimples appeared on her cheeks and neck as her metabolism spiraled out of control. "This disease would be so much more fascinating in the broader sense if I didn't have it."

"There's no possible action?" Jake asked, his good hand wrenching the dusty couch arm as if to rip it free. Though he remained blanked, his frustration-raw voice forewarned that he was on the verge of burst. "Nothing to be done?"

"Return. That is what must be done," she said. "Otherwise we may as well walk into the ocean, one by one."

The situation seemed so unbearable that I had to lose myself in anything else; the morning's rags lay near. Hauling them up, I gleaned the heads; read more carefully. They must have seen my stare.

"What's up?" Jake asked. "What's the word on the Big Boy?" he said, eyeing what I read. WHERE IS STALIN? the *News* asked. KREMLIN ADMITS PREMIER'S DISAPPEARANCE, read the *Times* in upper right; *Stalin Last Seen Friday Night*. In the *Mirror*: TOP RED VANISHES; frontpage-pictured were shots of the Big Boy, and of Amelia Earhart and Ambrose Bierce. Perhaps Oktobriana could have spotted the connection immediate, but I didn't. *Trotsky Keeps Mum.* SOVIET LEADER STALIN MISSING, REPORTS CLAIM, announced the *Herald-Tribune and Mail's* head. *Trials Suspended Until Further Notice.*

"Oktobriana," I said. "Did such as this occur in our history?"

"No," she said, studying the banners. "Stalin, in our world's June 1939, was secluded within the Kremlin, on one hand deciding to deal with Hitler in regards to Poland and the Baltic States while on the other hand making up lists of who else among his countryfolk should be killed. This is so unlikely as to—"

Clapping her hand to her forehead, she let the papers slide from her lap. When she took away her hand she showed a small black bruise left behind.

"You've connected?" I asked. "What's meant?"

"I've connected," said Jake. "Alek's behinding this fadeout."

"Such an *utter* fool," she said. "It must be Sanya. Took him three weeks to get through but he obviously did."

"Wait. What's inferred—"

"The Kremlin would not lose *Stalin*," she said, her eyes fury bright. "If they did they would never admit it unless, as is certain, they have no knowledge of how he got away. Sanya has done what he must have planned all along—"

"He's transferred this world's Stalin into ours?"

She nodded. "As we were leaving they must have been returning. *More* than a fool. He not only has brought enormous danger into our world but has committed deliberate retrocide in this one, destroying the future as it would have been by interfering with the past."

"There'll be no danger of political upheaval in ours," I said. "Krasnaya has no desire to hold a living Big Boy. They'll gulag him from now till—"

"Think, Luther," she said. "What is it that is killing me? Sanya must have been immune or else not picked it up or the disease would have spread through Dubna following his first return. But if Stalin carries the virus, and as he has lived through its ravages, then it is certain that he has brought it now into our world's air. Even as we speak, it spreads."

"Meantime in this one," Jake said, "with Roosevelt exed, Churchill gone—"

"And Stalin removed from the scene," she concluded, "Hitler remains to act as he pleases. The possibilities are enormous. Sanya has committed crimes against humanity in both worlds."

From outside sounded seagull cries, surf's steady beat.

"What's possible, then?" Jake asked.

"Hitler can take Europe in two years," I said, "including England. Inference from our history's progression suggests he may or may not hold on to western Russia; depends on when he invades and what strategy he uses under these changed circumstances. He'll certainly be able to take all of northern Africa, and Egypt. If he chooses to slow, if he heeds some among his group, Germany might invade the Middle East, move through Iran from Russia, join with Japan somewhere in India—" It was the old worst-case scenario as laid out, the difference here being that all was yet possible. "That in twenty years or so there might be only Germany, Japan and North America. If Germany develops the bomb—"

This world, suddenly, seemed even worse than ours.

"Luther," Jake said, pitching me the *Times*'s front unit. "Viz this." Frontpaged low was an article concerning a meteor's descent.

> . . . neither information detailing its nature, nor even size, which local residents estimate to be enormous. Several dump trucks have brought dirt to the area, where bulldozers are being used to build a ramp across the marsh from the site of impact to Route 3. Members of the New Jersey State Militia have erected an enclosed tent around the apparent meteorite and stand guard. . . .

"Deep cover," I said. "Meteorite. They've certified it's not contemporary flight-oriented—"

"Unless they've begun dismantling the controls they know only that they have in their possession a Russian plane of advanced capability outfitted with weapons. That they would make the obvious, if erroneous, connection seems certain. That would easily explain last night's events, with or without Skuratov's assistance."

"They think Stalin came with us?" Knowing Skuratov, he may well have told them that *he* was Stalin.

"It is the obvious inference," she said. "That the ones investigated brutally murdered all members of the investigating party might conceivably convince them entirely."

But what, I thought, feeling my own mind's line unreeling, if this tale of disappearance was nothing but disinfo in itself; Skuratov's scheme. Mayhap he'd broken or lost his tracker during his drop, and found himself unable to sight Oktobriana's glow as he earlier had. What better way to set a lure than to let fly a tale of a

problem's disappearance, knowing we would make the obvious
decision; to wish return quickly, to find him fast—

Ridiculous, I told myself. The love of plot is my disease.

"In any event, under these circumstances they must be quite
aware that Skuratov would seem to be, to someone, one of great
importance," she said. "And so, as it seems evident as well that
Sanya has returned to our world accompanied by his hero, our
hope of escape remains with Skuratov."

"If it's still in one piece," said Jake.

"There is one additional possibility to which I must give further
thought," she said.

"What?"

"We had a theory that with Tesla coils of great size conjoined
with resonating towers of equivalent power, the effect produced by
our device might be caused without any such device, that the
energies resulting could split the wall between worlds. We could
never test such theories, for we hadn't funding to build a coil and
tower of the necessary size. So Sanya developed his machine—"

"Where would such a coil be—" I began to ask; remembered her
odd silence of the night previous after passing the fair.

"Inferring what I can in these articles, I would say it is obvious that this Trylon and Perisphere are a tremendous Tesla coil
and resonating tower, and they will be switched on tomorrow
night."

"We may be able to use it to get back?"

"There are further calculations to make. The danger, neverthe-
less, will be much greater."

"Why?"

"There will be no control over the effect, if such an effect occurs.
The transferral may be imperfect. There are many awful possibilities but as last resort it is worth investigating," she said, curling
her feet beneath her to slow their unending jiggle, her face drained
of color by the effort's pain. "My mind is useful so long as I have
it. Let me use it." She suddenly paused; turned and looked at
Jake. "What was it you gave me after we crashed?" she asked him.
"Extamyl, was it?"

"Three hundred mils to lessen pain and shock," he said, his

voice seizing as if he needed lube. "The last of it. It would assist now, I know—"

"In such massive doses Extamyl decreases the immunity to transient respiratory ailments," she said, tapping lip with finger; she bled beneath her nails. "Of course. Certainly there would be no concern ordinarily but I'm afraid that this particular transient takes its vehicle with it when it reaches its stop. Examining the possibilities, I feel assured now that it was the dosage of Extamyl that likely assisted in my immediate infection, even if it has had no bearing on the speed of its progression, which I would gather is rapid."

"I had Diodin—" Jake said, his face drawn tight.

"There are no such side effects with Diodin," she said. "Who's to say that Diodin might not have lent you greater immunity? Or temporary immunity?" Bruises blotched her arms and wrists, where everflexing muscles forced capillaries to break. A vein had gone at elbow joint, leaving a Rorschach of desperate sign. "Jake, you showed wise concern and acted properly. There is no reason to blame yourself."

So, pronouncing sentence on Jake, she faced him full; in his own look he showed, through his lack of emotion, the strain of holding it within. Good intentions always killed, or killed often enough to give pause to any samaritan. I myself would have thereafter seen a murderer in any mirror, deservedly or not; what he might see, I never knew. He patted her hand clumsily, as if fearing he might be struck down for affection's show.

"This explains so many things," she said. "The untoward energy and euphoric feelings earlier on. I am so tired. Hand me something to write with, Jake. I'd better set down whatever I have to offer." Her left eye showed pink, where something else had given way. The head of a fullpage ad in the opened paper, lying at my feet, announced: WE ARE ALL INTERESTED IN THE FUTURE/*For That is Where We Will Spend the Rest of Our Lives.* So I hoped; it seemed evermore unlikely.

Wanda stood sole and only on the sun porch still, peering towards oceanedge through bulged-out, rusted screens. I walked across to where she was, leaving Jake and Oktobriana to be by themselves a short time longer.

"How're you?" I asked.

"I've been better," she said, avoiding my eyes. "Hurts being here."

Hurts us both, I thought, remembering the ambush suffered as we neared Southampton so long ago. Breaking formation, positioning roadside, we delivered our own messages, rocketing all within radius. Those hit with phosphorus fire popped up from their burrows as if from a Roman candle. We felt the earth wince with shellblast as we lay upon it. C-380s swept overhead, bearing napalm eastward to cauterize dissent's wounds. Ten lost there in the road, for no purpose, for no reason, to no effect.

"Luther," she said, stirring me from my reverie. "Where are you?"

"Sorry," I said. "Daydreaming."

"Wish I was like you all, in a way."

"What's meant?"

"I wouldn't feel any of this," she said. "It'd be so much easier."

"Feel? Feel what?"

"That's what I mean. You don't feel anything, do you? Emotions, I mean. You've all gotten rid of 'em somehow. Streamlined 'em away. It just seems like you get along easier without them."

"They're there," I said, speaking at least for myself; she was right, in the broader sense. "We bury them deep enough not to rise again."

"Can't get 'em down that deep," she said. "It's close in here."

"Let's take outer air," I said. She nodded. Opening the screen door, its spring shuddering loud as its rust flaked away, we exited. None rose from underbrush to meet and greet when we showed; no warning shots blew out our brains. We moved forward, careless as icebergs. The abandoned garden through which we passed was overgrown with kneehigh weed; the faint marks of path and a tilted sundial at center showed where a pattern once used, failed. Reaching an outcrop of rock at beachside, we sat. Blue-and-white butterflies drifted by like paperscraps tossed over fire; I'd not seen one living since youth. Birdsong rose; eyeing upward I sighted a boiling feathered cloud cross the sky, aiming inland, towards the east. No ornithologist, I.

"What are those?" I asked.

"Passenger pigeons," said Wanda. "They set up a preserve for 'em somewhere out here 'cause they say they're dying out. When I was little big flocks'd fly over ever' year and the men'd wait till they settled in the trees. Then they'd beat 'em down with long sticks. My grandparents told me they'd black out the sun for hours when they'd pass, back when they first came here."

"They're over a century extinct in our day," I said.

"That's life." She shrugged. "Nothing but damn birds anyway. Gave 'em a place to live just the same. Killed off the buffaloes. Killed off the Indians. They'd kill off all the colored folk, thought they could get away with it. But they try to save those damn birds." She shook her head. "Sounds like it's too late for them, too."

For a few minutes we watched waves folding in on themselves, rising again, striking the beach with seaspittle. Coastlight lent all a gentle gilt.

"You've seen the disease in progress previous?" I asked.

She nodded her head. "Ever'body's seen it in progress. Just not as fast as it's happening with her. Two of my brothers died of it."

"Sorry," I said. "Quickly?"

"Don't know," she said. "I wasn't with 'em and my sister never said much. They never left Georgia and I wouldn't go back there on a bet."

"Doc pastspoke only yesterday," I said. "Related early life tales."

She nodded, again. "Your grandfolks must of told you some kind of stories like that," she said. Father's father owned three mortuaries; mother's father was president of Citibank, until the Ebb.

"Some kind," I said. "He told me you were in Cuba. Didn't have chance to lend color and detail—"

Wanda lit a cigarette after rolling it between lips, wetting its end. "We weren't there long. Not as long as some."

"The description horrified."

"Being there was bad," she said. "Getting home nearly killed us. That was the worst of it."

"I asked Doc how you effected return, but he didn't elaborate."

Her smile suggested the remembrance of a lost one's beloved, if fatal, quirks. "He wouldn't have. Norman always thought he got the short end of the stick in the long run and maybe he did. We both had it hard getting back, but we made it back. Helluva lot of 'em didn't. Almost like it happened to somebody else, now," she said; drew in smoke as if to inflame memory's burned-out circuits. "That last morning they woke us up at five like they always did, lined us up in front of the barracks like they always did. We'd get our work assignments usually then and that'd be it. All they said that morning was, 'You're free.' Turned around and headed back to the office.

"Well. We all just stood there looking at each other like maybe we was still asleep and still dreaming. Longer we stood there the more we realized we weren't. What exactly they meant by what they said worried us, though, and so in a little while me and Norman and a few more went down to the office to find out just what they did mean. We were young, remember."

"Did they explain?"

"Once we talked to 'em. Said that since Mister Roosevelt set us free they didn't own us anymore. Said they didn't like it any better than we did, but they didn't have no choice. Couple of the fools asked if we could keep working for the company but they told us company'd been took over by the government. Wanted to make an example out of 'em, they said; Lord knows they couldn't of picked a better one. We said, well how do we get home? They didn't know. Said they was going to burn the barracks down so we'd better get out before they did. We said, where were we going to live, what were we going to eat? They didn't know. Told us some feds be coming down in a week or so to help smooth things out. See, Cuba wasn't a state yet, just a territory, and they said because of that it'd take longer than usual. What about in the meantime? I asked. What were we supposed to do? They said more of us died now, more room there'd be in the boat going home, once a boat went home. Then they told us to leave. Shut the office door, locked it. That was that."

"Then?"

"Some of us wanted to be done with it, leave all the shit behind. Decided to walk down to Caibarién, that was the closest port, see if we couldn't work something out getting a boat up to Florida. Took us two days to get there. Wasn't much of a road to speak of, just kind of a narrow clearing. Didn't eat much on the way 'cause we didn't see but a few trees or bushes growing anything we recognized. Folks living on the little farms we passed weren't much better off than we were, most of 'em didn't speak English and once or twice we got shot at and had to hightail it before they aimed right. Guess they figured we'd escaped and was hoping to get a cash money reward.

"None of the peons in town wanted shit to do with us once we got there, though. None of us had any money to pay 'em to take us across, nobody wanted us to work for 'em to pay 'em that way, and we didn't know what the hell we was going to do 'cause we sure weren't going to try and swim across. This one fellow down by the docks, name of Alfredo. Had the ugliest teeth I ever saw. He talked to Norman and some of the other men. They made a deal. Alfredo wanted to hop the one other woman that came with us, her name was Sophie. Big strapping girl, had forearms like a man but an ass you could serve dinner on. Fine looking."

She paused, as if to retrieve breath.

"Sophie wouldn't hear of it first. She loved her man Robert so much she couldn't even imagine going out on him, much less whorin'. I couldn't say much good for it either except it'd get us back to where we could at least walk where we wanted to go. Took a while but I finally convinced her it was our only choice. Her only choice. I never have forgiven myself for doing that.

"Alfredo owned a thirty-foot fishing boat, carried a crew of nine. When we got set to sail, first thing they did was lock all the men up down below for the duration. Sophie and me, we went to Alfredo's quarters and waited. He came down, took his clothes off. Vilest, filthiest man I ever saw. He took her. She just lay there with her eyes shut tight the whole time, she said. I don't know 'cause I couldn't stand to look. I was supposed to be there, see, to keep her company, and make sure she went through with it. He got up, unlocked the cabin door. Gave a whistle.

"They was going to go in groups of three, I guess. I tried fighting 'em off but two of 'em held me down while the other one was goin' at it. They kept pushing her face down in the pillow like they was trying to smother her." She coughed. "Sophie nearly bit her lip clean through, holding back." Without audible sob great tears rolled down her dark face; brushing them up, she threw them away. "They split that poor girl wide open. When they was done with her, the bastards, they started in on me."

The shore seemed always so cold, whatever the season.

"Wish old Jake'd been on that boat with us," she said, laughing with true pleasure at the joy of imagined revenge. "We finally got to Florida. Came into port just north of Miami. Threw us all off. Sophie's Robert knew one was going to get to it, but didn't know the whole crew would, and he treated her like shit ever after that. Started whipping her, talking to her like she was a dog. We'd just reached the outskirts of Waycross one night, made camp. We had a big pot of hominy boiling on the fire. Robert came over, started in on her. Sophie didn't say a word, just took that pot, flung it over him. Didn't have any skin left on his head or chest. Sophie ran off that night." Wanda smiled; frowned. "Never saw Sophie again."

"Doc didn't act that way—" I said, rather than asked; knew the answer already.

"Norman always was a good man. I told him what happened, afterward. He didn't hold it against me, never even talked about it. Thing that tore him up was that I lost the baby," she said. "Too many uncles, I guess."

"You mean you were pregnant—"

"Six months," she said. "If we could've had another we would have, but we couldn't."

"Why?"

"After he started that to-do in the Atlanta plant they gave him a two-part punishment," she said. "Least thing they did was ship him down to Cuba. Main thing they did was make sure he couldn't have any children. Much as they needed new ones, they didn't want any from bad stock, as they put it. Some of the owners were from Kentucky and they were used to horse bloodlines. Son of a bitch bastards, they didn't know I was already pregnant and I wasn't going to tell 'em." She sighed, her voice deepening as she spoke. "His voice had already changed but he never could grow a beard after that. Bothered him he couldn't. He said it didn't hurt

much as he thought it would but they shot him full of morphine to
do it and then kept him shot up for three weeks after just to be sure.
It was hell when they took him off it and he never did break loose
completely. Ever' Friday night he'd come home from the hospital
in East Orange, go in the bathroom and let fly. Never more than
once a week though. Just enough to help him keep going till the
next time."

"So you came north—"

"*Ever'body* come north except the ones too beat down already.
Ever'body found out once they come north that if they was going to
work they'd be working for the same people used to own 'em, 'cept
now you had to pay for your own shack." Her eyes burned as they
stared over the ocean, from a home never owned to a home never
known. "Shit. Steal us to come over here. Work us to death. Kill
our babies. Finally set us loose on a long, long leash. Start gettin'
too far off, they pull on it till we choke. Day the market fell was the
happiest day of my life. Let it all fall down, I thought. Let it all
burn. See how they like it."

She lit another cigarette; shot smoke through her nostrils.

"You know the future, Luther. What am I going to miss?"

"This September Hitler invades Poland," I said, deciding for
folklore's sake to follow our world's chronology. "Starts World War
Two. Conquers most of Europe. Sets up death camps. Kills millions of Jews. Many know but none act—"

"Figures," she said. "Haven't there been enough dead already?"

In God's plan, I doubted that Hitler had ever had a cold.
"Fighting Hitler's like makes us forever more like the fought," I
continued. "We abyssgaze overlong. That's Europe. Another front
opens in the Pacific. Japan attacks Hawaii in late 1941 with planes
built"— I had to laugh, remembering now —"with scraps of the
Sixth Avenue el. A bomb—"

"Japs?" she asked. "Good."

"Good?"

"They're colored people," she said. "True?"

10

WE HEARD A SUDDEN CRY COMING FROM THE HOUSE; TURNING around on the rock, we eyed Jake, stepping out so far as into the garden to give his call without direct interruption.

"He's moving," he called, his voice fading in the air. "She thinks she has something."

"What's shown?" I asked, reaching him.

"Aiming northbound," he said. "On rubber, as evidenced. Undoubtedly in the company of others."

"What's Oktobriana's word?" I asked as we stepped back in, coming through the sun porch. I realized how strongly the house smelled of mildew and must.

"Unclear," he said; morninglight showed wrinkles cut into his face, new-pouched eyes and drawn cheeks. For once he almost appeared as his age, ten years younger than I. "Let's ask—"

"Lord," said Wanda, seeing as we saw. Oktobriana's body, lying on the couch, had arched upward, describing a circle, the top of her head almost touching her heels. Her teeth sank into her lip; she was unable to give voice to pain; her arms flailed uselessly to either side of her self-made hoop.

"Her feet," I said. "Take hold and stretch them out." With my hands gripping her head, enough to hold though not enough to crush, I kept her positioned while Jake attempted to pull her sofaways once again.

"She's like iron," he said, struggling. "Wanda. Force her stomach down—"

"Gently," I said. "Not overquick. She might shatter."

Jake pulled, Wanda pushed, I held; slowly, carefully, we flattened her out once more, keeping her down once she'd settled. Bruises mottled her arms and ankles, showed at her neck, lent the appearance of flowered bracelets running up her legs. Adrenaline coursed through her body; her pulse raced like a marathoner's at finish line's end. With sinking stomach I noted that to touch her now was to mar her. Her eyelids fluttered like butterfly wings; as she strove to give word, froth bubbled over her bleeding lips. Then, from the depths of her lungs rose two sirenlike wails, echoing through the empty house, bearing in their warning nothing but full-body anguish.

"Calm," Jake chanted, again and again. "Calm. Calm, calm—"

"Lord," Wanda whispered, "please take her—"

"Not yet—" I said. As if limit had been reached, somewhere within, Oktobriana did begin to calm; the veins in her neck rose as she struggled to speak, and speak so that we might understand. Her hands shook as if they might shake loose from her wrists.

"Paper on floor," she gasped out; I suspected that the muscular contractions affected the lungs as well, and it seemed possible that her attempts to breathe might suffocate her. "Some things I have written down but let me tell." One of her knees shot up, driving towards her chin; Wanda and I kept it from striking. "Instructions worded so simple as possible. Get the machine if you can. Go to fair. When coil is switched on massive power will be released. If weather prediction holds true—" A sudden fit of hyperventilation kept her from finishing; her reddened eyes bulged from her blue-dotted face as she tried to force her aspiration again into normal pace.

"Calm," Jake said, from her opposite end. "Calm, calm—"

Her right arm struck the couch as in fury, spinning dust motes through the air. "If weather prediction holds, thunderstorm tonight should bring additional possibilities. Nothing to count on. There on paper written. But go to fair after retrieval. Get within range of coil as it is turned on. Timings and situation figured out—"

Without advance her legs flung themselves airways, knocking back Jake, sending Wanda rearward with a thud. As one of her Achilles tendons snapped she let out another long wail. Jake struggled again to lower her legs, and I cradled her head, brushing the loose hair from her face. She stared into my eyes, showing anger and incomprehension and scarifying hope; the blood on her lower lip had dried, and crusted as she smiled. As I looked at her, she slowly settled, her breathing quieting, coming lower and lower. Her visible body showed as a quilt of black and blue and greenish yellow. Her bloodshot eyes continued to look upward, flickering as if stirred by outside charge. She lay there, unmoving; Jake and Wanda pulled themselves closer to her face.

"Is she—" Jake began to ask.

"Not yet," said Wanda. "It's a blessing. Usually the fits keep up from here on out up till the end. Sometimes they get all quiet like this, though, and then stay that way until they have one last conniption—"

"Can she hear us?" I asked. "She's aware?"

Wanda nodded. "She won't answer, but she knows what's going on. They always know what's going on. Lord, Lord—"

The three of us rested for long minutes, feeling hearts pound away beneath chests, lungs aching with the gulp of air, the cooling feel of sweat as it dried upon the body. Jake stared at Oktobriana as she stared at him, or at any of us. He unpocketed the tracker, flicked it on and read.

"Unmoved, now," he said, his voice oddly calm, as if enough endorphins had passed through his own brain to bring a temporary peace unto him, or so at least it seemed. "Settled at First Avenue about Twenty-fifth. Righthand side."

"Bellevue," said Wanda. "They got him in the hospital."

"Bellevue," I repeated, thinking of our own day's germ-free Bedlam. "Why've they moved him—?"

"Let's find and discover," said Jake.

"There's a chance," I said. "If we get there in time—"

"Doom's certified, Luther," he said. "We've other purpose to serve as well." He gathered up the scraps of newsprint on which

Oktobriana had transcribed late thoughts. "Hold these. They'll essential later on."

"We'd best go in caution," I said. "By now they've investigated the apartment. Certain to have word on the watch. How safe do you judge an approach, Wanda?"

"Not safe at all," she said. "But I gather we got to do it. Let's get going. Longer we kill time here, more time they'll have getting ready for us."

"Jake," I said, noting his mask, his evident peace. "What's planned?"

"If not for him," he said, feeling beneath his jacket and coat for his securities, "we'd not have come. If he'd not incited, I'd not have thrown. If he'd not stolen, we'd have had and already tried. She'd shine with health," he said, laying no direct blame on Skuratov for the last specified. His face drew sheet white as his blood settled deep inside him. With both arms, good and bad, he lifted Oktobriana off the couch, pressing her against him as if to warm her. We left the house as we'd found it. In the west clouds showed; an oncoming front slowly taking the blue from the sky. The air was heavy with verdant flowerscent and seaborne salt.

"Why do you keep looking around?" Wanda asked me as we climbed into the car; Jake settled Oktobriana in the back, next to him. "I mean you know there's nobody around here—"

"Long Island unnerves me," I said. "I knew bad times here." Before she ignited, a sudden crash in the distance, the thump of waves shore-pounding shocked my mind into remembrance.

"Trouble?" she asked. "Had an accident out here or something?"

"Went to war out here," I said. We edged down the drive, our tires chewing at the gravel below. Jake drew out his pocket-player as he supported Oktobriana upright; her head sagged loosely on her neck, resting against her shoulder. He kept himself unphoned, so as not to lose himself too deeply—in event of Oktobriana's stirring, I supposed. When he switched on the player his music soaked us in acid's bath.

> *"Got to keep movin', got to keep movin'—*
> *"Blues fallin' down like hail, blues fallin' down like hail—"*

"War?" she asked. "What kind of war?"

"Prolonged war," I said. "Twenty-odd years. I was here for just one, but it served purpose—"

"Blues fallin' down like hail."

"On Long Island?" she said as we turned onto the dirt road leading us back to the highway. "Why'll there be war out here? War with who?"

"With Long Islanders," I said, too overcome by onrushing memory to detail overmuch. "At a point later on it becomes necessary"—in our world, it became necessary—"to declare martial law due to a variety of circumstances. Most people went along with it. They didn't out here. That's it in basic."

She shook her head. "That's all right. I don't have to know."

"How long a passage in?" asked Jake. Oktobriana's eyes drifted from side to side; I wondered what she watched. I looked at Long Island as we passed through its daylight, its perfect weather.

"Not more'n an hour, if we're lucky," said Wanda. "I'm going to go in a different way, avoid all the fair traffic. Got to stop somewhere soon and get gas." We reached the main road; turned back towards town. "You going to bring this guy back out with you once you find him?"

"We'll bring what's needed," said Jake.

"And the days keep 'mindin' me,
"There's a hellhound on my trail—"

On that perfect Long Island afternoon our unit had continued down Hill Street towards town. Seeing smoke rising from shore's direction, hearing the pop of distant gunfire, sounding as caps from a child's pistol, we realized that our fellow platoons were delayed at the beach, and so we marched towards the ocean to assist, nothing disturbing our ears but the wind's rustle, and the unending barrage. We crept across the rangy grounds of one of the neighborhood's older cottages, a blasted lowrambler that must once have held twenty rooms. Poised at the murky, brush-choked pool's patio were plastic flamingos of unusual heredity; each pink body

carried two heads. Muller approached them, pulling his nonissue
.44; he dropped to position and aimed at their dualities.

Yeeeah, he shouted. Ambients. Plug 'em.

He fired; they were boobied. Before the flashbulb splash, before
the air split with explosion's sound, I'd flattened, as had most of the
men, who generally did whenever they saw Muller act in moment's
heat; the twelve nearest hadn't, and they writhed on the ground like
fish blown from a barrel. Muller was beyond flattening. We
radioed in to obtain wounded's airlift and prepped to call down
vengeance on whatever we found.

"Hellhound on my trail."

"She's burning, Luther," Jake said, his hand pressing her forehead; he'd set his pocket-player's tune into recycling loop, so that
the song repeated without end. "Warming like she's microwaved."

"Increased metabolism, Jake," I said. "Her fever."

We pulled away from the Esso station at which we'd stopped to
refill; as we left its lot I looked beyond the tall, glass-domed pumps
to see the three rest room doors at building's side: men, women and
colored. The proprietors had no qualms over accepting our money.
"How much longer?" I whispered to Wanda; she kept eye on the
lane before her.

"Not over forty minutes, Luther. I'm going as fast as I can without getting pulled over—"

"I mean Oktobriana," I said. "How much longer, do you think?"

"Tonight," she said; the car's clock showed two-thirty. "Sooner,
maybe. Depends on when she goes into another fit. Can't be much
longer."

"No question?"

"She's lucky, under the circumstances," she said. "Man used to
live three floors above us came down with it. He had it three
months before he got to this point. Believe me, Luther, it's a
blessing she's going fast as she is."

"If she goes before we do—"

"Don't worry yet," she said. "That happens, they'll catch us
soon enough. We'll be going to meet her not too long after that."

"If today was Christmas Eve, if today was Christmas Eve,
"And tomorrow was Christmas Day—"

I'd sent Johnson up ahead to size the situation at closer range. Beyond a row of trees we heard shooting's sound come without pause. Drawing closer, we saw the house from which the snipers worked, ridgetopped just before the beach's stretch, standing at the edge of a wide field. The place was one of blankfaced neomodern, done with swoopcurved concrete, opaque glass and tubular steel pipe. Our compatriots had been pinned down on the beach as they landed, and slower ones lay scattered over the sand. I estimated Johnson was doing all right, though he hadn't yet returned. Under circumstance there was but one way to deal with such a threat as presented. At my word, Padilla directed two of his men to position rocket launchers. They awaited their cue. As I gave it, the house lights went up.

"If today was Christmas Eve—"

"Your friend hasn't gone anywhere else, has he?" Wanda asked after my next check of the tracker. We'd entered the outskirts; on either side of our street showed row houses and one-story shuttered shops, gas stations and brick churches, their names plain for all to read: St. Paul's Doctrinarian, the Valentinian House of God, St. Joseph's Holy Roman Catholic Church, the Albigensian Church of Jesus the Light, Reformed. Leaving city behind for the nonce, we drove past unending cemeteries, their stone markers stretched horizon close; I wondered how many had died like Oktobriana. In the rearview I eyed them, one losing, one lost.

"No," I said.

"I'll park close as I can to where he is," she said. "That thing can narrow it down for us, right?"

I nodded. "Once we're ranged."

"When you get out just go in through the front," she said. "Don't stop to sign in, nine times out of ten you don't have to anyway. Walk in like you own the place and you shouldn't have any trouble."

"Fine—"

"Not at first, anyway," she added. "Then it's up to you."

"Oh, wouldn't we have a time, baby."

From within the inferno we heard high-pitched screams. Fireballs rushed from the house, smoldering and snuffing once they'd flung themselves onto the field behind. Billowing black clouds dyed the blue sky, their smell rich with ash and frying grease, an excremental stench. My men neared the flames to judge the viability of housebound residents. Jets migrated above, flying in geese's formation. The ocean glimmered as if bejeweled, summerglory's light striking sparks from its waves.

They're small, said Klonfas, shouting back after examining one of the fielded.

"All I need's my little sweet woman,
"Just t'pass th'time away—"

Brooklyn and Queens showed so gray as the sky had become; it was ever harder to spot the skyline ahead between the everrising factories and apartments around us. Our approach seemed unreasoned; I wouldn't have thought the Midtown Tunnel had yet been built, but towards its location was where Wanda seemed to aim. Soon enough it evidenced that while there was entrance to Manhattan from this direction, it was not through the underground. From Greenpoint, or thereabouts, a suspension bridge ran into Thirty-fourth. Crossing the bridge, reaching Second Avenue, Wanda headed downtown and then over again. At First Avenue and Twenty-fifth, on the right, Bellevue's redbrick hulk rose, stretching north for several dismal blocks, all replaced by newer outdated hulks in our day.

"You can tell where he is in there with that?"

"North building," I said. "Not far in but somewhere on high. Can't tell the floor till we're inside."

Shutting off his music, Jake, with care, lay Oktobriana down onto the back seat as he readied to step out. She remained no less still than she had been for the last hour. Wanda curbsided the car on Twenty-eighth and cut the motor. The building in which he showed stood just to left. Looking about, we saw none of law's minions, or prints left by the long arm's hand.

"Anybody wants to see your papers, just show'em that passport," Wanda said, giving further guide. "Say you're visiting from Mount Sinai, you have to. They got foreign docs running through all the time. Whatever you're going to do, be quick about it, if you can."

The entrance was off First; we strolled around, aiming downstreet, seeming nonchalant as if we'd stepped out to take the air. Shoving through dark wooden doors resembling the el station's, we entered. In our time hospitals generally are lit so brightly that to open your eyes within them is to risk blindness. All within Bellevue was steeped in shadow. Through the shade we saw the bile green walls, the hissing light fixtures above and the dirty, worn tile floors; the all-Caucasian mass of patients milling about, dotted amidst its rush with white-capped nurses and white-suited doctors. Throughout the entrance hall many smoked; doctors and nurses smoked. Ceiling fans did little but spread heat and odor, those familiar smells of alcohol, of fresh gauze, of oncoming death.

"If asked," said Jake, "we're specialists."

"Doctor Zuckerman," an unbodied voice called from wooden loudspeakers wallbolted above us. From downhall came screams' sounds; Jake appeared not to notice. "Please report to the emergency room. Doctor Zuckerman—"

"Where's he kept, Luther?" Jake asked, striding ahead as if to the firing line; in his whites he appeared as might any surgeon adept at sliding the knife. Keeping the tracker hidden within my hand, I looked.

"Almost above us," I said. "Sixth floor."

"No higher?"

"No," I said, eyeing elevator doors. "Over here."

As Wanda predicted we'd experienced no interference; all seemed involved in their own matters of mortality too much to be concerned with ours. Some did eye Jake's suit overclose, as if admiring the cut and style. We stepped aboard the elevator as the door slid open; saw that it had been pulled open by the elevator operator, a short black man seated within.

"What floor, sir?" he asked me, a faint smile round his lips.

"Sixth," I said. "Thank you."

As we rose Jake stood silently, facing front, his mind somewhere distant. Whether Oktobriana would still be alive by the time we returned—if we returned—I had no idea, and I suspect that lack of certainty only made him all the more assured in his action. As the man twisted a lever to halt our ascent, we readied; I'd sized Skuratov's locale as being elevator-near. In a deep alcove close by, hidden from immediate view, showed an unmarked door with translucent window. A policeman slept in a chair just to door's right.

"Bottleneck," Jake muttered, moving ahead. "Let's unclog the drain."

"Move with reason, Jake," I said.

"As always."

The cop snorted himself awake, started rising as he saw us head for him. "Better have a good reason for wantin' in—" he started to say. Jake's right hand, palm up, flew out; landed on the nostrils with solid punch, sending the small bones deep within, pithing the brain. As the cop's eyes crossed, a blood strand dripped towards his lip. Jake shook his hand free of mucus and pushed open the door, looking in; a short hall led to another, unguarded door. Through my jacket's cloth I heard the tracker's beep.

"The best," Jake responded, dragging the late one off his chair into the hall as he entered, leaving him floored as we moved on.

"Jake," I reminded. "Careful."

"An enclosed space ahead," he worded, lowvoiced. "They won't attempt overkill even if they're prepped in this event." He readied something undercoat. "They expect communion. We give them surprise."

He surprised, kicking open the door and leaping in. Within, a middle-aged man wearing a brown suit sat upon a chair facing a curtained space. Before he could move Jake floored him, thrusting the Omsk into the man's mouth with undue passion. I shut the door behind me, quietly, so as not to disturb.

"Looking for someone?" Jake asked. "Where's the guest of honor?"

The man pointed towards the curtain, his eyes showing full white. Pulling the drapes away I found Skuratov, bedded flat, both arms needled with intravenous tubes. Another tube sent breath through his nose. Only his eyes showed awareness. His legs were bound thick with plaster; I saw no sign of those twotone shoes. Around his head a heavy pad and bandage were wrapped.

"Mal?" I said; he offered no more harm than a nursery's denizen.

"He won't answer you," said the suited man, his face tight as he awaited Jake's sentence. "He can't talk—"

"Can't talk?" I said. "Who took his tongue?"

"For God's sake get this guy off me—"

"Unarm him, Jake," I said. "Why can't he talk?"

"Poor bastard probably won't last till morning," he said. "Broken legs. Internal injuries. Fractured skull. Crash threw him sixty feet—"

Jake refigured. "Thirty," he said, taking the man's single pistol, keeping his own shooter straightaimed. Skuratov seemed so much smaller than he was.

"You guys must be the ones came with him," he said.

"You're FBI?" I said. "What's told, then. What did he say?"

"Nothing. Truck driver saw the wreck out there around dawn yesterday, told the Secaucus police. They found him lying out there in the swamp, found the plane. Called us, called the New York cops. Jersey claimed jurisdiction but Mister Hoover said as a Russian plane was involved it was a federal matter. And now, with this Stalin stuff—"

Skuratov's breath came in gasping spurts, as if it were being squeezed free by other's hands. Jake tossed me his Omsk so that I might continue live coverage. Stepping calmly over to where Skuratov lay, Jake bladed his longest switch, meal's companion; twirled it round his fingers and then slashed Skuratov's intravenous tubes. One recognized the other, undoubted. In the room's ill light I saw Skuratov's lips slapping wordlessly together as if to wet themselves. So small.

"Where you got Uncle Joe, anyway?" the man asked.

"We don't," I said, noting the bruises on Skuratov's face. "If legs are broken, doesn't that infer a particular landing pattern?" I asked the man.

"What?"

"How'd he split his skull if he settled footways?" I asked, pressing the barrel into his forehead, breaking the skin. "You'd beat an injured man?"

"God, don't. During the interrogation. City cops. You know how they are. They got kind of rough—"

"So you break his head like an egg? To what purpose?"

"He wouldn't talk—"

"You will?" I asked, taking his collar with my free hand, wringing tight but no more; no Jake, I. "I wish answers."

"You two came with him. From Russia—"

"AO," I said. "What was possessed?"

"You two must've been the ones in Harlem last night—"

"As you must be the one here, now. Where're his goods?" I asked, driving the barrel in even harder, choking him with greater vigor as I tried to keep back memory's blight. "What was on him? Where are they?"

"H-headquarters," he stuttered. "D-don't hurt me—"

Small ones? I asked Klonfas as I walked across the field, seeing the lumps there grounded. No sounds came from the house but those of crackling flames.

Kids.

In the new-mown field, its rich dirt unturned for planting, lay the black crinkles that preteens left. How many had been male, how many female—couldn't tell any longer; didn't matter.

See how many, I said, breathing through my mouth.

"On him should have been a plastic and metal camera," I said, clearing my mind, calming myself though stupidity ran rich around me. "Was it found?"

"It was a camera, then," he said; his face brightened, as if with victory. "Most of 'em didn't think it looked right, but I did—"

Jake stepped back, leaving Skuratov undisturbed in body. Unreeling and opening his jacket's line length, he looked round the room as if judging its proportions. Near the radiator a long pipe ran from ceiling to floor. Looping one end, he knotted it tight with doubled squares and a half hitch, saying nothing, listening to all.

"*Was* a camera?" I said. "Is or was—".

The door banged open; a new suit and a fresh cop entered, guns leveled.

"Get 'em—" yelled the agent I held. As if allowed by ones on high, I became as Jake, firing the Omsk with instinct's aim, blasting the cop's chest with a softball-sized blow. Jake, as figured, had swung round as the door opened; as I triggered, he sent his own regrets, blading the fed in the throat with quick-thrown switch. The G-man's machine gun dropped from his hands as he lingered, grasping neckways. Face first he fell with crunching thud. I looked out to see if the far door remained open; it didn't. Positioning the policeman with care I certified that the inner door could not be immediately reopened. Jake left his knife where he'd pitched it, an odd action; unreeled his line, assuring its firm fix upon the pipe, finding the opposite end, some thirty curled meters from the knot.

"This won't be long," he said, approaching Skuratov's bed.

"God," our more animate prisoner whispered. "Don't hurt me. Please don't. Please—"

Please, I heard; heard the calming shot, didn't turn to look. The day's count was seventy-nine; doubling the count as pro forma per HQ's wish, Klonfas tallied our success and forwarded records. Shards of blown containers within the rubble evidenced that there'd been a gasoline stockpile within. No adults turned up; the place was no traditional school. In a basement refrigerator two had crawled in, pulling the door shut after. Whether they'd suffocated or baked, we couldn't say. The Long Island War ran a twenty-year run before Mister O'Malley rang down the curtain; its residents would have fought to the last child. These, that afternoon, were among the first. Those within we left entombed. Those who'd made it onto the field I wanted buried; the beach seemed likeliest to allow a quick dig.

If we just leave 'em out, sir, they'll be gone before the month's out, said Sergeant Rich.

Bury them, I said, going to find my own shovel.

"Semantics are all," I said, settling us both by lowering my voice, showing I meant no harm. "Again. *Is* a camera, or *was* a camera?"

"Luther," Jake said, pulling terrycloth towels from dresser drawers; padding across the room he heaved open the window, knocked loose the screen and bent it in, removing it. Traffic's breath sounded clear. He leaned forward, looking down. "If he's not helpful—" With good arm he wrenched the line; it held. "—thumb out his eyes."

"Answer," I said.

"We couldn't figure out how to get it open," he said. "One of the guys decided to take a hammer to it. Just tap it, that's all. Damn thing flew all to pieces, like it was made in Hong Kong or something. Nothing inside it looked like anything, all those boards with the little things on 'em—"

"Within," I said. "A small blue box. Where?"

The man closed his eyes, undoubtedly certain they were about to be thumbed. "It wouldn't open either."

What he awaited, what he deserved, never came. Opening again, he saw; saw me staring at Jake, wondering if he'd even heard, so intent he seemed over whatever it was he did. As if ribboning a giftwrap Jake wound the line's loose end twice around Skuratov's neck.

"When we drop keep the towels tight round your hands or they'll burn," he said, slipping Skuratov's nasal tube loose, dragging him into vertical, grunting with the effort of lifting dead weight.

"You heard?" I asked. "That's it." Jake nodded, working his better hand beneath Skuratov's plastered legs.

"Heard plain. Stand aside, Luther."

As I watched I recalled the rest, unable to contain the flood. Three remained to be planted and I chose to be their farmer. They were no heavier than papier-mâché, I thought, carrying them one by one to the beach. As afternoon became evening I designed their final homes. We had time overmuch, now; orders were to hold position until dawn, when again we could attempt entry townways. Additional planes would toast aboveground survivors during the night hours. As I readied the last slot, Johnson appeared from beach's direction, shouldering a heavy bag, his stumble slowed by its weight. In the fading light I discerned that half his shirt was burned away; closer, I saw that he wore no shirt. The men of our unit and the survivors of the others had set camp beyond the ridge, near the ruin. We alone, alive, walked the beach.

Let me know it's fireworks hour before you give the AOK next time, he said.

You got inside? I asked. He nodded.

Then got blown out.

Lifting myself from the grave with shovel's support, finding feet again on unearthed ground, I stared down into the pit.

Why didn't you report?

Look here, Lieutenant. He unshouldered the bag, dumped its contents onto the sand. I saved one for you.

She was seven, perhaps, crowned with blond hair matted with sandy mud. But for her bloodied thighs her body remained whole, though covered with bruises and scratches. Her wide eyes, long cried dry, held no more life than Jake's. As she stared my way she held her breath, keeping it, at least, from attacker's touch. Johnson grinned when he looked at me, showing steel braces.

Lieutenant?

"Jake—"

While trying to haul Skuratov upward, Jake's foot tripped over his dangling line; inadvertently he crushed Skuratov's leg against the window frame, splitting the plaster. "I'm sorry," Jake said, balancing him on the sill so that his stiff extremities countered his seated weight. Guiding his torso forward and down, Jake took care not to strike Skuratov's broken head against the sash. He paused then, as if for effect; probably for thought. With good hand, he pushed. Skuratov sailed through Sunday haze. Inertia took its course; the line tightened as if to give tune, and then as quickly went slack once more. Jake wrapped towels round his hands, considered the view.

"Not a far drop," he said. "Let's slide, Luther."

I answered Johnson, swinging the shovel full-force against his head. Nothing gave; pitching forward, he whumped into the hole. The little girl sat on the sand, squeezing herself together; she looked on as if watching a puppetshow of uncommon design. The shovel's sound came as *shuff* as I rescooped what I'd thrown, lifting a load, tossing it onto Johnson. Sunset's colors inflamed the horizon; night tinted the sky's other side. Ocean's breeze ruffled our hair. Without warning Johnson rose from his uncompleted vault, turning in his grave, stretching out his hand; sand poured from his eyes, his mouth, his wound.

Nigger, he said. Can't keep a good man down.

Repeatedly I applied the shovel: swung it flatside, drove it in edgedown, clubbed and reclubbed until the sharp crack first heard muffled into the sound of a smashed melon. My arms free of ache, my mind clear of thought, I shoveled all the more quickly, heaving in sand atop blood, shortly building a fresh dune. Dropping the shovel I sank onto the beach, rolling over it as if to make sand angels, pressing my head between my hands as if to burst it. Looking up again, I saw the little girl, sitting there still, seeing and not seeing; she shivered, as though cold. I'd seen a tenth of what she'd seen, felt a twentieth of what she felt, knew nothing of what she knew but knew she shouldn't know it, so early on. There was one thing to do, I knew, for mercy's sake. I unholstered my sidearm. There remained but one mercy more to grant.

"Drop, Luther," said Jake, having already grounded. As I slid down I refused to feel my rib's ache, the bandage's boalike clutch; landing, I collapsed, unbroken. Seeing blood soaking the towels as I unclutched my hands, I thought momentslong that I'd harmed myself without noticing; realized when I dropped the cloth away that another's blood wetted them as I reached the end of the line. His foot-first landing was so hard, driving his broken legs up and against his chest, that his knees might have shattered his jaw had his head not been pulled away at the conclusion of his drop. He lay in twain on the ground, to either side of me in the empty courtyard in which we stood; his teeth's metal shone through his grimace. One eye was shut, as if to wink us luck.

"Which way?" I asked, staring round at the courtyard's multi-eyed walls, the heavy stone trim and iron bars. Jake gestured towards an archway, behind us, that led onto one of the side streets. Twenty-eighth, I hoped.

"There," he said, almost, but not quite, running. "I eyed from on high."

Deciding for one, for eighty, for a thousand or for a million; in strategic theory no difference should show, which kept it all the more problematic when it did. Crawling towards her, gun readied, I burned inside, raging at this world that was no world for anyone any longer, and especially not for little ones. Katherine never understood how deeply I felt that rage which prevented me from wishing to bring life to the world, no matter how often I tried to give the feeling word. If that caused her decision to be done with me, then it couldn't have been helped after all. Raising my pistol, trying with barrel tip to brush back the hair from the side of her head, I repeated to myself: mercy, mercy, rain mercy down on us; no need to suffer them overlong. Staring at me as if she knew me, making no move to run, crying no plea to deaf-eared heaven, seeming satisfied that I would decide the most suitable conclusion, the little girl lifted her hand and pushed her hair away. In theory, no difference; one decision, one solution, no choice—

"There's the car," I said, seeing its blackness, vizzing Wanda sitting within, filling the interior with smoke. None had yet noticed the scene above but for the one we'd left untrammeled. For another minute, we were preserved.

"Any luck?" she asked as we climbed in, pulling the doors shut quickly behind us.

"None."

Whose decision? Who decides? By distant word I'd killed children before; killed children after. Jake never killed at distance, and always faced the adults he plucked, as if to honor their end. Whether it was deliberate or pure chance, that was his method, so merciful as might be allowed. I hadn't mercy enough to kill the little girl; wrapping my shirt around her, I carried her back to camp.

11

"Slaughter on Eighth Avenue," the Journal-American's late edition's head read; Jake laughed, scanning highlights. Oktobriana lay alongside him as if awaiting the last incision, indigoed arms crossed upon her chest. Her country's color darkened her half-shut eyes; when she breathed the sound was as wind rustling reeds. In the front Wanda and I studied a fairground map. Earlier in the month she and Doc had visited the fair; those of darker shade were admitted on Tuesday and Thursday afternoons so long as they left by nightfall. Pinned now to my lapel was another souvenir, a small blue-and-white tin button Doc had been given at GM's Futurama, warning, *I Have Seen the Future*.

"It's so twentieth century," said Jake, continuing to read as if there were nothing else to be done. "Naught ragged here but sensation and braindiddly."

"They'll tell of nothing essential," I said. "Keep lipshut on any supposed Stalin connection. Now that they'd been worded about Bellevue I'd think they'd only expand on their design—"

" 'Quack's wife missing—' "

"*Quack*," said Wanda, angered. "Not a medical school would've took him even if he'd gone to college. Bastards."

"You're imagined dead," Jake said, reading further, sounding envious.

"Probably imagined eaten," I said, "considering article's tone towards us—"

"New's shock," said Jake. "The unfamiliar upsets them."

We'd parked on Rodman Street above Fifty-seventh Avenue, close to the fair's Flushing gate. Rising directly behind its stiles was, according to the map, the Soviet Pavilion, its Lenin's Tomb–maroon tower capped by some oversized worker clutching a red star. Beyond, the far-flung buildings stretched out before our view, their multiform roofs capped with white domes and narrow shafts, their curving walls heavy with mural and abstract design. To our left, in the distance, rose what on the map was referred to as the parachute jump; almost directly before us, much nearer, the Try-lon aimed towards the sky. Through the gate's stiles passed hun-dreds, returning exhausted into the world of the present, making their break before storm settled in; clouds washed the sky with deep gray as sunset's time approached.

"According to what you've said," Wanda remarked, studying the map, "if ever'thing happens like she seems to say it might happen, then we're going to want to aim for here."

On the map she fingered a spot marked Washington Square, be-yond Constitution Mall, past Borden's and Heinz's, next to the World of Fashion pavilion and almost directly before the spire and ball.

"Where's the ceremony taking place?" I asked. "Will we have to cut through?"

She shook her head. "That'll be over here on the other side of the thing, in City Hall Square. You won't even have to see 'em. It's still going to be hard walking in, under the circumstances—"

"Lights go up when?" Jake asked. "When's the show?"

"Eight-thirty," I said. "Duskbreak. Soon as the charge starts we'll have to run for it."

"Running for what?" he asked.

"I'm not sure," I said. "But we'll know it when we see it." The dash's clock read seven-fifty.

"You ever figure out from those figures of hers just how this thing's supposed to work, anyway?" asked Wanda.

"No," I said. "It's above my head. Something to do with the amount of electricity produced in regards to the frequency of the resonator. But if all goes as theorized then we should be prime to go—"

"Think it'll work?"

"Maybe," I said. "We're at ultimate option and that exes debate under circumstance. If all doesn't happen, we'll just toss ourselves into police's arms and have them waltz us to the cutter."

Beyond the Trylon and Perisphere a host of bright balloons rose as a flock of birds, disbanding as they ascended; part of the ceremony, I estimated. Studying the people departing, watching them move past us, uncomprehending of how they kept so cheerful, living in such a world where war would so soon erupt, where poverty never ended, where the plague's shadow had forever darkened all. They seemed such happy Martians.

"You've decided your actions?" I asked Wanda.

She shoved the map aside as if tossing off a blanket. "No. Don't have much left here anymore, but what've I got over there? Why would I want to go, Luther—"

"For new life," I said.

"That is, even if this thing works like you hope it's going to work. If it doesn't it won't make no difference. If it does, well, I just don't know—"

"Fear's felt?"

"Hell, yes," she said, her voice near-inaudible, as if to admit such loud would call down lightning on its own accord. "If you all are from the future like you've been saying then it's a hell of a lot different place from anything they've come up with." She gestured towards the gateposts of the World of Tomorrow. "Judging from how you act, anyway. How you talk. Sometimes you act like us. Sometimes you don't. I don't know which's scarier."

"We're adjusted to the familiar," I said. "Our fear's been so great here, but even now we're adjusting. In time all here would show true to us as in time all of ours would show as well to you."

"Yeah, well. Somebody born without an arm never misses it but ever'body still calls 'em stumpy," she said, a near-smile softening her face. "Norman was the one who oughta been able to come along. He was always hot to trot talking about the future. He'd've gone along in the blink of an eye. Anything to get out of this."

By *this*, had she meant this world, this country, this life; meant the relationship so demanded by others and lived with thereafter? Would anything have brightened him, I wondered; who nurses the doctor?

"I don't know, Luther," she continued, embracing the wheel as if for support. "You all don't need me along. You can walk over there and once you get through the turnstile you can just go on through. Forget about me—"

"Even if the authorities judge you as noninvolved," I said, "say no persecution awaits. Even then, what's left?"

"Nothing."

"So accompany," I said. "I can assist, once we've homed. You'd adjust—"

"You mean I'd turn into you all."

"People change," I said. "It's nature's way."

With care she groped for words as if fumbling with foreign tongue, mindful of translation's pitfalls, fearful of gesture's giveaway. "You all don't even act like people," she said.

"That's unreasoned—"

"Not like people I know," she said. "Way you look at things. Way you do things. Killing people like you was fixing breakfast. It's just not—" She paused. "I'm not trying to insult you, I just want to explain and it's hard—"

"Understood," I said. "Dayplain."

"I mean doesn't life mean anything to people anymore?" she asked. "Means something to us here, Luther. Ever'body's seen too many people they love lose theirs. What is it to you?"

"Something to live with," I said, responding as felt.

"But is it important or not—"

"Important." Important, the lives of those known, loved and lost; the lives of the millions or the life of the stranger in the street could never be so important, for you couldn't overmuch dwell on the all-surrounding tragedy without knowing madness. There

could be no saving of all, and no sense in trying; all to be done was
to protect those you could.

"But not in the same way," she said. "Least that's the impression I
get. How'd we turn into you all, Luther? What went wrong?"

"Nothing," I said. "No one notices the changes until they
happen."

"That's even worse, then," she said. "Turning into something
awful and not even knowing it. Jekyll and Hyde."

"You find me so awful—"

"Luther," she said. "Look what's happened. I can tell you're not
bad at heart but there's just something not there. I think it's something must have happened a little bit at a time. One day something
happens and you don't see any way around it but to do something
you wouldn't have ordinarily done, then the next time around, you
do something a little worse. Next time, a little worse. Time you've
finished up . . ." Her voice trailed away, faded into star's static.
"You got the faintest idea what I'm talking about?"

As she eyed me I wondered what she saw. "Overmuch," I said.
"All'll happen here as well."

"Maybe not," she said. "I think it's just a way you've taught
yourself to act, but it's no way to live—"

"I know no other," I said.

"Then things shouldn't have happened way they did," she said,
here where so much had happened as it hadn't. "Lot of things
shouldn't have happened way they did."

"Luther." Jake's voice came whisper loud; I turned, to see
what was needed. He held Oktobriana's arm, its skin glossy dark
with bruise's sheen; with her fingers she petted air. "She wants to
code."

Taking her hand, feeling her fingers press slowly down into my
palm, I listened to her finalities.

"If she's coming out of it," said Wanda, barely heard, "that's
curtains."

LIGHTNING WILL ASSIST, she said, referring, I supposed, to the
tower and coil once the switch was thrown. IF OPENING SEEN GO
THROUGH AT ONCE.

Jake patted her forehead with his own hand, seeming neither

relaxed nor accepting. Evening's gloom settled deeper, darkening all within and without.

TELL JAKE, she tapped; her fingers shivered, as if stricken by chill.

"Yes?" I said, holding them, awaiting conclusion.

HE IS LOVE OF LIFE. I nodded. Her eyes opened, barely seen in dusklight. Afterthought: BLESS ME.

"What's passed?"

Once I told him he took her up within his arms and lifted her; her head wobbled on her neck, her eyes rolled back beneath her lids, a thin cord of spittle trickled from her mouth. Looking upon the two of them made me feel as if I were betraying a scene of deepest intimacy, yet I couldn't turn away from the sight of the nearly dead.

"Ya lyuba—" he began to say; stopped. "Ya lyub—"

Somewhere he'd attempted to learn to say "I love you" in Russian tongue, as if to tell her in natural lingua would give away the game; he'd not, needless to say, mastered its phrase.

"Ya," he began, more slowly. "Ya ly—"

Before he might finish her arms squeezed round him as if to hug; tightening, they set to crush. With difficulty he struggled free from her coils. Oktobriana's limbs began wrapping around themselves, drawing tight as she curled herself together. As her chest contracted she gasped for breath, her mouth stretched wide until it bled at the corners; blood flowed from her ears and from her eyes. As her arms and legs gave under muscles' torque the sound of snapping bones echoed throughout the car. She fell down onto the seat, her vertebrae twisting as they were shattered by her flesh's grip. Her silent gasps came as if she were being leapt upon.

"Jake," I said. "You know what's essentialled. Move."

"I can't—" he said, sounding as if he were no more than six.

"It's a reasoned act," I reminded. Her lips quivered as she tried to give word to her pain; her bones' crunch pierced my ears. Fairleavers streamed past us, oblivious to the scene within our car. "Help her, Jake. You have to."

He couldn't.

"Lift her, Jake. This way."

Gripping her tight he raised her from the seat, leaving deeper bruises wherever he lay finger, bringing her forward, resting her shoulders against the back of the front seat. He turned away. Oktobriana's bleeding eyes squeezed shut as if not to see the last.

"Luther, please—"

"There's no choice, Jake," I said, lifting my hands. "None."

Wrapping my fingers around her head, I closed my own eyes as I twisted. She left before she slumped; my fingers burned with mercy's scorch. Jake stared at her as she tumbled back into the seat, her eyes half-open. From fair's direction I heard faint cheers and applause. Wanda looked away from all of us, staring off into a parking lot just to our right as if hoping to see someone she knew. Jake hugged Oktobriana's body, making no more sound than did she, showing no tear.

"Let it go, Jake," I said. "It's over. Come on."

Unresponding, he slowly pulled himself upright, staring into her stillness, clutching her without cease, looking in wonder as if realizing what was lost. His face showed no more than it ever did. I eyed the dash clock as I caught my breath; I couldn't stop my hands from shaking. It was eight twenty-three.

"How quick can we foot it over?" I asked.

"You can't," she sighed, starting the engine.

"You'll drive us through?"

She nodded. "No other way. They don't allow cars in, so you're going to have to play by your rules, going in. I can't believe this—"

"Trouble's handleable," I said. "Jake can cover our approach."

"It'll take a minute or two once we're through to get over to the mall," she said. "How close you got to call this if it's going to work?"

"I don't know," I said. "All we have to do is aim for what appears, and I'm uncertain as to what's supposed to appear—"

"Shit," she said, staring towards the gate. A police car had pulled up and parked. Two patrollers stepped out, looking idly around as if searching for those attempting to beat the admission. "You all better be ready for anything."

"As ever," I said. Lightning's strobe lit the clouds overhead; thunder's drumroll came no longer muffled by distance. "Weather's holding as forecast. Just start pulling forward. Don't worry yet—"

They looked towards us; perhaps saw our shadows moving within the car, several hundred meters away from where they lingered. Patting their sidearms, they moved our way.

"Jake," I said, worrying. "You prepped? Action's coming."

No answer came; I turned, looked around.

"Jake?"

He held Oktobriana, stroking her shoulders as if to return life with death-soaked hands. Looking towards her without sight, he listened to me without hearing. The lights went up across the way; the fair showed in full illumination, in crystalline light. Our investigators drew closer, unhurrying, as if time were all they had in the world.

"Weapon me, Jake."

Without word he drew the Shrogin from beneath his jacket; after he handed it across, I slipped it over to my right, between the seat and the door. So nonchalantly as I could I rolled down the window and unclicked the gun's safety. Wanda had slowed the car to a snail's run as I'd readied myself; the two policemen prepped their own toys. The fair's lights glowed now against the dark, lightning-lit sky, showing in multihues; blue and orange and red and purple. The Trylon and Perisphere glowed in purest ivory white.

"They'll shoot, Luther," said Wanda, quickening our roll towards the gate.

"So'll I."

They lifted their guns and readied. The Shrogin held three clips and could send forth a thousand bursts; thrusting myself out the window, raising and aiming, I triggered before they could shoot. The recoil was so unnoticeable, the feel and hold so smooth and balanced. They burst into spray, dropping streetways; I barely felt a thing. Perching myself on windowedge, with left hand gripping the underside of the roof, with right I set my charge.

"Go through the stiles. They'll give when I send warning."

"They've got the lights on already, Luther—"

"Go."

As if freed, I fired without cease for a moment or so, aiming not to strike with death but with fear. The gatekeepers scattered into the safety of the fair; those leaving or entering did so more quickly.

Raindrops began pelting the car, began washing my face as we crashed through, scraping by. I slid back inside, keeping the Shrogin aimed without and forward.

"We too late?" Wanda asked, steering us through a curved alley dividing two smooth-sided buildings; a caterpillarlike tram, its passengers sheltered from the rain by a brighthued top, crawled out of our path as we eked through.

"Don't think so. Go, Wanda. Come on."

As we pulled onto Constitution Mall, its aligned trees glowing screen green with the lights positioned beneath their branches, its pink-shaded buildings rising from either side, we saw the lights round the fair's centerpiece fade from white and return again as sun yellow; the Trylon gleamed like a golden javelin, the Perisphere glistened like a boiled egg's yolk. Around the iron ring beneath the spire's apex, bolts of artificial lightning crackled, shooting along the metal wires supporting the ring; along the needle's length blue flashes of unimaginable voltage ran wild. Greater applause than previously heard rose from the distance as we headed towards the light.

"This is it," I said. "Floor it, Wanda. I'll keep us cleared. Aim straight. Stop for nothing."

Jake's hand appeared from behind; he began dropping his arsenal into the front seat as we rushed forward. On top of all he placed his pocket-player. Why he had chosen such a moment to disarm I couldn't guess and couldn't take time to ask even had I expected answer.

"I don't believe this shit," Wanda said, her hands tight upon the wheel except when she shifted; by the engine's roar I gathered we'd entered highest gear.

"Keep driving," I said, firing again to drive any crowd from our onrush. Beyond the trees' long line the Trylon showed as a maypole bedecked with ribbons of lightning swirling round; the Perisphere glowed more brightly, its shine rising from within as if it prepped to blast. Bolts flashed upward into the rain-drenching skies. Without warning a great flash shot from cloud to peak, the real electric meeting the sham; a waterfall of charge cascaded downward, one stream angling to right, coming to ground directly in our path, hundreds of meters distant. When it struck it showed as a high white curtain rising from the earth.

"Luther—"

"That's it."

"Drive into that?" she asked, not slowing. "We'll be cooked."

"Drive."

The curtain's white edges tinged with blue; ozone's scent perfumed the air. On our right I noticed a long reflecting pool lined with statuary; the water seemed aflame with reflected light. Ahead, between us and the curtain, red revolving lights suggested that our progress might be interrupted. I readied to aim again, not noticing pain, not feeling fear, knowing nothing but a feeling exhilarating in its effect, horrifying in its implications as I prepped to kill.

"Road's blocked, Luther," said Wanda; with my free hand I reached over to assist her guidance of the wheel. Keeping my eyes low to avoid the blinding light ahead, I knew we couldn't stop at this point. Even as we raced forward, the ones officiating surely were trying to shut off the coil and bring this unexpected polytechnic to an end. There'd come no further chance.

"Aim left. Clip them if needed. I'll keep them down."

Guns fired our way; with free finger I released the trigger, firing at optimum, uncaring of who or what might be hit, feeling within my hand the warming shake of death as I flung it forward. On the left was room enough to pass, just; the rear of our Terraplane struck the squad car that nearly blocked our path, catching its front bumper. We skidded away from the light, towards the trees. Dropping the Shrogin, its handle burning, I reached across, aimed the wheel towards the glow and pressed Wanda's foot down with my own upon the accelerator.

"Lord help us," she shouted. "Luther—"

No sooner had we entered the light than silence surrounded us; the white painted all before and behind. My stomach roiled with nausea; the hair on my neck's nape rose. Knowing that we would experience some location displacement, wondering how far our speed might shoot us through, I hoped that we would not emerge in the Hudson River's midst, or break through full speed into the side of Grand Central.

As the light faded, the rear door opened.

"*Jake!*" I turned; watched them sliding into unoccupied airspace, without sound falling out between worlds, leaping into light.

"Luther!" Wanda screamed. "Hold tight—"

At once the white vanished; scenes showed once more. We were airborne, or so it felt. Having landed at bridge's arc and bounding upward, we crashed again onto its slope, striking the Fifty-ninth Street ramp. The rear tires broke away as the axle gave. Sparks flew up from beneath the car as the underpan scraped the long-neglected pavement, slowing us but slightly as we skidded towards the wall defending midtown from the Queensboro Bridge's sealed approach, heading straight for the guardpost on First Avenue. The city rose around us, its heights lost in nighttime smog. We slowed before striking the wall, spinning as if loosed by top-string before finally coming to a stop. No sooner had we come to our rest than the guards reacted, firing into the windshield as we ducked, sending glittering shards onto our backs with wind chime's ring. I fumbled for my wallet; finding Valentino's passport, I threw it aside. The bootsteps neared; I held my true ID up on high, hoping they might read it before they termed us; hoping that they could read. A barrel pressed into my temple as my wallet was snatched from my hand. Eyeshut, I wondered if death at home seemed truly preferable, after all.

"Dryco," I whispered, as if to my lover.

"Sir," the soldier asked, unaiming, shouldering his toy. "Are you AO, sir?"

Heaving myself upward, hauling Wanda with me, I smiled, seeing the city as I knew it to look; stared childlike at the soldier's visor mirror, the glass bluffs rising round us, the razorwire cornice topping the graffitied wall, the searchlight's unending slash at the moon and stars. Cityroar resounded round, warning all weak-hearted away. Wanda opened her eyes and stared into her new abyss. Her lungs spasmed at first breath; her cough ran for five minutes full as she adjusted to the air. I breathed deep, knowing home.

"Hospital us," I said, looking back, but Jake was still gone.

12

HEARING WATER BEATING GLASS I AWOKE; ROSE, STUMBLED across darkness that I might retrieve my plants from the balcony before the rain killed them. From pelting damp I reentered, scratching blindly at the itch the drops left on my burning skin. Standing in four-A.M. calm, I scanned the nightlit room, knowing without solid reason that another kept near. A wallhanging fell floorways, dropping without weight, lending no sound as it landed.

Bending, feeling old aches left from bones broken and rebroken, from ill-knit ribs and oft-concussed head, I lifted the frame, ran fingertips along the unbroken wire there attached. Stroking the wall, feeling its coolness, finding the holder still set secure, I rehung the photo and stared at its look while my eyes adjusted to dark. It was an ancient colorshot from a more accessible 1939, showing an evening pose of the Trylon's clean needle; the Perisphere ashine with blue and dabbled white. The picture stayed where I'd hung it; one fall was enough.

Between worlds Jake wandered yet, I supposed, good arm forever supporting Oktobriana's stillness. Where he walks others must also beat the walls that they might make some sound, there in the space through which panthers leap from Canada into England, crocs from Florida to Boston; the void through which little girls slip without warning from mother's clasp; somewhere in the fence.

The Flushing Window—its present monicker, as per Dryco's word—remains open, though the guard keeps its surroundings perpetually closed; not so much to keep theirs from entering as ours from leaving, a matter solely of perspective. Little danger exists now from viral transmission, at least of the particular virus; in the initial pandemic DS followed a like pattern in our world, though since its housebreaking by new-developed vaccines few have been lost to its purges. As Oktobriana feared, when Alekhine returned with his prize his gift brought more than was desired. By word of our informants, Alekhine received definitive treatment for his efforts. Word passed, too, that the Big Boy himself lived into elderly's years, safe from all upon a state-supplied dacha—Skuratov's, I'd like to think. Krasnaya always tried to do the right thing. Even in Russia it was a matter of greatest humor that only the Big Boy could have killed millions of his countryfolk during two different centuries.

Awakened full now, I stood ready to meet and greet; imagined that as through a windblown drape his hand might reach. Did he, then, still float there, lost beneath the ice, forever seeking the hole through which he'd flung himself? When he screams, who hears? In revenge, does he light the fires of unknown origin; thumb shut night drivers' eyes; scotch the readings as planes ready to land? With incubus charm does he lure those whose bodies never after know grave? Jake never showed; I never knew.

It wasn't night's most rational hour. Needing reality's blow after so long I gazed outward, across Bronx hills and buildings, sighting distant Manhattan's towers through cloud and falling water. All looked so normal as it ever did. I shifted my glance, sizing my holdings. Upon retiring from Dryco after long officebound years and receiving all gratuities forthcoming, I wished to invest as desired, and so gathered timekeepers as my budget allowed, scattering them round me: the photo that had fallen, a tin maple-syrup can in log cabin's guise, a pack of unopened Lucky Strikes, its Christmas colors fresh; a green shirt of radium silk free of harmful isotope, a Terraplane's hubcap—

Jake. Jake, Jake, twenty years gone.

I asked Alice once to bring up the city's residential files for the

appropriate years so that I might know of our world's Doc. Here,
too, Norman Quarles had been a doctor, undoubtedly one of more
professional background; his wife's name was Wanda and they lived
on Eighth Avenue, just below 133rd, and surely slept as fitfully
through the el's all-night rumble. When they died, in the early
seventies—Doc first, and then Wanda—they left no survivors; for
different reasons, undoubted. I told Wanda of what I found, but
she didn't wish to hear of it. Perhaps she feared that if she were
to more fully acquaint herself with her counterpart, the half
would become whole and she might vanish. Whether this world's
Quarleses knew a happier life, I can't say; I hope they had a
quieter one.

Thoughts rushed to me too rapidly as I stood there, awaiting
word, seeking omens, watching for signs, listening to hear a code
tapped out above the rain's rhythm. As on every night when I
awoke before dawn, the old uncertainty crept up. Switching on
kitchen light, taking up a jar of pennies, I shook them onto a table
and stared at their pile, praying to all unlistening that the kraken
within me hadn't yet awakened as one day, still, it might. No
numbers glowed as neon within my mind as I looked upon them; I
counted, one by one. I counted one hundred and twelve.

Were there any answers? With two worlds in existence, each
following a like trail along a different path, does it follow that an
interactive God drew the map for each? Did having to keep eye on
two instead of one account for such seeming senselessness, that too
much went on for even God to follow? Would this distraction
become madness; provide at last the reason for why the beloved are
snatched away, why the faintest hopes are dashed, why only waste
brings knowledge? If all is predestined, then, does God choose
lesser vessels, through which It delivers Its evil so that It might take
credit for only the good done in Its name? What does God grant Its
killers in return?

One by one, numbering the count again to reassure, I at last let
my fear fall away until the next night's malaise. Rain-wind rattled
windowpanes, drummed its beat without cease, sent its tears into
darkness. Heading bedways I slipped in where, until November
last, Wanda lay. She died of old age; so few do.

Lying down, inserting phones so that with music's graze I might rub my mind to sleep, I paused to deliberate choice of hands. Leaving Jake's tape boxed as it lay, in no mood for Ives or Penderecki or Lalo, I picked Elgar's *Sea Pictures*; slept away to lost voice's song singing across long-gone years, carrying comforts penned by one lost longer. In daylight I awoke, rinsed in memory, washed by distance, hearing only time's breakers crashing onto a new day's shore, feeling the beach as it forever slipped from underfoot into tide. I dressed by Johnson's song. The waves broke; the water rushed away.

ABOUT THE AUTHOR

JACK WOMACK was born in Lexington, Kentucky, and currently lives in New York City. *Terraplane* is his second novel, following *Ambient*.

THE BEST IN SCIENCE FICTION

THE TOR DOUBLES

Two complete short science fiction novels in one volume!

THE BEST IN FANTASY

☐ 53954-0   SPIRAL OF FIRE by Deborah Turner Harris $3.95
     53955-9   Canada $4.95

☐ 53401-8   NEMESIS by Louise Cooper (U.S. only) $3.95

☐ 53382-8   SHADOW GAMES by Glen Cook $3.95
     53381-X   Canada $4.95

☐ 53815-5   CASTING FORTUNE by John M. Ford $3.95
     53826-1   Canada $4.95

☐ 53351-8   HART'S HOPE by Orson Scott Card $3.95
     53352-6   Canada $4.95

☐ 53397-6   MIRAGE by Louise Cooper (U.S. only) $3.95

☐ 53671-1   THE DOOR INTO FIRE by Diane Duane $2.95
     53672-X   Canada $3.50

☐ 54902-3   A GATHERING OF GARGOYLES by Meredith Ann Pierce $2.95
     54903-1   Canada $3.50

☐ 55614-3   JINIAN STAR-EYE by Sheri S. Tepper $2.95
     55615-1   Canada $3.75

Buy them at your local bookstore or use this handy coupon:
Clip and mail this page with your order.

Publishers Book and Audio Mailing Service
P.O. Box 120159, Staten Island, NY 10312-0004

Please send me the book(s) I have checked above. I am enclosing $_____
(please add $1.25 for the first book, and $.25 for each additional book to
cover postage and handling. Send check or money order only — no CODs.)

Name _____

Address _____

City _____ State/Zip _____

Please allow six weeks for delivery. Prices subject to change without notice.

THE BEST IN HORROR

☐ 52720-8	ASH WEDNESDAY by Chet Williamson	$3.95
☐ 52721-6		Canada $4.95
☐ 52644-9	FAMILIAR SPIRIT by Lisa Tuttle	$3.95
☐ 52645-7		Canada $4.95
☐ 52586-8	THE KILL RIFF by David J. Schow	$4.50
☐ 52587-6		Canada $5.50
☐ 51557-9	WEBS by Scott Baker	$3.95
☐ 51558-7		Canada $4.95
☐ 52581-7	THE DRACULA TAPE by Fred Saberhagen	$3.95
☐ 52582-5		Canada $4.95
☐ 52104-8	BURNING WATER by Mercedes Lackey	$3.95
☐ 52105-6		Canada $4.95
☐ 51673-7	THE MANSE by Lisa Cantrell	$3.95
☐ 51674-5		Canada $4.95
☐ 52555-8	SILVER SCREAM ed. by David J. Schow	$3.95
☐ 52556-6		Canada $4.95
☐ 51579-6	SINS OF THE FLESH by Don Davis and Jay Davis	$4.50
☐ 51580-X		Canada $5.50
☐ 51751-2	BLACK AMBROSIA by Elizabeth Engstrom	$3.95
☐ 51752-0		Canada $4.95
☐ 52505-1	NEXT, AFTER LUCIFER by Daniel Rhodes	$3.95
☐ 52506-X		Canada $4.95

Buy them at your local bookstore or use this handy coupon:
Clip and mail this page with your order.

Publishers Book and Audio Mailing Service
P.O. Box 120159, Staten Island, NY 10312-0004

Please send me the book(s) I have checked above. I am enclosing $_____
(please add $1.25 for the first book, and $.25 for each additional book to
cover postage and handling. Send check or money order only — no CODs.)

Name _____

Address _____

City _____ State/Zip _____

Please allow six weeks for delivery. Prices subject to change without notice.

THE BEST IN SUSPENSE

BESTSELLING BOOKS FROM TOR